DEAD END

They kicked their horses into a gallop and rode through the entrance in single file until entering the small clearing. A short distance away they could see smoke rising from campfires. As they approached the circle of teepees near a steep bluff, they saw only a few women milling about. Only then did they realize that they had entered a box canyon with but one way in or out.

Barclay leaned toward Taylor as he brought his rifle to his shoulder. "Don't see no horses," he said just as the first shot echoed through the canyon. The soldier in front of them slumped in his saddle, blood pouring from a hole in the back of his neck. The Indian women hurriedly disappeared into the teepees.

Two dozen Comanches, wearing full war paint and screaming battle cries, approached from the same entrance through which the soldiers had traveled. Instead of hiding in the rocks above, they had waited until the soldiers had entered the canyon, then followed, blocking the only exit. . . .

Ralph Compton

COMANCHE TRAIL

A Ralph Compton Novel

by Carlton Stowers

A SIGNET BOOK

SIGNET
Published by the Penguin Group
Penguin Group (USA) LLC, 375 Hudson Street,
New York, New York 10014

USA | Canada | UK | Ireland | Australia | New Zealand | India | South Africa | China
penguin.com
A Penguin Random House Company

First published by Signet, an imprint of New American Library,
a division of Penguin Group (USA) LLC

First Printing, August 2014

ISBN 978-0-451-46824-6

Printed in the United States of America
10 9 8 7 6 5 4 3 2 1

THE IMMORTAL COWBOY

This is respectfully dedicated to the "American Cowboy." His was the saga sparked by the turmoil that followed the Civil War, and the passing of more than a century has by no means diminished the flame.

True, the old days and the old ways are but treasured memories, and the old trails have grown dim with the ravages of time, but the spirit of the cowboy lives on.

In my travels—to Texas, Oklahoma, Kansas, Nebraska, Colorado, Wyoming, New Mexico, and Arizona—I always find something that reminds me of the Old West. While I am walking these plains and mountains for the first time, there is this feeling that a part of me is eternal, that I have known these old trails before. I believe it is the undying spirit of the frontier calling me, through the mind's eye, to step back into time. What is the appeal of the Old West of the American frontier?

It has been epitomized by some as the dark and bloody period in American history. Its heroes—Crockett, Bowie, Hickok, Earp—have been reviled and criticized. Yet the Old West lives on, larger than life.

It has become a symbol of freedom, when there was always another mountain to climb and another river to cross; when a dispute between two men was settled not with expensive lawyers, but with fists, knives, or guns. Barbaric? Maybe. But some things never change. When the cowboy rode into the pages of American history, he left behind a legacy that lives within the hearts of us all.

—Ralph Compton

Prologue

There was a clean sweet smell to the predawn air as the man stepped from the cabin porch and walked toward the barn. Inside, his wife and children still slept, warmed by the fire he'd just stoked.

The time before the sun rose was his favorite, the autumn solitude broken only by the sounds of early-rising birds. With the soreness of his muscles relieved by a night's sleep, he contemplated another day's work. He would feed his mules, milk the cow, and spread grain for the laying hens before the aroma of biscuits and brewing coffee lured him back to the house. Then there would be wood to cut, the field to till, and repair of a wheel on the wagon to be tended.

In the year and a half since they had arrived from Arkansas and staked their small claim, the work had been hard, the harsh frontier environment a daily challenge. But now times were better. He'd finished building the cabin and barn, dug a well, and removed rocks in order to plow a small sandy loam field where stands of corn and grain were beginning to flourish. The family, like so many other ambitious pioneers moving west, had begun to feel they were home.

He was emerging from the wide doorway of the barn, milk pail in hand, when he saw shadowed movement in the nearby stand of trees and heard the impatient pawing of unshod hooves. Even as he dropped the bucket and raced to get his rifle, the clearing filled with a dozen mounted Comanches, their faces lined with war paint. A yell was followed by the leader's first wayward shot, which struck the wall with a loud thud.

The farmer kneeled behind the wagon and returned fire as the horsemen moved in his direction. A round smashed into the chest of the nearest attacker. As the Indian fell from his horse, a volley of return fire ricocheted through the barn.

With only the interior darkness for cover, the man was trapped as the attackers began to circle the building, their war cries growing in volume.

Inside the cabin, his family was wakened by the shouts and gunshots. His wife directed the children to hide beneath the bed, then raced toward the front door where her husband's pistol hung. She had just taken it from its holster when the door swung open and a bare-chested form filled the entryway. Holding the gun with both hands, she closed her eyes and squeezed the trigger. A rifle fell from the hands of the Comanche as his face turned red with blood that gushed from one eye.

Even as he was falling, another stepped over his body and shot the woman. From the barn, her husband heard the screams of his children. He left his makeshift fortress and raced toward the house. A hail of bullets and arrows struck him and he fell forward after only a few steps. He managed to get to his knees, dizzy and gasping for breath, before one of the raiders kneeled beside him and drew a knife across his throat.

The Comanches dragged the bodies of the woman and children into the yard and laid them beside the man. Then they pillaged the two small rooms, collecting the few items of value they could find. That done, they lit torches from the fireplace and set the cabin on fire. Across the way, others had led the two mules and the cow from the barn, spread coal oil from the farmer's lantern, and set the building ablaze as well.

Angered by the deaths of their own, the savages scalped the man and woman, then set about mutilating their bodies. The Indians formed a circle around their victims and began to chant their war cries as they repeatedly shot arrows into the remains. The children were thrown down the nearby well.

Then, with their two fallen warriors lashed to the stolen mules, the Comanches rode away as black smoke curled against the rising sun.

No neighbors were close enough to hear the gunfire or the death screams. It was the smoke that alerted the dead man's brother, whose cabin was on the other side of the valley. By the time he arrived, his horse lathered in sweat, only smoldering ashes remained.

When he found the tortured bodies that lay in the dusty yard, he fell to his knees and retched. He searched frantically for the children, fearful that they had been abducted. Only when he saw the girl's rag doll near the well he'd helped his younger brother dig did he know where to look. What he saw as he peered into the cool darkness caused him to let out a pained cry that echoed across the valley.

He dug through the ashes of the barn and found a charred

pick and shovel. With them he dug graves in the shade of the nearby trees.

He knew no words to say once his work was done, so he stood alone in the morning silence, his tears a final farewell to the only kin he had.

Part One

Chapter 1

Kansas, summer 1873

Thad Taylor's lanky body throbbed with pain and the bright morning sun forced him to shield his eyes as he stepped from the front door of the jail. His recollection of the previous night was hidden away in a drunken fog—too many whiskeys and an argument in Stubby's saloon down the dusty Independence, Kansas, main street, a flying chair or two, then a full-scale free-for-all. The fact that one eye was almost swollen shut, his knuckles were raw and blood-crusted, and his ribs felt as if an anvil had been dropped on them was all the hungover Taylor needed to realize he'd been on the losing end of whatever fight he'd likely instigated.

It wasn't the first time.

He was making a futile attempt to smooth his tangled rusty brown hair and wipe the dried vomit from his torn shirt when he saw his sister glaring at him from a nearby buggy. Once again the sheriff had called her to fetch him and, despite earlier vows that she would never again do so, she had come to take him home.

Thad nodded in her direction, aware that a tongue-lashing was soon to come.

"Get in, Thaddeus," Sister said, hoping passersby would not take notice and quickly spread the word that the doctor's boy had again gotten himself in trouble with the law.

He ran his fingers through his hair again. "Gotta find my hat," he mumbled through swollen lips.

"Get in . . . *right this minute*." Her tone made it clear that finding his hat would have to wait.

They rode in silence on the trip out to the Taylor Farm, sweat beading on Thad's forehead despite the cool morning breeze. Sister kept her eyes focused on the mare in front of her, her knuckles white as she held tightly to the reins and her temper.

The weathered old farmhouse was in view before she finally spoke. "Thaddeus," she said, careful not to look toward him, "you're past your twentieth year and still whoring and drinking and carousing, doing absolutely nothing worthwhile with your life. It's a shame, if you ask me. Are you *ever* going to amount to anything?" A tear ran down her cheek as she spoke.

"Reckon not." He was sorry for his response as soon as the words escaped his mouth. "Where's my horse?"

"Unlike you, he came home last night," Sister said. "I unsaddled him and put him in the barn." She gave him a stern look. "Just like I always do."

"He okay?"

"Much better than you. I'm just glad Daddy's away and not here to see what a frightful mess you are."

After cleaning up and pouring himself a cup of coffee from the pot that hung above the fireplace, Taylor declined

Sister's offer of breakfast. His stomach churned at the very thought of food. Instead he headed toward the barn and the small room he'd converted from what was once a place for storing saddles and tools back when the home place was still a working farm. It had only a bed and a small chest, most of its faded paint peeled away. But the place provided him solitude, away from the big house that he'd stormed out of three years earlier, following yet another argument with his father.

He fell onto the bed, resting an arm across his eyes, hoping the dizziness would soon go away. And, as was his routine following each of his boozy misadventures, he took stock of his miserable station in life. As was always the case, he didn't like the scenes that played in his mind.

His father, Independence's only doctor, was one of those bigger-than-life characters. He'd lost count of how many children, his own included, he'd helped bring into the world, how many broken bones he'd mended and lives he'd saved. If the stories Thad had heard since boyhood were true, Dr. Winslow Taylor, a portly Scottish immigrant with a booming voice, had been a fun-loving man in his younger days. He was quick to help out friends and neighbors, ever ready to buy the first round on Saturday nights, loved dancing, playing the fiddle. And, above all, his wife.

That he had been unable to save her life when complications developed following his son's birth had changed Dr. Taylor forever. His good nature disappeared, his delight in the company of others waned. While he continued to carry about his medical responsibilities in a professional manner, he was never the same after Maggie Taylor was buried. Doc Taylor became a bitter man. Often, on late nights when he sat alone in his library, sipping whiskey and smoking his pipe, he would quietly talk to himself. His words, part curse, part an expression of haunting disbelief, were always the same: *I can heal others but couldn't save my own.*

The only thing that brightened his spirits was his daughter, Peggy, whom everyone had begun calling Sister even before her younger brother was born. She had her mother's features—high cheekbones, eyes so blue as to be almost hypnotic, shiny auburn hair—and a warm, generous nature. In Sister's company, Dr. Taylor was able to think back on happier times.

Thad, on the other hand, was a constant reminder of the darkest day in his life. And, while the doctor had never said as much, his son was certain that he was blamed daily for the death of his mother. Thad had long since resigned himself to being the family curse, robber of all of his father's joy. He'd so balked at the doctor's insistence that education was the path to a man's success that when he'd stopped going to the schoolhouse, no argument was offered. Whatever small effort at guidance the elder Taylor had tried ended in such grand failure that he'd long since halted the useless exercise. By the time Thaddeus reached adulthood, he couldn't even remember when he'd finally given up on any effort to win the doctor's approval.

In exchange for doing handyman jobs around the farm—milking, mucking out stalls, carpentry when the roof of the house leaked, clearing brush, and tilling Sister's summer garden—he lived on the family place and enjoyed his sister's cooking. Otherwise, he and his father were as distant as strangers, seldom speaking, seeing each other rarely, and then only from a safe distance.

What little money Thad earned came from odd jobs he did

for folks in town who occasionally tried to reach out to the young man whose life they perceived to be painfully lonely, filled with anger, and without real purpose.

If Independence had a bona fide outcast, it was Thaddeus Taylor.

The day was nearing an end under a gray sky that was forewarning a thunderstorm by the time he was wakened by a gentle knock at his door and the sound of Sister's voice. "You feeling good enough to eat something?" On her arm was a basket that held a plate of tomatoes, corn bread, beans and bacon, and a large slice of apple pie.

"Looks like I'm gonna live," he said as he realized that his appetite had returned.

Sister sat silently watching her brother as he began to eat ravenously. He wasn't exactly a handsome man, she thought, but if one looked beyond the bruises, swollen eye, and unkempt hair, overlooked his need for a shave and new clothes and another ten pounds on his skinny frame, there was something about Thaddeus Taylor that she assumed women might find attractive. Not just whores, but good women like those who attended church at the Calvary's Cross Baptist. She was certain she wouldn't always be the only one to love her brother—if he straightened up.

"I'm sorry about what I said today," she said.

Thad smiled for the first time since he'd been released from the jail. "I've heard worse," he replied as he buried his fork into the apple pie.

After gathering the emptied plates, she sat beside him on the bed. "You up to talking for a bit? I've got something on my mind that—"

"I know I've said it before, but this time I swear on the Good Book that I ain't going back to Stubby's."

"That's not what's worrying me."

"What, then?"

"It's been over three weeks since Daddy left to go visit Uncle Dalton in Fort Scott. Dalton's getting up in years, you know, and he's not at all healthy, so Daddy felt it was time to look in on him, maybe talk him into coming here to live with us. But he told me he wouldn't be gone more than two weeks, since Julie Simpson—you know her, she works at the grocery in town—is going to be having her baby soon. It's not like him to delay his return and ignore her needs."

"Didn't even know he was gone," Thad said.

"Anyway, the last couple of nights I've been having these awful dreams. In them, bad things are happening to Daddy, like Indians getting him or some outlaws knocking him in the head and robbing him. I know it sounds crazy. But the truth of the matter is I'm getting really scared."

"And just what is it you want me to do about it?"

"I want you to go find him."

A bright eruption of stars had filled the moonless, cloud-free sky after the rainstorm. It was still a couple of hours before daylight and there was a clean, newly washed smell in the prairie air as Taylor stood at the entrance of the barn, a packed saddlebag draped over one shoulder.

He'd slept little. Instead he had listened to the gentle rhythm of the rain on the roof as he contemplated his sister's request. *Go find him.* Where? How? And, perhaps most puzzling of all to him, why?

He was saddling his sorrel, Magazine, when he sensed that he was not alone. In the flickering light of a nearby coal oil lantern, he made out the image of his sister standing in the doorway.

"You're going to do it," she said.

Her brother shrugged. "Got nothing better to do."

"Come up to the house before you leave. Coffee's about ready."

Carefully laid out on the kitchen table was a knotted bandanna filled with freshly baked biscuits, a hat her father wore when he was making his rounds to visit patients, and his hunting rifle.

And there was a small gold-framed photograph of their mother and father. "Could be that you might need this if you need to make inquiries," Sister said. "Of course, it was taken when he was considerably younger, but it's the only likeness I have."

Taylor gave the picture only a glance. Instead he focused on the Winchester and laughed. "I couldn't hit the side of a sizable barn with that thing. I ain't exactly got a reputation as a gunfighter, you know." The fact was, he'd never even owned a sidearm.

"I doubt it would be a barn you'd be aiming at if you found yourself facing some kind of serious trouble." She handed him a pouch filled with ammunition, then reached into her apron and produced a small white kerchief knotted around a fistful of coins.

Her brother sipped from his coffee cup and shook his head.

"You take it and don't argue," she said. "But don't you

dare go spending it all on whiskey and foolish amusements." She put her arms around him, burying her face against his shoulder. "I'm expecting you back real soon, you hear?"

He reached for the doctor's hat and wasn't surprised when it fell across his bruised forehead and rested against his ears. He sighed. "Figures that it'd be too big."

Sister put a hand to her mouth to hide her smile.

Chapter 2

Aside from a lone coyote that appeared from an alley and stopped in the middle of the muddy street to watch him pass, Independence was quiet as Taylor began his northward journey. Even the morning birds had not yet begun to sing, and no rooster's crow had signaled the arrival of a new day. Whoever might have taken his place in Sheriff Henry's jail was still lost in tortured sleep, and the saloon was dark and quiet. Thad welcomed the solitude as he passed the deserted general store, the livery, and the hotel, making his way toward the open plains.

He was without any real plan, aside from following the trail that led north toward Fort Scott. Once the route of Indians following buffalo herds, it would take him along the Kansas-Missouri border, across miles of flatlands, past an occasional way station and a few small communities established by ambitious settlers. Depending on Magazine's willingness, Taylor judged that it would take him three days to reach the home of Uncle Dalton, a man he'd not seen since he was a child.

Likely as not, he would arrive to find his uncle and the

doctor sitting on the front porch, sipping whiskey, talking of old times, and arguing the virtues of Dalton taking leave of his home to make the trip back to Independence. Taylor would make his father aware of Sister's worry, urge that he consider a prompt return, and offer to help with the loading of Uncle Dalton's belongings in the event he'd decided to take the doctor up on his offer.

Once the sun rose, its warmth felt good on his aching body, and he'd begun to sense a small measure of purpose to his journey. While he didn't share his sister's concern for the well-being of his father, believing that his delayed return was nothing more than a matter of his own choosing, the rider was enjoying the sights and sounds of the flatlands through which he was traveling. He'd not seen another person or even a settler's cabin since sunup.

By noon he reached a small creek and dismounted to allow Magazine to drink and graze while he sat in the shade of a small stand of mesquites, eating a couple of the biscuits Sister had sent with him. Taylor had closed his eyes and was about to doze when he suddenly felt the presence of someone standing over him.

It was a boy, no more than ten or twelve, wearing overalls and a frayed straw hat.

"That's a mighty big hat you're wearing, mister," the youngster said.

Taylor smiled. "Borrowed it off a giant. What brings you here?"

"Been fishing since sunup. Pa said it would be okay if I promised to bring home enough catfish for supper."

"Catching anything?"

"Come on, I'll show you."

The boy introduced himself as Jakey Barstow as they made their way down the creek bank, where he lifted a length of rope from the muddy water to display half a dozen fish.

"By the look of things, I'd guess you're a pretty fair fisherman. Where'd you come from?"

"Our cabin's 'bout a mile past that ridge," he said, pointing to the west. "Me, my pa, and Ma come here from Tennessee."

"Well, then, welcome to Kansas, Mr. Jakey Barstow. We're glad to have you and your folks settled in our fine state."

"My pa says we're likely to have neighbors real soon, maybe even a town one of these days. He says there're gonna be lots of folks moving this way."

"You got no worry about Indians, being out here all by your lonesome?"

Jakey shook his head. "Pa says the soldiers moved 'em all down south to the reservations where they'll mind their own ways and leave civilized folks alone."

As the boy chewed on one of the biscuits offered him, he cast an eye toward the rifle strapped to the back of Taylor's saddle. "You fearing you might come up on Indians along your way?"

"Nope," Taylor said as he mounted Magazine. "But I am gonna be on a careful lookout for rabbits and squirrels intent on making any trouble."

Jakey grinned and waved as Taylor tipped his oversized hat and rode away.

Fort Scott, Kansas, had changed dramatically since the days when it was garrisoned by army troops charged with protecting the frontier and negotiating treaties that called for Indian tribes to take leave of their land and move farther west. For years there had been more fighting than negotiating as the Removal Act, which President Andrew Jackson had signed into law, dissolved into all-out war.

Finally, after a great amount of bloodshed, the spirit of the tribes and their leaders was broken, and most survivors had been driven away. All that remained were scattered bands of angry young warriors who continued to occasionally raid white settlers, stealing livestock, burning homes, and leaving unspeakable death in their wake.

The danger, though still real, was no longer considered grave enough to keep Fort Scott active.

Long before it closed in 1853, Dalton Taylor had resigned his position as legal attaché for the military, convinced that the Indians were being treated unfairly. A gentle, well-educated man who could not embrace the bloodlust of either the soldiers or the Indians, he sought to distance himself from what he perceived as unchristian cruelties by all parties.

He opened a law office, and when the military buildings were eventually sold at auction to discharged soldiers and newly arriving settlers, he purchased one of the clapboard officers' quarters and made it his home. And from that vantage point he'd spent two decades watching Fort Scott grow into a thriving community.

Thad Taylor was pleased to see the town on the horizon. He'd stopped only to spend a night in the settlement of Parsons, sleeping in the loft of the livery after seeing that fresh hay was laid out for Magazine. In the morning he'd bought a bowl of stew and a cup of chicory coffee from the owner and was on his way. The following night he'd slept under the stars.

His empty stomach was growling as he rode along the main street, searching for a place that served food. A sign positioned on the wooden walkway in front of the hotel caught his attention: FRESH BREAD AND GRAVY, 25 CENTS.

The proprietor waited until he'd finished his meal before initiating a conversation. "Will you be needing a room during your stay?" he asked. "For a dollar a day I can give you one of the upstairs rooms with a window and a nice view of the town. A heated bath is fifty cents extra."

Taylor said, "I don't expect to be staying here long. I'm here to see my uncle, Dalton Taylor. Don't reckon you might know where he lives."

"Oh my, yes. Everybody knows Mr. Taylor. A real gentleman, he is, and a fine and honest lawyer until various illnesses caused him to close down his business. He still comes in here every Sunday after preaching's over to have his lunch. It's always a genuine pleasure to see him. You're mighty lucky to have him as kin."

Then, pouring more coffee into Thad's cup, the hotel owner gave him directions to his uncle's home.

As he prepared to leave, Taylor reached into the pocket of his jacket. Wiping dust from the small gold frame, he handed it to the owner. "You seen this man here lately?"

The owner studied the photograph, then shook his head. "Can't say as I have."

It was the same response Taylor had heard earlier from the man who ran the livery stable back in Parsons.

A frail-looking old man stood in the doorway of the small cabin located near what was once the hub of military activity. He looked at his visitor over glasses that rested on the end of his nose. His hair was white and he leaned against a cane. In his free hand he held a book, a thumb marking the place where his reading had been interrupted.

"So," he said after clearing his throat, "you're my brother's boy. Can't recall when I last saw you, but I'm guessing you weren't more than knee-high." He invited Taylor inside.

The interior of his home was sparsely furnished but neat, the front room resembling a library more than a place for greeting guests. On the rows of makeshift shelves that covered each wall were carefully arranged books on a variety of subjects. A welcome aroma wafted from a small kitchen.

Dalton Taylor put aside his book—*Malaeska: The Indian Wife of the White Hunter*—and poured coffee for his nephew.

"It appears you do a good deal of reading," Thad said in an attempt to make conversation.

His uncle glanced at the small volume on the arm of his chair. "It passes an old man's time, though I can't say this one here is worth the dime it cost me. All these folks back in New York City are writing about life in the West like they've grown up out here when the truth is they don't know anything about this part of the world." He set the book aside. "So, what is it that brings you this way?"

Thad explained his father's planned trip and its purpose. And his sister's worrisome dreams that had sent him on his search.

"I've not seen him," the old man replied. "Last time I heard from him was a letter that came maybe a month or more ago. We correspond on occasion, just to let each other know we're still breathing, but he made no mention of coming here. And if he had suggested it was to convince me to return with him down to Independence, I'd have told him not to waste his time. I'm quite satisfied where I am and plan on dying right here. Sooner than I'd like, I expect."

He put a handkerchief to his mouth to muffle a hard, rattling cough. "Tuberculosis, in case you're wondering," he said.

The simplicity of Taylor's mission vanished as the dying old man spoke. The likelihood of Sister's dreams coming true sent a sudden chill along his spine.

So sure had he been that his father had safely reached Fort Scott, he hadn't bothered to pay careful attention as he followed the trail northward. Now he would need to visit every way station and farmhouse along the way as he retraced his route. As he contemplated his task, he reached into his pocket and felt the coolness of the small picture frame.

What, he wondered, would he tell Sister if he wasn't able to find their father?

"I suggest you stay the night here," his uncle said. "Get some rest before you start out again. There's a grove of trees out back and a small stream. You can tether your horse there. I've got a bed that's fairly comfortable." Before Thad could argue, his uncle added, "I'd enjoy having the company."

The sun was going down as the two men sat on the shaded front porch, Dalton Taylor steadily puffing on his pipe despite the fact that it increased his coughing spells, Thad lost in thought about what the next few days might bring.

It was the elder Taylor who broke the silence. "One of the few benefits of getting up in years," he said, "is that you're allowed to express yourself as you please. That being said, I've got something I want to ask you about."

"Ask away."

"I'm wondering why it is that in his letters, your daddy has never once mentioned you, good or bad. He'll always say something about your sister and how pretty she is, but nothing about you."

Thad smiled. "I guess he don't think I'm pretty."

"I take it you and he don't exactly get along."

"That's a kind way of putting it. Truth is, me 'n him have never had much to do with each other, least not since I got old enough to talk back when he was scolding me."

"Your daddy mean?"

"No." After a brief silence, he added, "Mostly, he's just sad. Folks who know him say he's been that way since my mother passed."

Dalton tapped the ashes from his pipe. "And you're thinking that all these years he's blamed you for what happened, I suppose. An angry man has to have someone to hold responsible for his misery, and it sounds to me like you got elected."

Thad didn't respond. He stared toward the road, where someone's dog was hurriedly trying to beat the darkness home.

"I knew your mama, even back when your daddy was courting her," Dalton continued. "She was as fine a woman as you could ever hope to meet. She made every day of your daddy's life a pleasure. When she died, more than a little of him did too, I expect. Being a bachelor all my life, I can't claim to be an expert on the love shared by a man and a woman, but what I saw between your folks was special.

"It's no wonder that he changed once she was gone. But, boy, none of that was your doing. That she didn't survive giving birth to you was no fault of yours. Call it the course of nature or the will of the Almighty, but don't go blaming yourself like he's done all these years. No need for you to be as unfair as your daddy's been."

Thad pulled the small photograph from his pocket and handed it to his uncle. Dalton studied it carefully for several seconds. "A happy time," he said. "Unfortunately I fear that the days ahead might not be."

Chapter 3

For adventuresome settlers dreaming of a better life, the Osage Trail, extending westward from Missouri through Kansas and into New Mexico, was the route increasing numbers followed in search of prosperity. A steady caravan of wagons, loaded with meager belongings and high hopes, traveled the rutted and dusty pathway originally blazed by massive herds of migrating buffalo.

Now, with the Indians moved westward or onto the Indian Territory reservations to the south, the spacious plains of Kansas had become a new and welcoming frontier, offering pioneers free plots of land simply for the claiming.

Among those staking claim to a hundred-and-sixty-acre plot in an isolated region of Labette County was a large, bushy-eyebrowed German immigrant named John Bender. Older than most who had made the hard journey, he had arrived with his son and set about building a small cabin and barn, dug a water well, and planted a small orchard and garden before summoning his wife and daughter from the Michigan mill town where they had waited for word that their new home was ready.

Bender's wife, Kate, a lumbering, overweight woman who spoke little English, had immediately recognized that the untilled land her husband had claimed would hardly yield a living for the family. And it was she who soon devised a plan to improve matters. With the help of her grown daughter, Kate Two, she set about rearranging the interior of the small cabin, stretching the canvas from her husband's wagon across the middle and placing a table in the front half of the room, leaving only a small area in back for the family's living quarters. She instructed John to build a small row of shelves across one wall, and began canning the produce from the orchard and garden.

Soon a hand-painted sign hung above the doorway, visible to those traveling the Osage Trail, proclaiming that GROCERIES, FOOD, AND LODGING were available. Crude though it was, another way station for weary travelers was in business.

In time, a steady stream of settlers stopped in. Some purchased a meal, a few bought sacks of ground corn and canned pears, some only stopped to water and feed their horses. Occasionally an exhausted traveler would take restful advantage of a night spent in the Benders' barn.

And Kate Two, a pretty young woman who had not inherited her mother's girth or ill humor, would entertain guests. If a male traveler arrived alone, she would invite him to the bed in back of the cabin while the rest of the family excused themselves to the barn to tend the visitor's animals.

It was another talent, however, that most intrigued travelers. Kate Two claimed the mystic ability to communicate with the dead. For a dollar, the same price she charged for a visit to her bed, she would conduct séances once a meal was finished and the table cleared. With a flair for the dramatic, her eyes would roll and her head would jerk as she reached out to passed loved ones and communicated their reassuring thoughts to mesmerized onlookers.

Along the Osage Trail, Kate Two was becoming something of a celebrity.

Thad Taylor had felt a growing sense of uneasiness as he traveled back southward, stopping to ask settlers and townsfolk if they might have seen his father. None, however, recognized the man in the picture he showed. It was as if Doc Taylor had simply vanished.

Thad spent a morning in the small settlement of Thayer, getting no positive response from shopkeepers or passersby. The town marshal was asleep in his tiny office when Taylor entered and roused him. He grumpily said he'd not seen the man in the photograph before, placed his booted feet back atop his desk, and was again snoring even before his visitor left. Down the street, an elderly gentleman, repairing the broken axle of a traveler's wagon, had suggested that he might want to make a stop at the next way station. "It's only about five miles down the way, where you meet up with the Osage," he said, pointing southward. "You'll see it just 'fore you get to Big Hill Creek. Likely there'll be a number of folks to inquire to once you get there.

"If nothing else," he added with a smile and a wink, "I hear tell you'll find a mighty pretty young lady living there."

It was nearing noon when Taylor saw John Bender hoeing in the garden. "Young fella," Bender called out as he tilted his hat back and wiped his brow with an oily bandanna, "it looks as if you're headed the wrong way. Most folks are traveling west these days. Why don't you get down and come on into the house? You look like you could use something to eat and something to wet your whistle."

As he issued the invitation, a young man who appeared to be close to Taylor's age peeked from the corner of the cabin, a grin on his freckled face. "Howdy, howdy, mister. Howdy, howdy," he shouted, then broke into laughter as he began flapping his skinny arms. Then he disappeared.

"That there's my boy," Bender said. "He's a bit touched, as you can see. But he's a hard worker and does what he's told, so I ain't complaining none."

The inside of the cramped cabin had the odor of lard too often used, boiled turnips, and a faint metallic smell Taylor didn't recognize. Kate Bender stood at the woodstove, sweat beading across her forehead and a dip of snuff protruding from her bottom lip as she removed a pan of corn bread and placed it on the table. She ladled a cup of water from a barrel that sat near the doorway and handed it to the visitor.

"It vas jus draw from vell," she said in broken English. "Maybe it still can be cool." She motioned for him to sit at the table.

"You're more likely to feel some breeze if you sit on the side by the curtain," her husband suggested.

Just before Thad took his seat, the canvas parted and Kate Two appeared. Her long black hair fell across shoulders that were exposed by a white peasant blouse, her blue eyes quickly settling on the visitor. "Can't say I've seen you here before," she said. Her voice had a lilt to it, free of her mother's accent.

"Never been here before," Taylor said as he sipped at the turnip soup, which proved to be foul-tasting.

"So, what is it that brings you this way?"

Taylor pulled the framed photograph from his pocket and pushed it across the table. "I'm looking for this man," he said.

He looked so intently at the face of the young woman seated across from him that he didn't notice the quick exchange of glances between the elder Benders.

"Yes, I do recall him," she said. "He stopped in a while back to water his horse and purchase a jar of Mama's peaches. A fine old gentleman, he was. We exchanged words for a bit and he seemed seriously interested in taking advantage of my gift."

"And what gift might that be?"

"I, sir, am a spiritualist." She smiled. "Blessed with the special ability to make contact with the departed."

"You mean you talk to dead folks."

"That's exactly right," she said, ignoring his skeptical tone. "I felt there was someone he wanted me to reach out to, but he said he was already late arriving at his destination and took his leave. I urged him to stop in another time when he was of a mind. It was my opinion I would be seeing him again.

"Is it your fear that he might have run into deadly trouble with Indians? Maybe you'd like me to try to make contact with your friend."

"I don't recall saying anything about him being a friend."

Kate Bender began wiping crumbs of corn bread from the table and looked across the room at her husband. "Time for you get back to working," she said. John Bender reached into his trousers pocket, pulled out his watch, and nodded.

Taylor's pulse quickened at the brief glimpse of the gold pocket watch. It looked exactly like one his father had carried for as long as he could remember. His first thought was to rip it from the old man's hand and challenge him about the whereabouts of the doctor. Instead he took a deep breath and said, "Mighty nice-looking watch you're carrying." He tossed two of Sister's dimes on the table.

Without reply, an ashen John Bender turned and was out the door, moving swiftly in the direction of the barn. The two women stood silently, their faces vacant stares.

"Fact is, I found that watch to be familiar-looking," Taylor said, "and it makes me wonder a bit what else might have taken place here when my father visited."

Though neither of the women responded, he was overcome by a feeling of uneasiness. The sweltering cabin suddenly felt cold and threatening. Would the old man return from the barn with a gun?

"I reckon I'll be stopping back again real soon," he said as he quickly made his way out the door and mounted his horse.

He nudged Magazine into a trot and as he rode away he could hear a high-pitched voice chanting, "Howdy, howdy, mister. Howdy. Howdy," then an insane laughter that was now far more chilling than amusing.

Taylor hurried back toward Thayer as storm clouds rumbled along the horizon. Something, he was certain, was wrong. Some manner of harm had come to his father during his stop at the strange way station he'd just visited.

He needed to talk with the marshal.

Brantley Thorntree was slight and bony, half a foot shorter than the man who had already interrupted his morning sleep once that day. An unruly beard hid much of his face, and his clothes hung on him like a scarecrow's as he rose from his chair on the boardwalk in front of the jail. Only the deep growl of his voice hinted at the authority one might expect of a lawman.

"Mighty short trip," he said. He looked westward toward the approaching cloud bank. "I reckon you've come to seek shelter before the storm arrives."

"Truth is, I'm in need of your help," Taylor said as he dismounted.

"Come have a sit and tell me what's troubling you."

Taylor recounted his journey and its purpose, ending his story with the fact that he was certain the watch he'd seen in John Bender's hand belonged to his missing father. "Marshal, there's something strange going on down at that foul-smelling place," he said, his words coming more rapidly. "Seems to me everybody there is half-crazy or worse. There's a dim-witted son and a sister who claims to have special powers to talk with dead folks. The old woman barely speaks the language and the old man, he seems to just do whatever pleases her."

"They's a lot of strange folks moving out this way these days." The marshal spat into the street. "Can't say what you're describing is all that unusual, though I have heard tell of the pretty young woman who offers a variety of special favors. Not that I know about them firsthand, mind you.

"Let me think on it," he said. "Can't do nothing till this storm clears anyway. Best you hurry on down to the livery and get you and your horse a dry place to stay the night. My old bones tell me we got us a frog-strangler coming our way."

The storm hit with a vengeance. Loud claps of thunder rattled the walls of the stable where Taylor lay, head resting on the saddle he'd removed from Magazine. Though he was weary and distraught, rest evaded him as his horse nervously paced the small stall. Outside, the sky had blackened long before sundown, and the rain beat against the roof with a roar.

He could not rid his thoughts of the scene that had played out at the way station.

Or of his father. Was it possible that an educated man like him could have believed the claims of a young woman boasting powers to reach out to those who had passed? Had he, in desperation and sadness, been convinced that, for a dollar's price, he might hear the comforting words of his wife one more time? And, if so, had it led to yet another family tragedy? What, he wondered, would he say to Sister upon his return if his dark concerns proved true? If there was real truth to the dreams she'd told him about?

The questions raced through his mind late into the night.

There was a squeak of the hinges on the livery door and a figure appeared, a lantern flickering at his side. Rain dripped from the brim of his hat and down the slicker he wore. "You in here, boy?" It was the voice of Marshal Thorntree.

"I figured the thunder was most likely keeping you awake," he said. "Me, I don't get much sleep nights, no matter what the weather. I reckon that's why you caught me snoozing earlier in the day. We need to do some more talking."

Taylor rose, brushing hay from his pants, but made no response.

"Truth is," the marshal said, "you ain't the first to come to me with a concern for lost kinfolk. People been disappearing along the trail now for some time. I didn't give it much mind, thinking there was all manner of explanation. Maybe they lost their pioneering spirit and turned back or fell ill or got themselves killed by savages who still take leave of their reservations now and again.

"I never made no connection to the Bender place till you brought it to mind. But now that I've thought on it, seems all the bad things I've been hearing about took place down that way." He cleared his throat and shook rain from his hat. "Anyways, as soon as this storm passes, I'm gonna deputize me a few men here in town and go down there for a look-see and some conversation with those folks."

"I'll be wanting to go along," Taylor said.

"In that case, consider yourself rightfully deputized." With that he turned and walked back into the watery night.

The driving rain, the likes of which eastern Kansas had seldom before seen, continued for two days.

Four men were already waiting with Marshal Thorntree when Taylor arrived in front of the jail to finally begin the morning ride to the Benders' place. Though a clear blue sky greeted them, the three-day storm had left the street a chocolate quagmire. Standing pools of rainwater made the street look like a stagnant riverbed. There were no wagons or buggies in sight and few other people aside from idle shopkeepers stirred.

"Gonna be mighty slow going, I'm afraid," the marshal said as the newly deputized men sat along the boardwalk, scraping mud from their boots.

"This here's my deputies," he said after a brief nod to Taylor. "Tater Barclay here, he's kinda my full-time, part-time deputy when he ain't drunk or tending his place." The burly man with oversized arms that strained against the sleeves of his flannel shirt nodded at him. "These boys are

Jason and Mason Weatherby, fairly good for nothing mostly, but they'll have to do."

The twin brothers flashed identical smiles. "Reckon you get what you pay for, Marshal," Mason Weatherby shot back.

"And this," Thorntree continued, "is Brother Winfrey. He does our preaching."

Though surprised that a man of the cloth would be riding with them, Taylor only nodded in the direction of the slightly built man whose long, prematurely silver hair reached to his shoulders.

Brother Winfrey stood to extend a handshake. "I've not always had the calling," he said. "Rode with Sterling Price and the Missouri State Guard back in the day." He tapped a hand against the handle of a ten-year-old army-issue Colt that hung at his side.

"Now that we've made our proper acquaintances," the marshal said, "we'd best mount up and be on our way."

He rode point, followed by the twins, Barclay, and the preacher. Taylor brought up the rear.

"Anybody rides hisself off into a gully and gets drowned," Thorntree yelled back at his posse, "we ain't stopping for you."

Chapter 4

The six riders remained in their saddles, staring toward the ramshackle cabin's open doorway, the sign that had promised food and lodging swinging in the gentle breeze from the one nail that still held it in place. The snorting of their mounts was the only interruption to the silence.

"Hello, the house," Marshal Thorntree called out.

When there was no response, he instructed Barclay and the twins to check the barn. He, the preacher, and Taylor headed toward the cabin.

Inside, debris was scattered across the dirt floor. Footprints of scavenging coyotes crisscrossed the room.

"Don't look like there was much for the critters to find here," the marshal said as Taylor pulled back the canvas that separated the single room. "Cleaned out back here too," he said. Only the frame of the bed remained.

Barclay joined them. "Only thing out in the barn is a milk cow badly in need of tending. I give her some hay and seen she had fresh water. By the looks of tracks, there was once a wagon there, but it's gone."

Thorntree looked around the deserted cabin. "Appears to

me these folks took their leave in a bit of a hurry." He pointed toward the shelf where rows of Kate Bender's canning jars were still in place. "Me, if I'm planning to move on, I'd figure on taking some food along."

Taylor called out from the opposite side of the curtain, "Something here you need to see, Marshal." He'd pushed the bed aside and was standing over a hole that led to what appeared to be a cellar. A ladder disappeared into the darkness below.

"I seen a lantern out in the barn," Barclay said.

"Go fetch it," the marshal said.

Even before the deputy returned, Taylor was aware of the metallic odor he'd been unable to recognize on his earlier visit. Now, though, it was stronger, more cloying. Once he and the marshal had made their way into the cramped cellar, the stench was so strong that both men placed a forearm against their faces. Thorntree was holding the lantern above his head when the preacher joined them. The three stood shoulder to shoulder, filling the small earthen room.

"I know that smell all too well," Brother Winfrey said. "It's not one you'll likely ever forget."

Taylor looked at the preacher. "From your soldiering days?"

He nodded, silently pointing to dark spots on the wall and floor that were visible even in the lantern's faint glow. "The Devil's work has been done in this godforsaken hole," he whispered. "Folks have died here."

Bile rose in Taylor's throat as he hurried up the ladder and away from the cabin. Outside, hands against his knees, he heaved as the muscles of his stomach knotted and the ground around him spun.

* * *

The Weatherby twins had made an even more chilling discovery. Their boots caked with doughy mud, their faces suddenly white, they urged the marshal to follow them to the orchard located no more than a hundred yards from the cabin. "We was trying to follow the tracks of their wagon," Jason said, "when we come upon something strange."

"Yessir, mighty strange," Mason added breathlessly.

The deluge had washed soil away, baring the roots of many of the trees. Pears and peaches lay scattered, knocked from limbs by the pelting rains. In several places there were sunken areas where loose dirt had settled.

"Right yonder." Jason pointed toward one of the indentations. A decaying arm reached up from a shallow grave, its discolored hand wrapped into a clenched fist.

Brother Winfrey fell to his knees and began to pray.

The marshal tugged his hat tighter as he began to count the number of low spots that were visible. "Looks like we're gonna be needing us some help," he said. He helped the preacher to his feet and instructed him to ride back to Thayer. "Gather up some folks for digging. And alert Doc Libby we'll need his wagon and some burlap for wrapping soon as he can get it here."

Taylor was already walking toward the barn to see what tools old man Bender might have left behind.

In the following days word spread quickly of the horrific discovery on the Benders' place. In addition to a dozen men from Thayer who had returned with Brother Winfrey, neighboring settlers began arriving on horseback. Some came by wagon, bringing picnic baskets and spreading blankets wherever they could find a dry spot that afforded a good view of the gruesome drama being played out.

Joining those who returned with the preacher was Ashley Ambrose, editor of the *Thayer Observer*, who mingled among the onlookers and workers to gather information for a story he was sure would be unlike any he'd ever written.

By the end of the third day, ten bodies had been exhumed. Among them was that of Dr. Taylor, the back of his skull shattered and his throat slashed. In another grave, workers found a man an onlooker identified as George Loncher, who had last been seen a month earlier, leaving for a trip to the nearby settlement of Harmony Grove. Most of the bodies examined by Doc Libby as they were brought to him in the barn were so badly decomposed that it was unlikely they would ever be identified.

Before their grim chore was completed, workers also found skeletal remains of several body parts in a brush pile in a nearby ravine. In an abandoned water well, a human skull floated among a tangle of water moccasins.

It was nearing sundown when Marshal Thorntree found Taylor seated near the barn. His face caked with dirt, he looked out onto the nearby prairie with a dazed expression. Thorntree placed a hand on his shoulder. "I'm mighty sorry, son," he said as he crouched down beside him. "Don't rightly know what else to say."

Taylor turned to look at the grizzled old lawman. "I've never seen anything like this. Never even imagined . . ."

"Ain't nobody could have imagined civilized folks doing this kind of evil. I reckon we're all in for a long spell of night terrors 'cause of what's been seen here."

He explained that the bodies, each wrapped in burlap, were being loaded onto Doc Libby's wagon and would soon be on their way to Thayer. "You got any thoughts on what you want to do about your pa?" the marshal asked.

Taylor closed his eyes. "It was my sister's wish that I find him and bring him home," he said. "I suppose that's still my duty."

"In that case, you'll be wanting the doc to prepare him for the trip."

With the twins out front, carrying torches to light the way, the somber procession made its way northward deep into the night.

The marshal and Taylor rode side by side behind the slow-moving wagon. Thorntree said, "Soon as everybody's had fair time to get some rest and see their families, we'll form up a posse and be on our way. This matter won't go unattended, I can promise you. Likely as not, they're headed south and I doubt they can get too far what with all the mud and flooded creeks. We'll catch up to them soon enough."

"And when you do?"

The marshal looked straight ahead. "We can hope they decide to make a stand and put up a fight," he said. "That way we won't have to bother bringing none of them back to waste good hanging rope on."

"I'm still deputized, ain't that right?"

"I reckon so."

"Then, soon as I get my father home, I'll be catching up to the posse. Never in my life have I been of a mind to claim revenge, much less to take a life, but given the chance now, that's what I'd dearly like to do, be it man or woman or a laughing half-wit."

Thorntree didn't respond. The two men made the remainder of the journey in silence.

* * *

The headline on Ashley Ambrose's article in the *Observer* spared none of his flair for the dramatic. DEATH AT THE DEVIL'S INN, it read.

A horror so unspeakable that it caused some who discovered it to fall faint in disbelief had been played out just a short distance from our own community. It happened at a cabin way station south of Thayer. The property belonged to folks known as the Bender family and had been the darkly evil site of many murders and the desecration of bodies of unwary travelers along the Osage Trail for an unspecified amount of time.

Ten dead have been discovered, and it is believed there might be that many more who fell victim to the murdering ways of the family.

It is the speculation of Marshal Brantley Thorntree that the Benders would take quick measure of those who stopped in to determine if they had any sizable amount of money or valuable goods worth stealing. If such was the case, the likelihood of their surviving the visit was slim. Otherwise, if travelers were seen as ordinary poor folks, they were allowed to go on their way unharmed after making payment for their purchases.

This reporter, who witnessed firsthand the horrific sights that Thorntree and his deputies were forced to deal with, wishes never again to view such ungodly carnage.

Brother Noah Winfrey was seen praying over the lifeless bodies as they were being removed from shallow graves located a short distance from the deserted cabin.

The Bloody Benders—a mother and father, son and daughter, all who are assumed to not be right in the head—had taken flight before the arrival of Thorntree and his men, leaving behind only a single cow badly in need of food and bawling to be milked.

The marshal says that a posse will soon be formed to hunt them down and return them for hanging, which, to this reporter's thinking, is the proper justice due.

The one-room cabin, apparently built by the father upon settling there, was divided by a canvas taken from his wagon. In the front portion, this reporter observed a cookstove and table where visitors were invited to sit. In the event they were folks with money or other valuables, they were urged to take their place on the side of the table that would cause their backs to be to the canvas.

While the Bender women served and entertained the customers, father Bender and his grown son, claiming need to tend to livestock in the barn, would sneak around to hide themselves away behind the curtain, one or both wielding an ax handle that had been used to knock the victims in the head.

Once that foul deed was accomplished, they would drag the unconscious bodies down into a cellar that was dug beneath the cabin, and there the innocents' lives would be ended by a quick knife slash to their throats.

Marshal Thorntree supposes that once they were dead and their valuables taken, they were carried out to their final resting place, most likely under the cover of darkness. With apologies for the vileness of this report, it must be said that some of the bodies had been cut into pieces, apparently to make the chore of carrying them from the cellar a bit easier.

It was a gentleman named Taylor from Independence, traveling in search of his missing father, who alerted Marshal Thorntree that something was amiss at the Benders' place, causing the lawman's visit that resulted in the gruesome discovery.

Sad to say, Taylor recognized his father among the deceased and says he now plans to return him to Independence for proper burial.

Thad Taylor stayed drunk for two days in an effort to wash away the sights and smells of the Bender place and forestall thoughts of what he would say to Sister when he returned home. Tater Barclay, dealing with what he called "memory tantrums," matched his new friend, whiskey shot for whiskey shot, and saw to it that Thad made it back to the livery once the saloonkeeper had sent them on their way.

Though he had not yet been asked, Doc Libby had taken it upon himself to order the building of a casket. "I cleaned and wrapped your pa as best I could," he told the finally sobering Taylor. "The casket is made of a good, sturdy wood and the top's nailed down tight. There's enough salt and charcoal covering him so that you won't likely be offended by foul smell as you make your trip.

"My condolences to you, my good man, and it is my sincere hope we meet again under more pleasing circumstances."

Taylor shook the doctor's hand and paid him for the casket and care with the last of the money Sister had provided him, grateful that Barclay had offered him free use of his horse and wagon.

"My ol' mare ain't likely to get you anywhere in much of a hurry," Tater told him, "but she pulls a wagon more steady than your own pony is likely to. Axles been fresh greased, so I 'spect you're ready as you're gonna be."

"I'll get your horse and rig back to you soon as I can," Taylor said as they lifted the casket into place and tied it and his saddle to the side rails. He gently scratched behind Magazine's ears, then tethered him to the back of the wagon.

"All you'll need to do this time is follow along and see to it you keep the doctor company," he whispered.

Chapter 5

Taylor had lost track of the number of days that had passed since his journey began. He lazily rocked with the lurches and sways of the wagon, his hat pulled low to ward off the sun. And he found himself thinking of the cargo riding along with him. Whatever chance there might have been for him and his father to ever find common ground was now gone forever. He strained to summon any memories of good times between them, a moment of praise, an embrace, or a time of shared laughter, but couldn't. And the knowledge both saddened and angered him.

As he neared the short trail that turned toward the Bender place, he hurried Barclay's mare along. Glancing toward the way station, he saw that several people mingled outside the cabin and barn and down by the orchard. The Bender Farm, he suspected, was to become a dark landmark, a destination for scavengers and the morbidly curious.

Someone had already posted a crudely made sign that pointed the way to "the Homestead of the Bloody Benders." Taylor muttered a curse and rode on.

* * *

The rains had given new life to the sprawling Kansas grasslands. Parched and brown during his dusty ride northward to Fort Scott, it was now an endless sea of green and there was a fresh smell to the air as he retraced his route. Taylor marveled at how quickly things could change.

He was still two long days away from Independence before his strength began to return and he felt any real urgency to reach his destination. Delivering the unwelcome news to his sister, he decided, was best done and over with as soon as possible. Then there was the matter of Marshal Thorntree's posse, which he was determined to soon join.

The need for vengeance that had begun to stir in him the moment his father's body was lifted from its muddy hiding place might have been puzzling had he given it more careful thought. Instead he simply kept his course, carrying out his responsibility to bring the doctor home.

So lost in thought was he that he was unaware the sun had disappeared and dusk was fast approaching. Taylor steered the wagon toward a stand of trees and stepped down to stretch his legs. He unhitched the mare and freed Magazine and they quickly moved side by side toward a shallow pool of water left from the recent downpours.

While the horses leisurely drank and grazed, Thad stood near a wild blueberry bush, filling his hat with the fruit. It was the first time he'd felt a need for nourishment since leaving Thayer. Soon he was lying beneath a star-filled sky, his sleep filled with raw and ugly dreams.

He woke at dawn to the warm breath of Magazine nuzzling his face, the high-pitched arguing of a pair of nearby crows, and the faint smell of smoke and the sound of gunfire.

Beyond a distant rise he could see a black cloud rising

against the mottled gray sky. Thad saddled his horse, tethered the mare, and reached into the bed of the wagon to retrieve his father's Winchester. He placed a hand on the wooden coffin. "We'll be back soon," he said.

As he rode into the valley, Taylor saw the smoldering remains of a small cabin. Only the frame of the doorway was still standing, flames still spitting from its charred wood. It too crumbled into the heap of embers as he neared. The barn had also been destroyed by fire, and the gates of a corral and hog pen hung open. Nothing moved as he called out.

Shouldering his rifle, he surveyed the destruction. A garden had been trampled and near where the barn had once stood were the skeletal remains of a buckboard, a dark mass leaning against one of its wheels. Moving closer, Taylor was able to make out a human form. The swelled body, tied to the wheel and badly blistered by fire, was that of a man. Arrows protruded from his bared chest. He had been scalped and his tongue cut away.

Taylor had heard stories of raids on settlers by renegade bands of Kiowas and Comanches. Instead of going quietly onto reservations, they wandered the plains to kill and plunder. But he had never before seen their savagery firsthand. And for the second time in a matter of days, bile welled in his throat and he knew he was going to be sick.

Afterward, standing in the eerie silence, a gentle breeze swirling the smoke into wispy patterns, he let his eyes roam over what had once been an idyllic setting. Nearby was a creek, ashes settling onto its surface before being carried away.

It was, he realized, the same stream on which he'd encountered the boy fishing on a day that now seemed a lifetime ago.

Taylor searched the rubble but found no sign of other family members who had once called the destroyed place home. He assumed they had somehow escaped or, more likely, were carried away by the attackers.

He mounted Magazine and nudged him toward the water's edge. Moving slowly along the creek bank, he refrained from calling out for fear Indians might still be nearby. Instead he watched the still-damp ground for signs that someone might have managed to flee from harm. He was hardly a trained tracker, and was surprised when he saw a series of small footprints. Only then did he remember the youngster's name.

"Jakey . . . Jakey Barstow . . . You here, boy? I reckon it's safe to show yourself. The Indians are long gone."

Nearby, bushes rustled and the boy appeared, cold and shivering, the same overalls he'd been wearing days earlier now covered in mud. He was crying as he looked in Taylor's direction.

"You here to help me, mister?" he asked.

"Reckon I am," Taylor said, hoping there was reassurance in the sound of his voice. "You here by your lonesome?"

"They took my ma with them," Jakey said.

Taylor extended a hand and pulled the boy onto Magazine's rump. The two rode in silence toward the campsite where Tater Barclay's wagon and mare waited.

Jakey sat against a tree, wrapped in a flannel shirt Taylor had pulled from his saddlebag, watching as his rescuer hitched the wagon. "Where you heading, mister?"

"Home. And, unless you're of a mind to stay here, you're welcome to come along."

"I don't want to stay here, that's for certain."

"Then I reckon since we'll be traveling together, you ought to be calling me something 'sides 'mister.' Name's Thaddeus Taylor. Most call me Thad and you can feel free to do the same."

"It's mighty nice to meet you again, Mr. Thad. And I thank you kindly for your willingness to help me. I wasn't at all sure what I was planning on doing till you came riding up."

"Best we get on our way. You can ride the horse and trail behind or sit up on the wagon alongside me."

Jakey approached Magazine and rubbed his hand along his flank. "If it's all the same," he said, "why don't you relieve him of his saddle and I'll ride up in the wagon?"

Taylor, who had spent little time in the company of children, was surprised by the adult manner in which the boy spoke.

"How old are you, boy?" Taylor said in an attempt to break the silence as they made their way toward the trail.

"I'll be nine on my next birthday."

"Seems to me you're mighty well-spoke for being so young."

"My ma's been teaching me. It was her plan that whenever a town got built and a schoolhouse was opened, she would make it known she wanted to be the teacher." At the mention of his mother, a look of despair filled the boy's face. Despite the fact that the sun had dried his clothes, he again began to shiver, pulling Taylor's shirt tight against his slight body.

They had been on the trail almost half a day before he spoke again.

"I was up before daylight, planning on doing some more

fishing," he began. "I had just made it to the first brake of trees when they came riding in, all painted up and screaming and firing their rifles into the air.

"It was when they set fire to the house that Ma and Pa came running out, not even fully dressed from their night's sleep. One of the Indians shot my pa two or three times and a couple of others grabbed Ma and started dragging her away. She was screaming and begging them to let her go see to my pa, but they paid her no mind.

"They put her on one of the horses while some others began herding our milk cow and the pigs and Pa's team of mules down toward the creek. . . ." He told the story in a halting manner, staring straight ahead as he spoke.

"How many of them?" Taylor asked.

"I was so scared I don't rightly know, but I figure there were six, maybe eight. Some had feathers on their heads and they were all riding bareback, even the woman who rode up with them."

"You seen a woman among them?"

Jakey nodded. "But I don't think she was an Indian even though she had long black hair. She was right pretty and was dressed like white folks. All she did was sit on her horse, smiling and watching as the commotion was taking place.

"I'm not sure what else might have happened. I just took off running fast as I could, looking for a place I could hide."

Taylor bit against his bottom lip as he listened. "I reckon I might know who the woman was," he finally said, his thoughts flashing back to the foul taste of turnip soup, the long shiny black hair, and the peasant blouse worn by a woman who had claimed to be a spiritualist.

"Who might that be?"

"Somebody more evil than the Devil himself. Somebody who I suspect likely watched the killing of my father as well."

For the first time since they'd begun their ride, Jakey glanced back at the wooden coffin tied down behind them. "Don't seem neither one of us is having much good luck these days," he said.

"That, son, is about as right a statement as I've ever heard," Taylor said. "And it's my thinking that something sorely needs done to see that things change."

Sister took the news of the doctor's death far better than Thad had expected. She cried and excused herself to her room to spend some time alone, but soon reappeared to begin making a fuss over the youngster who had accompanied her brother home, seeing to it that he had a bath and a hot meal.

Long after Jakey had fallen asleep in their father's bed, Thad and Sister sat on the front porch, the full moon overhead causing playful shadows to dance in the yard. It was the first peace Taylor had experienced in days.

"I've been preparing myself, you know," she said. "I figured when neither you nor Daddy returned directly that my prayers wouldn't be answered and something bad must have happened. I'm just glad you made it home safe." Her disturbing dreams, she told him, had ceased.

Thad spared her details of the discoveries at the Bender Farm, telling her only that their father had been robbed and killed by a family of murdering thieves. He was a bit more graphic in his description of the scene he'd ridden up on following the Indian attack but avoided the manner in which the raiders had desecrated the body of Jakey's father. He was relieved when Sister did not press for more information.

"I'd admire to hear your thoughts on what I should do about the boy," he said. "I don't reckon he's got any other kin, least not until somebody catches up to his mother and sets her free from her captives. He's a lot more scared than he lets on."

Sister reached across the porch swing and placed her hand on her brother's shoulder, then leaned forward to brush a kiss against his cheek. "He's welcome to stay right here," she said.

He smiled. "I got a strong impression that he liked your cooking."

They talked late into the night. He told her of his plan to soon leave again, this time to return Tater Barclay's rig and join Marshal Thorntree's posse. "I'm thinking," he said, "that if we can catch up to those who killed our father, we might also learn the whereabouts of Jakey's mama."

"But you'll be staying here until we can have a proper funeral for Daddy," she said. "First thing tomorrow, I'll see to it that things get set in motion."

Her brother slapped his hands against his knees, nodded, and rose. "Fair enough."

He had taken only a few weary steps in the direction of the barn when Sister called out, "Seeing as how you're now the man of the family, maybe it's time you moved back into the house."

Taylor waved an arm in response. "I'll think on it," he said as he continued walking toward his makeshift room.

The funeral of Dr. Winslow Taylor was the largest anyone in Independence could remember. A caravan of buckboards and horses made its way to the farm, where people gathered in the shade of two spreading oak trees. Women fanned themselves, men shuffled uncomfortably, and children whom the doctor had helped bring into the world played nearby. Members of the church choir sang "Old Rugged Cross" and "Amazing Grace" and the preacher read scripture and used words like *beloved* and *respected* as he eulogized the departed.

After the casket was lowered into the ground, guests were invited to the house, where ladies of the church helped Sister serve lemonade and cake.

Jakey, attending his first funeral, stayed close to Thad's side. "Seems folks really admired your pa," he said.

"Seems so."

"I wish my pa could have had himself a proper burying."

Taylor placed an arm across the youngster's shoulders. "Boy," he said, "I'm gonna see to that right soon. Come first light, I'll be heading out to tend some business. And it's my plan to stop by your folks' place on the way."

As he spoke, Stubby June, having closed his saloon to come pay his respects, approached. "I'm mighty sorry 'bout your daddy," he said. In his hand was the hat Taylor had lost in his last drunken skirmish. "It's a bit stomped on, but I was thinking you might be needing it."

Taylor smiled. "Won't be," he said. "I've got me another."

Chapter 6

The smell of charred wood still hung in the hot air and buzzards glided in lazy circles over the small clearing where Jakey and his parents had lived. Coyotes and rats had also visited, leaving little more than a grotesque skeleton for Taylor to find upon his arrival.

He tied a bandanna over his face in an effort to mask the stench, then lifted a pick and shovel from the wagon and walked toward the soft ground where the family's garden had been before it was trampled by Indian ponies. There, in the eerie quiet, he began to dig a final resting place for a man he'd never known.

He cut the leather bindings from what remained of the body, wrapped it in a tarp he'd brought along, and dragged it to the grave site.

His father had been a devout Presbyterian, but Thad was not a religious man, so he knew no scriptures to recite, no prayer or proper words to say. Instead he silently went about filling in the grave, anxious to have the task done and be on his way.

He was halfway back to the wagon before he stopped,

turned, and slowly returned to the fresh mound of dirt that rose where vegetables had once been grown. "I promise to see to your son as best I can," he said.

As he rode into Thayer, he was surprised to find Marshal Thorntree sitting in his chair outside the jail, a large chaw protruding from the side of his mouth. "I see you've brung Tater's wagon back," he said, "thus making me into an unholy liar. Told him he wasn't likely to ever see it or you again."

Taylor climbed down and rested one foot against the boardwalk. "Didn't figure on interrupting your rest, Marshal. I must say I'm a bit taken aback that you ain't out on the trail."

"I was. We just come back last evening. Seems our work got done for us."

The marshal and his posse had wasted little time beginning their pursuit of the Bender clan. "We'd gathered provisions for a long ride," he said, "but we wasn't but a day and a half out before we caught up to 'em. We rode up on the Fall River down south and seen their horseless wagon stuck up to the axles out in the middle of the water. They had to be plumb crazy to try to ford when it was on such a rise from the recent rains.

"That's where they met their due."

"You saying they drowned?"

The marshal shook his head. "That would have been too kind an ending to their story. They were attacked and killed by a party of renegade Indians."

The posse had found John Bender and his son lying side by side on the riverbank, both scalped, skin peeled from their naked bodies. A dozen arrows had been shot into each one. "They also had their arms cut off," Thorntree added. "The old lady, we found her floating in a shallow downstream, gutted like a boar hog, her eyes poked out." The marshal turned and spat off the porch. "Given their murdering history, I'd say they got a more proper justice than we could have provided."

Taylor pondered the surprising turn of events. "And the daughter?"

"The pretty one you spoke of? She wasn't among the dead. Probably got herself taken away to a life of grinding corn, scraping hides, and pleasuring young savages. I don't relish thinking what's to become of her. At any rate, what's done is done. I reckon we can now set the matter to rest and go back to tending to more ordinary business."

"I ain't so sure." Taylor began to tell the marshal about the raid on the Barstow cabin. He ended his story with young Jakey's description of the woman he'd seen. "From what he says, it didn't appear she was no Indian and wasn't likely being held hostage."

"And you're figuring this was the other Bender woman?"

Taylor nodded. "Kate Two, she said her name was. Spiritualist with a talent for talking to the dead."

"Even the spirits of Indians who have passed on to their happy huntin' ground, you reckon?"

"I'm guessing that's the very thing she wants them believing."

The two men fell silent.

"I suppose we've all been reminded of a lesson we might should be taking to heart," the marshal finally said. "It's for certain you've had enough misery of late. This here's still hard country, despite all the government's promise. Too many scalawags and outlaw types coming this way to take advantage of honest folks by stealing and killing. You seen that firsthand with what happened to your pa." He turned and spat again. "And what we seen down by the river got me to thinking that it makes no matter what they offer the Indians to leave folks be. It ain't likely to happen till every last one of them savages is dead and gone."

Taylor nodded.

"Truth be known," the marshal continued, "I can't rightly say why a man would take leave of a safe place to come out here, bringing a wife and young'uns to this godforsaken country. I've taken to wishing I'd never come West myself."

The marshal leaned forward and spat another stream of tobacco juice into the street. "Now, son," he said, "I'm hoping you're here to tell me you're planning to return that rig and then be gettin' on back home without delay."

"Reckon you could direct me to Barclay's place?"

"Sure." The marshal paused. "Did Tater tell you much about himself?"

"No . . . why?"

"Well, there're a few things you should know about him."

Tater Barclay had just finished dressing out a deer and was hanging meat in his smokehouse when he heard the clatter of the wagon approaching. Bare to the waist and sweating, he wiped his hands on his leather apron and waved to Taylor.

"Wasn't expecting you back quite so soon," he said.

"I figured you might be needing what you were kind enough to lend me."

Taylor surveyed the landscape of Barclay's spread. There was a small, weather-beaten cabin, built of native wood, a barn barely large enough to accommodate the cow and two horses he owned, the smokehouse, a well, and a garden. There was no sign of a woman's hand or the presence of children.

He had never been married, the marshal had told Taylor. And none who knew him were aware of his life before he'd come to settle in eastern Kansas. Aside from his once-a-week visit to Thayer's saloon where he routinely imbibed to a point where most doubted his chances of finding his way home, Barclay preferred his own company. He never participated in town dances or holiday celebrations and rarely spoke unless spoken to.

It was during his occasional visits to jail for sobering up that he and Marshal Thorntree had established a friendship. The marshal was in need of someone he could swear in as a deputy from time to time, a man who would strike fear in and demand respect from rowdies and lawbreakers, and Tater Barclay fit the bill. His huge arms, barrel chest, and a no-nonsense stare that could wilt a live oak made him an able sidekick for the slight and aging marshal.

Only Thorntree knew of his previous life as an Indian fighter and buffalo hunter. Or of the turn of events that had caused him to choose to homestead outside Thayer. Barclay had only spoken of it once, on a snowy winter night as he'd sat on the bunk of the marshal's jail cell.

There had been a pretty young woman up in St. Joseph, Missouri, the daughter of a ranking army officer, whom he had courted with great enthusiasm. He'd begun to think of asking her to become his wife but realized he had little to offer a bride used to life's finer comforts.

To make himself a proper husband, he had set out on a yearlong pursuit of buffalo. Despite dwindling herds, he'd managed to collect enough pelts to earn himself over five thousand dollars. He'd hoarded his money, slept in the open, and eaten only the meat of the animals he'd killed and skinned.

Finally, with what he judged a proper stake, he had made his way back to St. Jo, intent on proposing. So grizzled had he become during his travels, the woman didn't even recognize him when he appeared on her front porch. He'd grown a beard that was tangled and unattended, his clothes were ragged, and his foul smell caused her to demand that he be gone; then she slammed the door in his face. He soon learned that in his absence she had agreed to marry a young man under her father's command.

Barclay had stayed drunk for weeks before finally beginning an aimless journey westward that had brought him to the settlement of Thayer. With no plan and weary of traveling, he had decided to stake a claim and call it home.

"I was just fixing to fry up some venison," he now said. "Climb down and make yourself to home. I bet I got an extra plate somewhere."

After they had unhitched the wagon and freed the mare and Taylor's horse to graze, the two men entered the cabin, where they ate in silence. "Ain't real proud of my cooking," Barclay said as he brought two cups of coffee from the stove.

"You got no need to apologize," Taylor said. "The task of boiling water's a bit of a mystery to me."

"I'm guessing you didn't come all this way just to bring my rig back and taste my cooking," Barclay said.

"I was planning on joining up with the posse that was going looking for the Benders, but the marshal tells me that situation's done taken care of." He paused. "But it appears there're other things that still need tending." He told the story of the raid that had occurred at the Barstow place.

"So it's your belief that the Indians made away with two women, one who likely joined them willingly and another they captured?"

When Taylor only nodded, Barclay continued. "You know, when we was riding down to Fall River, the marshal expressed his concern for you. Said he'd taken a liking to you but figured you had no experience at such things as tracking outlaws and felt it best you stayed out of harm's way. The reason we set out after those folks as quick as we did was to get on the trail before you could get back.

"Now, son," Barclay said, "I'm wondering what your current plan might be."

"I'm gonna try to find them."

"Save one and kill the other, I suppose."

"Something like that."

Taylor was in the barn, grooming Magazine, when Barclay appeared and leaned against the doorway. "Most likely, it was Comanches who killed the Benders and probably was responsible for the other raid you spoke of," he said. "A bunch of young renegades who haven't taken kindly to the government's notion that they should live in peace on land parceled out to them. They roam these parts and even down into Texas, causing their destruction just for the pure meanness.

"My guess is that they're headed south now, down into Indian Territory, to see if they can sell the livestock they stole. There's plenty of a sorry kind in those parts who wouldn't bother to ask questions about where a cow or a horse might have come from. After that, ain't no telling where they might have gone."

"You know something of Indian thinking?"

"A mite. Only thing I can say for certain is that they have no remorse about killing white folks, be they man, woman, or child. And that includes anyone of a mind to go seeking them out." Barclay approached Magazine and began to scratch behind his ears. "Fine animal you got here," he said.

"Truth is, he's not rightly mine," Taylor said. "He's the property of my father. He just allowed me use of him."

"As I recall, your daddy's dead now, ain't he?"

Taylor nodded.

"Then I 'spect that horse is now rightfully yours by inheritance."

The barn fell silent except for the horse's occasional impatient pawing at the hardened sod floor.

"If you're of a mind to make this fool's journey," Tater said, "it occurs to me you might find some company of use."

"I can't be asking you to do that," Taylor said.

"Didn't hear that you did," Barclay said. "I got nothing and nobody keeping me here. I figure in exchange for what's in the smokehouse and ripening in the garden, not to mention the half jug of whiskey I got hid in the house, a neighbor across the way will agree to tend things in my absence. We can be on our way at first light tomorrow."

"And you're right sure about this?"

"Of that, and one other thing."

"What else might that be?"

Barclay broke into the first smile Thad had seen since his arrival. "Most probably," he said, "we're gonna get ourselves kilt dead before we can ever get back home."

* * *

The early-morning sun was just beginning to erase the shadows from Thayer's lone street as the two men rode side by side. Neither had spoken since saddling their horses and leaving Barclay's place. As they passed the jail, Taylor was relieved to see that Marshal Thorntree, who would no doubt argue his disapproval of their plan, had not begun to stir.

It was not until they neared the small clapboard church on the edge of town that they heard a voice. Brother Winfrey was hurrying from the doorway, waving in their direction.

Taylor reined Magazine to a stop. "Morning, Pastor."

"I can see that the marshal was right when I spoke to him yesterday," Winfrey said. "He figured you were planning on going looking for some Indians who are likely hiding out one of the people who caused all that evil down the way. Against his strong warning, I understand. That right?"

Taylor nodded.

"A dangerous mission, I must say. But it appears you've got your mind set." He glanced at Barclay, a man who had never set foot in his church or heard a word of any of his sermons. "Seems you've enlisted help that's most qualified. I'm highly pleased to see it."

Barclay grunted.

The preacher approached Taylor. "If you're going to carry out your plan," he said, "it might be that you could use this." He held out the Colt he'd carried on the posse's visit to the Bender Farm. "Truth is, it isn't particularly Godly for a man in my position to have it. I think members of my congregation will be pleased to know it's gone from my possession."

Taylor looked at the holstered pistol, wrapped tightly in a

wide leather belt. "I done got a Winchester," he said, nodding toward the rifle strapped behind his saddle.

"It was my experience, long ago in another life, that a sidearm can be more useful," the preacher said. He handed it up to Taylor. "I'll be praying daily that the Almighty accompanies you on your journey."

Chapter 7

Indian Territory

Big Boone Stallings sat beneath the shade of a large pecan tree, frowning as the small band of Comanches disappeared into the shadows of the winding trail that led away from his camp.

"Look at 'em," he said to the two heavily armed men who stood nearby, watching the visitors leave. "They're so happy you'd think they had good sense." As if on cue, they laughed. In his ample lap was a pouch filled with small pieces of jewelry—watches and rings mostly—for which he had negotiated a paltry payment. A couple of riders were moving the livestock the Indians had sold him in the direction of a corral that sat at the base of a nearby bluff. Two aging horses, a pair of mules, and a milk cow, none of great value.

Bargaining and trading with renegades was not the way Stallings had planned to spend the remaining days of his life. Rarely was there a sober moment when he didn't long for the times before he had been forced to hide away in the Cookson Hills, sharing his dismal world with savages and others like him who were hoping to elude the law and a hangman's noose.

It was hardly a fitting end for one who had ridden with the legendary William Clarke Quantrill. As part of a guerilla unit along the Kansas-Missouri border during the early days of the Civil War, they had ambushed Union patrols and attacked the homes of pro-abolitionist civilians. Stallings had never understood the reluctance of Confederate leadership to embrace their efforts, instead referring to them as cowardly bushwhackers. In his mind, the bloodshed for which he and his fellow raiders had been responsible for had been a patriotic service to the South.

Still, for Big Boone, his days with Quantrill had been a valuable education and served him well once he'd assembled his own small gang of social misfits and begun to boldly rustle cattle, steal hides from buffalo hunters, and hide in wait to rob stagecoaches. He had been *somebody* back then. Maybe not famous, like the James brothers or the Youngers, but a man of some reputation. Always with money in his pocket, he drank good whiskey, had whores whenever he wanted, and took great pleasure in being feared by all—even those who hired out to ride with him.

Then, on a long-ago night in Lawrence, a drunken argument had erupted during a card game. Pistols were drawn and soon the saloon was filled with the acrid smell of gun smoke and the screams of men being shot. Before killing those who had accused him of being a cheat, Stallings had been seriously wounded, bullets tearing into his chest, leg, and shoulder.

Well after one of his men had helped from the scene of the carnage, it was learned that among the dead left behind was a highly regarded Kansas City politician. With the shot that had killed him, Stallings had earned the reputation for which he'd long strived. Wanted posters went up throughout Kansas, offering a reward for his capture, dead or alive.

He'd slowly healed, tended by a rural doctor who cared little about who paid for his services, and had lain in the bed of an old chuck wagon, spirited away to a hiding place in the Indian Territory. "Boss," one of the men who had accompanied him on the torturous journey said, "you're mighty lucky to be alive."

Stallings wasn't so sure. His breath had come in sporadic bursts and even the constant sips of whiskey his companion provided had failed to dull the pain. One arm had no feeling. The doctor had warned that in all likelihood he would be an invalid for the rest of his life

And so it had come to this.

In a small hillside clearing sat a cabin hastily built from native timber. From its front door one could look out on a row of shabby tents where his men slept, a weather-beaten barn, the corral, the chuck wagon stolen long ago from cattle herders, an outhouse, and a still. The most unusual structure stood on stilts, towering above the trees. Atop it was a platform from which sentries stood constant guard, watching for intruders.

Old before his time and infirm as he was, his wounded body bloated to the point where he could no longer even mount a horse, the only remaining thing of value to Stallings was his own miserable life. Selling rifles and whiskey to Indians, buying their stolen goods, and directing one of his few trusted men to resell them for small profits, this had become, in itself, a form of imprisonment.

In truth, the day and night guard was an unnecessary precaution. The legend of the Cookson Hills was such that no law-abiding citizen would venture along their trails. Most lawmen considered the region too dangerous to approach. Few Indians even dared go into the Hills. It was a no-man's-land, an isolated parcel of the frontier that had been given over to the most desperate and feared of society.

There Big Boone had grown into a pained and constantly paranoid man.

He was not the only one in the Indian Territory struggling with paranoia. The young Comanche warrior who had just left was also troubled by self-doubt. Members of his tribe called him Hawk on the Hill, but Stallings knew him only as Hawk, an ill-tempered renegade with an enormous hatred for the white man and a dwindling following.

Were it not for the need he served, Stallings knew he and his men would long ago have been killed, probably in the dead of night, scalped, their bodies left for scavengers.

Hawk had chosen to ignore the treaties his elders had agreed to. He had initially banded a sizable number of like-minded young tribe members to his cause. He stirred their anger with whiskey-driven rants about the broken promises of the white man's government, the theft of their homeland, the weevil-infested grain and spoiled meat parceled out to their weak elders who had agreed to retreat to the reservations, the killing off of their buffalo. The only good white man, he insisted, was a dead white man. And to that end he had led raids on settlements north into Kansas and south into Texas, leaving death and destruction in his path.

And with each act of revenge, the legions of his nomadic

followers had grown. He soon become one of the most feared and respected members of the Comanche tribe. Army scouts were never swift enough to keep up with his movements. Hawk on the Hill was like smoke, a ghost, here one minute and gone the next, always leaving flames and death in his wake.

His savagery was making him into a legend and he reveled in the recognition.

Then another face emerged from the Indian rebellion. His name was Isa-tia, and he possessed an evangelical skill that Hawk was unable to match. The stocky, broad-faced Isa-tia was a medicine man, equal parts shaman, *brujo*, and magician. Traveling through what remained of the fragmented Comanche Nation, he spoke of how he had ascended into the clouds to a place far beyond the sun, where the Great Spirit had spoken to him, providing a plan that would not only destroy the white man but restore the Comanche tribe to its former glory.

It was just what many of the angry young warriors wanted to hear.

Isa-tia claimed miraculous healing powers, even the ability to raise the dead if he chose. The white man's bullets, he said, could not harm him. As proof, he would belch up cartridges he said had been fired into his body by soldiers. On command, he could send lightning, hail, and thunder down on his enemies. When a brilliant comet appeared in the western skies, Isa-tia promised that he could make it vanish in five days. And it did.

To demonstrate his ability to pay visits to the Great Spirit, he would gather a group of warriors and demand that they look directly into the sun as he began his skyward journey.

While his followers were temporarily blinded, he would steal away to hide in a nearby cave, only to reappear the following day with new promises brought from on high.

Gullible warriors were promised eternal life in exchange for their loyalty. They quickly fell under his hypnotic spell. Many of Hawk's men were among them, and he had no idea how to combat the mystical hold the new leader had gained.

Until the woman named Kate Two had spoken to him of powers that she also possessed.

It had been his plan to sell both of the women taken during the recent northern raids to buyers in Mexico, a profitable practice he'd employed since his early days of leading raids on white settlements. The pretty one with the long black hair and piercing eyes had shown no fear when she was taken from the wagon in the middle of the swollen river. A woman of such strength and beauty, Hawk was certain, would bring as much as four hundred dollars. The other, plain and frightened, would earn him less.

Aware that Hawk had been taught some English at the reservation school as a boy, Kate Two had asked to speak with him. Assuming the captive woman would plead for her life, he had entered the teepee where she was being held.

He had remained there for several hours, listening to her claims of being a spiritualist.

"If you will allow me," she said, "I can be of great help to you. I can contact the great chiefs who are now gone, and they can provide wisdom and guidance as you battle against the white man.

"I will ride at your side and help you to become the mightiest of all leaders."

After he had agreed to remove the bindings from her wrists, she reached out to him, placing a cool palm against his forehead. Soon her eyes were rolling and her body convulsing as she identified the spirit voice of Hawk's dead father. "He has been gone since you were a small child," Kate Two said, "but he has watched with great pride as you have grown into a strong and smart warrior. He wishes you to know that he is in a happy place, where large herds of buffalo roam as far as the eye can see and everyone lives in peace.

"And," she said, "he urges that you continue to fight for the rights of your people."

Hawk was mesmerized. "Ask him of this man named Isatia who is guided by the Great Spirit."

Kate Two was silent for a time, her eyes closed. Then her head began moving from side to side and beads of sweat formed across her brow. "Your father tells me that the Great Spirit knows of this man who speaks false promises. He says he is one who should soon die."

She let her hand fall to her side and looked at Hawk. "If you will allow me but a sharp knife and lead me to him, I will put it to his throat and kill him for you."

Hawk silently rose and left the teepee, then stood in the warm evening breeze. His eyes roamed the small encampment. He slowly walked toward a nearby stream, where he cupped water into his hands and bathed his face. Perhaps, he thought, he had found a way to regain his lost standing.

Returning to the woman, he extended a hand, helping her to her feet, and led her from the teepee and toward the water's edge.

"Wash yourself clean," he said. "From this time forward you will be called Talks With Spirits. And you will be one of us."

Chapter 8

The days of summer had seemed to lengthen, the heat scorching the red clay landscape of the Indian Territory long after the sun had gone down. As Taylor and Barclay rode southward, the flat Kansas terrain gradually changed to rolling hills. There was ample water and vegetation for their horses but no hint of other humans. Most of the reservation land where the Indians had settled was on the eastern side of the Territory, leaving the route they were following quiet except for the occasional sounds of wildlife and the occasional rustle of hot wind through the trees.

At Tater's suggestion, they had begun their journey at the burned-out Barstow Farm, the last place they knew the raiding party had struck. "Even if I was a tracker, which I ain't," Barclay said, "they been too long gone for the reading of any signs. And most likely, they never travel the same route twice, coming one way and leaving another. We're lookin' for a needle in a sizable haystack."

"So, what's your suggestion as to what we best do?"

"Just keep ridin'. Looking and listening. On down a ways, we'll be getting into the Hills, where I know peoplc to be.

Maybe, if they aren't of a mind to shoot us just for the amusement, they might provide us information that can give us proper direction."

"The Hills?"

Barclay grunted. "Cookson Hills," he said. "Hiding place of half the bandits and ne'er-do-wells in this part of the country. Some of 'em have even taken up with Indian squaws, raising half-breed kids and barterin' with the Devil on a daily basis just to avoid the law."

"And you're acquainted with these people?"

The big man looked away. "I suppose you could say that . . . a few of 'em, a long time past."

They rode at a steady pace for three days. Packs of wolves roamed among the timberlines in an endless effort to sneak up on the small herds of mule deer that grazed in meadows and drank from the streams. Squirrels played chase in the trees as coyotes watched them hungrily.

With two quick pistol shots whose accuracy amazed Taylor, Barclay killed two rabbits, which would serve as their dinner once they camped for the night.

Strapping the carcasses to his saddle horn, Tater spoke for the first time in hours. "We're still a day's ride, maybe a little more, before we get up into the Hills. Daylight's about gone, so I 'spect we ought to be looking for a place to rest our bones and cook up these critters."

Taylor's thoughts flashed back to home and the sweet smells of Sister's cooking wafting from the kitchen. And at that moment he wondered if it had been a mistake to embark on what his companion had called "a fool's journey." *Why go in pursuit of revenge for the death of a man who never for a minute cared about me? Why is it my duty to find Jakey's mother, a woman I've never even laid eyes on?*

Had Tater Barclay not invited himself along, Taylor would likely have already turned back. But he'd now come too far to admit his misgivings. While Barclay seemed at home in this wilderness, he was lost. And more afraid than he would dare admit.

He woke from a restless and nightmare-filled sleep and lifted his head from his saddle to see the forms of two men standing over him. For a moment he thought he was still dreaming. The campfire where earlier the rabbits had been cooked was reduced to glowing embers, and the hoot of a nearby owl was the only break in the silence. With only a sliver of moon above, it was impossible to see the faces of the intruders.

He was still not sure they were real until one spoke. "We had not expected the good fortune to meet up with a fellow traveler," the smaller man said.

As Taylor attempted to get to his feet, the end of a rifle knocked him back to the ground. He said, "What is it you want?"

"Our mounts are tired and we have no money. Perhaps you would be kind enough to help us." The man added a high-pitched giggle. "We're headed north and have been moving at night to avoid interference from those who wish us harm. We find that in these parts it is a wise thing to do."

Taylor was now fully awake. He rubbed his shoulder. The second bandit, the one with the rifle, stepped forward and placed a boot against his chest. In his hand was a large bowie knife. Even in the darkness Taylor could see a grin on his bearded face, and his breath smelled of whiskey and rotting teeth. "Course," he said, "if you ain't of a mind to politely lend us a hand, we gotta do what we gotta do." He moved the knife close to Taylor's throat as his companion searched the saddlebag that lay nearby.

He spilled its contents to the ground and bent forward to retrieve a small leather pouch. Shaking it, he giggled at the sound of coins jangling.

"It ain't much," Taylor said, "but you're welcome to it if you'll just move on and let me be." He was aware that his palms were moist with sweat and his mouth had gone dry.

Both men laughed. "Wouldn't be no fun in that," said the big man looming above him. "What we'll do instead is take your money and your fine horse and leave you dead."

A few feet away, Magazine snorted, and a third form moved swiftly from the shadows of a nearby stand of trees. Two rapid blasts from a shotgun echoed into the night. The coin pouch flew from the hand of one of the bandits as he went to his knees, then lurched forward onto the dying campfire. The man with the knife fell across Taylor, suddenly deadweight, blood pouring from where his grin had once been.

"Bein' one who don't sleep too good can be a blessing," Barclay said as he approached. "I heard 'em coming, so I fetched my horse and hid away to see what their intention might be. Turns out they were the no-goods I expected. Nothing more than roaming thieves."

Taylor had pushed the dead man from his chest and climbed to his feet. "Appears my indebtedness to you keeps growing," he said. "Now you've saved me from getting my money stole and my throat cut. It's the latter for which I'm most thankful."

Barclay just smiled.

* * *

It was dawn by the time they had dragged the two lifeless bodies to a nearby ravine and covered them with rocks and brush. "Ain't hardly what you'd call a Christian burial," Barclay said, "but I had no indication that they was exactly the God-fearing kind. I 'spect this is better than they rightfully deserve."

Taylor shook his head and sighed. "Seems all I been doing of late is burying folks."

In the stream he washed the blood of his attacker from his shirt and hung it on a bush to dry while Barclay collected the bandits' weapons and rounded up the mules they'd been riding.

"I've a mind to just leave 'em here to tend for themselves," Barclay said, "but chances are the wolves would get to 'em before the day's out. Might be we can use them for tradin' along the way. They're pretty broke down but still worth something." He mounted his horse. "Best we be on our way."

They rode in silence for several hours, their hats pulled low against their faces to ward off the sun's glaring heat. For the first time since their departure, Barclay kept his shotgun resting across his saddle.

"I'm guessin' you've had time to do some thinking on what took place back there," he finally said. "Likely, you're wondering why I didn't fire a couple of shots into the air and just warn those men away."

"The thought might have crossed my mind."

"Woulda been no use. If they'd run, they would eventually have come back at another time to carry out their thievin' plan. Or, if they weren't the cowardly type, they would have stood their ground and raised their guns for a shoot-out that mighta left the both of us dead. As I seen it, the situation called for fast and simple fixin'."

"Am I guessing right that it wasn't the first time you've shot a man dead?"

Barclay chuckled. "And it ain't likely it's gonna be the last. From here on, we'll do our sleeping with one eye open." He pointed toward Taylor's hip and the preacher's holstered Colt. "Better figure on usin' that sidearm soon."

By nightfall, they were nearing the base of the Cookson Hills.

As they made their way along a powdery red trail that ascended into an endless canopy of trees, they became aware of signs of life. Whispery clouds of smoke rose from cabins so deeply hidden in the woods they were barely visible. As they rode higher, the faint sound of children playing could be heard.

"Welcome to the back end of nowhere," Barclay said. "Know that we're bein' watched. I'd advise your best behavior from here on and let me do the talking if it's needed."

A mile away, on the highest of the hills, a sentry climbed from his post and rushed to find Big Boone Stallings. "Strangers coming," he said. "Two riders with a couple of mules trailing."

"Indians?"

"White men, it appears."

"Ride down and tell them I ain't in the market for more mules," Boone said. "If it's a place to hide out they're seeking, tell them to go looking elsewhere. If they're wearing badges, shoot 'em and feed 'em to the hogs."

Chapter 9

The hilltop clearing appeared abruptly as the riders emerged from the tree-sheltered trail. Word had already spread that strangers were being brought along, and several gathered to see who they might be. "Ain't Indians," one boy whispered to another. A woman standing over a large kettle making lard stopped her stirring to watch the arrival. Big Boone sat silently on his porch, arms across his chest, his thick fingers interlocked as he watched a bantam hen and her chicks peck at the hardened ground. A large Mexican sombrero shaded his eyes.

Taylor and Barclay were led to Stallings's cabin and told to dismount. Thad had been surprised that his traveling partner had willingly agreed to hand their weapons over when they were stopped.

"I'm guessing your purpose here ain't to be bringing my mules back," Stallings said. "Though I appreciate the gesture, truth is I got no use for the stupid animals. Or the men who was riding them when I sent them on their way. I hope you boys seen to it they didn't get far."

Barclay nodded.

"They made the poor decision of getting drunk and trying to steal from me," Stallings said. "If they hadn't been kin—cousins, I'm told, though I ain't sure I ever believed it—they'd never have left these hills. Being generous in my old age, I sent 'em riding out on those broke-down mules with a warning never to come back.

"I'm guessing that they tried to rob you as well and are most likely now dead. If I'd had a say, you would have stripped 'em buck naked and barefoot and sent 'em walking among the wolves."

He nodded to one of his men, who hurried to the porch to help him to his feet. The simple effort stirred a wheezing deep in Stallings's chest.

Barclay's eyes had not left his face. Big Boone steadied himself against a cedar post that held a corner of the porch roof in place and returned the stare. "Should I recall knowing you?"

"I reckon not," Barclay said.

He had been even younger than Taylor, tracking the buffalo herds across the northern plains of Kansas. On the hunt for months, killing and skinning the lumbering animals, spending the last hours of daylight scraping and salting the hides before stretching them to dry in the next day's sun. It was a hard and lonely undertaking, which Barclay endured only by focusing his thoughts on the money his efforts would bring.

One night, as he sat near a small campfire, bone-tired and dreaming of the time he could return to St. Jo as a man of means and marry Jolene Cavanaugh, half a dozen men rode into his camp, guns drawn. He'd not even had time to reach for his rifle before one of the riders' horses was spurred to lunge toward him, its sharp hooves cutting into his flesh and snapping his collarbone. He was beaten and knocked unconscious by the time the robbers gathered his hides and rode away, leaving him for dead.

Before passing out, Barclay saw that the leader, sitting astride a big bay, wore a sombrero, his long black hair hanging well below his shoulders. He laughed as his men pounded and kicked the hunter.

Before his swollen eyelids closed and he began to vomit, Barclay had heard one of his attackers call the leader's name. Boone.

For several days he was near death. Had it not been for a spring near his campsite where he sipped water and bathed his wounds, he would not likely have found the strength to retrieve his rifle and position himself against a tree trunk where he could watch for any further attacks from man or beast. There were days and nights—he couldn't recall how many exactly—of fevered dreams and a constant ringing in his head. Finally his body healed and his mind cleared.

His first thought was to immediately seek revenge against those who had robbed him. Then, as the rage subsided, his focus returned. He had come to hunt buffalo and collect their hides, and even if hindered by the makeshift sling he fashioned to protect his collarbone, he would begin to rebuild his lost fortune as soon as he could ride. Finding the man called Boone would have to wait.

And in time the raw memories of the assault and robbery waned. When Jolene had rejected him, he became a man without purpose, all feelings gone numb. Even summoning anger over what had been done to him was difficult. Months later, when he'd seen the Wanted poster for Boone Stallings and was told that he had likely fled into Indian Territory, Barclay had little interest in tracking him down. All he wanted to do was forget the past. And over the years the wounds, both physical and of the spirit, slowly healed, all but forgotten.

Until the young man from Independence returned his wagon and spoke of his own need for revenge.

Now whatever remnant of hatred he still held to had vanished the moment he saw the old man, his body bloated, his sunken eyes watery, and his stringy hair now white. Taking his life would be a kindness, releasing him from a misery far worse than death.

Instead, as he'd chosen to do so long ago, he concentrated on his new purpose.

"Our apologies for comin' to you with no invite," Barclay said. "We'll be on our way as soon as you'll allow me a few questions. It's only information we're seeking."

"I've got little of that I'm willing to part with."

"My understanding is that from time to time the Comanches visit these hills to do selling and trading. What might go on in these parts ain't of our concern, or wasn't until a short time back when they rode away from Kansas with a couple of womenfolk we're now in search of."

"I buy no women," Stallings said. "Too much trouble. Other items of interest, maybe, but no women, white, Indian, or half-breed. It ain't smart business. The only market for them is way farther south, past Texas and down into Mexico. It's there you should be headed."

"These Indians who visit, where is it they come from?"

"A few travel from the reservations to the west, mostly to buy whiskey. They're the older ones, like me, wanting strong medicine that will help them forget how bad their lives have become. The younger ones who refuse to stay put on government-given ground and make trouble, they roam, never staying in one place for long."

"How often is it that these renegades pay you visits?"

"I don't recall admitting that they do." For the first time since their arrival, he smiled. "But I reckon you boys ain't dumb." He focused his gaze on Barclay. "For the sake of continuing this enjoyable conversation, let's say it could be I do a bit of business with them now and again. Not long ago one might have spoken of a white woman he wanted to know if I was interested in purchasing."

"Just one?"

"That's my recollection. That and the fact that I quickly told him no."

"Any thoughts on where we might locate him?"

Boone shook his head. "My suggestion would be that you leave him be. He's a mean and crazy one, even without benefit of my whiskey. I'm being honest with you when I say it would suit me fine if he never set foot here again. But when a body least expects it, he rides up the hill with a few of his friends, wanting to do some business. Can't say there's much that scares me these days, but he does. They call him Hawk and he's an honest-to-goodness *bhoot*."

Taylor said, "A *bhoot*?"

Stallings nodded. "One of them Indian ghosts that's here one second and gone the next."

Barclay reached for his saddle horn and lifted his boot into a stirrup. "We thank you. We'll be on our way if you'll kindly return our property."

"Leave the mules. You'll find your guns down at the bottom of the trail. Does that seem a friendly exchange?"

"Thought you wasn't wanting the mules."

"I wasn't," Stalling said as he returned to his chair, "but somebody's likely to."

"I don't reckon I learned much back there," Taylor said as they rode away from the Hills.

"Except maybe the fact that it appeared you once knew the man."

Barclay told him of his long-ago encounter with Stallings and his band of outlaws, careful to leave out any mention of Jolene Cavanaugh.

"Did it cross your mind as we visited that you might still want to kill him for what he did?"

"Nope. He's done dead already. He just ain't accepted the fact yet."

In truth, they had learned something during the strange visit. "What we'll want to do is find us a place to make camp," Barclay said, "somewhere far enough away from the Hills so as to be out of sight of those men manning the guard tower and anyone who might be coming to pay a visit. We'll just hunker down and wait."

Taylor gave him a puzzled look.

"We could hope to stumble onto the site of the Comanches' camp. No telling where they are, and I ain't of a mind to spend the rest of my days wanderin' around these parts. I figure Stallings was being truthful when he said they come to do business with him, so what I'm suggesting is we just wait and let 'em come to us. Then when they take their leave we can follow at a safe distance."

"How long you think we'll have to wait?"

Barclay grunted. "Could be a while. Or maybe not. We'll just have to give our patience some exercise and see what develops. Meanwhile, maybe we could pass some time teachin' you how to properly shoot that Colt they just give back to you."

Taylor rubbed his hand against the holster belted to his waist. "I suppose."

"If you ever read any of them dime novels," Barclay said, "they're filled with gunfighters claiming to be fast draws, fannin' their guns with one hand while shooting with the other, always hittin' their target without so much as aiming. I'm here to tell you that ain't the way of the real world. I'll do what I can to teach you."

That evening, just before dusk, they stood facing a steep ridge where they had lifted a rotting tree trunk into place. They were well out of earshot of the Cookson Hills that now loomed in the distance. Barclay described the proper stance to take, the way to hold a pistol with not one hand but two, and how to sight down its barrel. "If time permits," he said, "it's a good idea to take a deep breath and hold it before you shoot. Keeps the hands steadier and gives you a better chance of hittin' your target. You always want to squeeze the trigger real slow."

"And if Indians or outlaws are suddenly bearing down on us and time is of the essence?"

"Then forget all the fancy stuff I'm telling you. Just point and start shootin'."

Their ammunition was limited, so Taylor's first lesson consisted of only six shots. Five raised small puffs of red dust well away from the target. One hit the old tree with a pleasing thud. "Now what you'll want to do," Barclay said, "is think on what you just done. Let your mind's eye take aim and shoot, over and over again, until it begins to feel a natural thing to do."

That night as he slept, Taylor fired shot after dream shot, reducing the tree trunk to nothing but pulp. It was when the target suddenly turned from a rotted tree to a smiling woman with long black hair, wearing a peasant blouse, that he woke, sweat beading on his forehead.

Hidden in a grove of trees atop the ridge, they took turns watching the landscape while their horses lazily grazed nearby, content with the inactivity. Dust devils raced along the flatland, and heat patterns danced from the surface as the sun rose high into the sky. That aside, there was no movement to see.

It was early on the third day when tiny dots appeared on the southeastern horizon. Slowly they came closer, finally taking the shape of four riders. Following behind were three packhorses. Barclay and Taylor shielded their eyes and watched as the small single-file caravan turned in the direction of the Hills.

"I think it's them," Barclay said.

Chapter 10

Had Barclay and Taylor been closer and able to view the faces of Hawk on the Hill and his followers, they would quickly have recognized their fatigue. Heads rolled and bobbed with the gait of their horses, bodies slumped forward in an effort to stay atop their mounts.

Their most recent raid had taken them south below the Red River, to a small trading post in Texas. With white soldiers armed with high-powered Sharps rifles now patrolling the northern and western parts of the Territory in search of those who had not remained on the reservations, the dwindling number of renegade bands had begun moving their encampments toward the southern border, the targets of their raids more far-reaching. And with greater risk.

The four buffalo hunters who had defended the small trading post—nothing more than a makeshift saloon, a blacksmith, and a tent where hides were being tanned—had put up a fierce fight before their defeat. Two of Hawk's warriors had been killed, along with three horses.

In recent days his anger had boiled into rage; the savagery he ordered heightened. The dead traders, the blacksmith, and the saloonkeeper had been scalped and decapitated, their heads mounted on poles to make them easy prey for the buzzards. It had been the idea of the woman who had ridden with them to cut out their hearts and burn them. She and the raiding party drank whiskey found in the saloon and hungrily ate from its small larder of dried buffalo meat and cold biscuits. Then they set the building afire.

As they left, the newly stolen horses piled with hides and rifles, only Talks With Spirits seemed pleased. She had argued against returning the bullet-riddled bodies of the two warriors to their camp. "It will only slow us," she said. "Their happy spirits are now in the clouds and they will understand. I will soon speak with them."

Hawk had begrudgingly agreed. He didn't like the fact that the white woman was becoming increasingly forceful with her demands. But as word of her special powers spread, new followers continued to come into his camp. For that reason she was valuable to him, and he chose to tolerate her efforts to influence his decisions.

"When you go to the Hills," she told him, "the hides should be traded for more rifles, not whiskey. If you are to be a successful war chief, you must have the proper firearms."

Taylor rose from his prone position and stretched his legs as the Indians disappeared into the trees that sheltered the trail leading into the Cookson Hills. "You figure that's who's gonna lead us to where we're wanting to go?"

"Maybe it is, maybe it ain't," Barclay said. "But I'm betting they'll take us in the right direction. These renegade bands might not like each other all that much, but they most often make their camps close by one another. If one bunch finds what it considers a safe place, the others ain't likely to be too far away."

"You never told me how it is you came to know so much about their ways," Taylor said.

"Back before my buffalo hunting days I joined up for a spell to help the army fight Indians. They talked about how we'd make the new frontier safer for settlers, all high-minded and noble about their intent. But what I seen was just a lot of murderin'. Killing Indians for killing's sake. Old men and womenfolk, children even. Seemed to me we wasn't no better than the savages we were hunting down. It boiled my stomach and one night, after everyone was sleeping, I just rode away from it. I ain't never looked back." He paused. "'Cept for a bad dream every now and then."

"So, what is it you see different about what we're aiming to do?"

"We ain't huntin' Indians," Barclay said. "We're just looking for two women. There's a difference. A big difference." There was a sharpness to his reply that Taylor had not heard before.

Taylor said, "You ain't thinking what we've set out to do is—how'd you say it?—high-minded and noble, are you?"

"No, I can't rightly claim that. But seems it needs to be done."

"I figure that's close enough."

It was nearing dusk when the Indians emerged from the Hills and headed southward. "Night ridin' is slow goin'," Barclay said as they watched the small caravan disappear into the soft haze of the horizon. "The rattlesnakes come out when the ground starts cooling, so be on the lookout for them. And there're prairie dog holes dug everywhere. The minute a horse steps in one of 'em, he's gonna be lame and useless. And that's if he ain't broke a leg.

" 'Bout the only thing you can count on from an Indian," Barclay said, "is that he's gonna seek the shortest distance to his destination. They're headed south and that's the direction they'll keep. The other thing to remember is we ain't lookin' for any confrontation, just the knowledge of where it is they've set up camp."

"And once we know that?"

"Best we wait and worry on that when the time comes."

Taylor pointed in the direction of the Hills. Three riders emerged from the shadows, headed in the same direction as the Indians.

Barclay shook his head. "This ain't good," he said. "Get your horse. We gotta figure a way to cut 'em off."

"What's their intent, you reckon?"

"If I had to guess at what Stallings is thinking," Barclay said, "I'd bet he's sent his men out to take back whatever it is he traded. And if the man he was dealin' with was the crazy one he told us about—this chief named Hawk—I'd guess he's finally decided the time's come to be done with him."

Riding along the ridge, they quickly put distance between themselves and Stallings's men before moving down onto the flatlands in search of a place to hide and wait. "Long as they ain't expectin' us, we've got the chance of surprise," Barclay said. "What it is we need to do is just block their way. And do it without shots being fired and sendin' a warning to those up ahead."

When they reached a wooded area where only a narrow

trail offered passage, Barclay dismounted and kneeled to examine the ground. "Don't take a tracker to see that the Indians passed this way not too long ago. Their mounts ain't shod," he said. "This'll be the way Stallings's boys will be comin' as well." After hiding their horses deeper into the trees, they returned, rifles in hand.

"Now," Barclay said as they waited in the shadows, "what we need to hope for is that these folks scare easy."

They could hear them long before they arrived. When they came into view, Barclay stepped from behind a tree as the riders approached in single file. He pointed his shotgun at the leader. "That's far enough," he said. When one moved his hand toward his holster, Taylor cocked his Winchester and aimed it at him. The rider withdrew his hand from his holster as the others raised their arms above their heads.

"We ain't aimin' to kill nobody unless it becomes necessary," Barclay said as Taylor collected the men's handguns and rifles. "We'd appreciate it if you boys would get down from your horses and take a seat on the ground."

As the three sat shoulder to shoulder, Barclay recognized them as the men who had taken their weapons at the base of the Cookson Hills before escorting them to Stallings's camp.

"What is it you're wanting?" asked one, an older man with several teeth missing and a scar across one cheek.

Barclay looked at Taylor and nodded in the direction of one of the men's horses. Thad took a rope from the saddle and, using the bowie knife that had been held to his throat only a few nights earlier, began cutting it into lengths. He tied the men's hands and feet.

The man spoke again. "I recall you being the ones who paid Big Boone a recent visit. I don't know what it is you want, but you can be sure he ain't gonna be pleased none by this."

"I'd be mightily surprised if he cared one way or another what happens to you, so long as you do what he tells you." Barclay cocked the shotgun and moved it to within a few inches of his head. Nearby, Taylor drew his Colt and aimed it in the direction of the others. "What is it you boys are intendin' to do roamin' out here in the dark? Explain that and maybe we can end our business."

"The boss wanted us following some Indians who came into the Hills today. They've got something of his and he wants it back."

"The payment he made for what they had to sell?"

The man nodded. "Big Boone acts all friendlylike when he comes around, sharing his whiskey and offering him a good exchange for his goods, but the fact is he has a particular dislike for that Comanche who calls himself Hawk. After they left, he called on us and said we was to track him down."

"And I suppose you was to shoot him dead?"

Puzzled, the man looked at Barclay, then Taylor. "Am I to think what you fellas are doing is *protecting* those savages?"

"I reckon you could put it that way." Barclay continued to point his shotgun in the direction of the captives while Taylor left to retrieve their horses. "What's now gonna happen is this. We'll be taking your horses—and your guns, of course—along with us. After we've properly distanced ourselves, we'll let your mounts go. If they're smart, maybe they'll make their way back home."

"What about us?"

Barclay shrugged. "That's more your worry than mine.

Likely, Big Boone will eventually send someone looking for you. If he don't, well . . ."

"He'll see you dead for this."

With the back of his right hand Barclay smacked the man's face and he went tumbling. "Now, that ain't a polite thing to say to your hosts," he said. "You need to learn some manners."

Taylor leaned down, his face just inches from the man. "If you're lucky enough to see him again, you can tell that fat old man that it ain't gonna happen unless he's willing to make a mighty long trip to get it done. 'Cause we ain't never passing through this godforsaken part of the world again."

They dismounted and rode away, the curses of three voices echoing into the still night. By then, the Indians were too far away to hear them.

On the bank of McGee Creek, Hawk's followers awaited his return. A dozen teepees circled fire pits where women prepared food in cast-iron pots that had been taken from the homes of white settlers. With no buffalo to be found and even deer having grown scarce, they prepared thin soups made with the meat from squirrels, rabbits, and turtles mixed with roots and nuts. It had been weeks since the warriors had returned with a steer cut from a rancher's herd or even a milk cow. Only when one of their horses came up lame and was slaughtered did they come anywhere close to a feast.

Some of the men sat making arrows and sharpening lances while others led horses to the creek for water. Naked children with swollen bellies gathered mesquite branches for the fires and played games. A few dogs, their ribs showing and fur dirty and matted, searched for scraps of food.

July Barstow, still wearing the threadbare gingham dress she'd had on when abducted, stood near one of the fires and let her tired eyes wander across the bleak encampment. And as was her daily habit, she thought of her son, Jakey, as she watched the children.

For a time she had counted the days that followed the morning her husband had been killed and she was taken from her Kansas home. It was a way, she thought, to keep her sanity. But soon they turned to weeks, then months, and she'd given up. Also gone were any thoughts of escape. It was that resignation that finally freed her from her imprisonment. In exchange, she became a slave, doing whatever labor was ordered. Even when they traveled to their next destination, she rode one of the mules, her hands free. And why not? She had no idea where she was or where the wandering band might be headed. The only hope left to her was that her son was safe and that she might be allowed to live another day.

Kate Two emerged from the teepee she shared with Hawk, wearing buckskins and a black hat that had belonged to her brother. A rifle rested on one shoulder. On each of her fingers were rings that had been taken in raids. In truth, her view of the shabby encampment was no more positive than that of the Barstow woman. She disliked its foul smells and the cloud of dust that hung over everything. The sad-eyed women irritated her, as did the children. The only bright spot in her life was the fact that she was now Talks With Sprits, and she enjoyed the reverent glances young warriors would steal as she walked among them. Each evening, as members of the small band gathered around a fire to hear her make contact with the dead, their eyes would be so fixed on her performance that they appeared hypnotized.

For now, she decided, the adulation of savages would have to suffice—until she could come up with a better plan for the remainder of her life.

"A quiet morning," she said as she approached July Barstow. Kate Two had no real interest in the white hostage aside from the fact that she served as someone to talk with and might eventually be worth a few dollars should a buyer be found. Hawk knew some English, but it came in strained phrases and misspoken words. July Barstow, on the other hand, was an educated woman with a command of the language.

"The men haven't yet returned," Barstow said.

Kate Two watched as July added wood to the fire. "I've seen the children gathered around you, listening to the stories you tell," she said. "Why is it you are trying to teach them to speak our language? Were you once a teacher?"

"It was something I had hoped to do. As to my teaching the children words of English, it seems to me that one day after all the hatred has died and peace comes, they might find themselves in a world where it will be necessary for them to be able to converse with white people."

Kate Two laughed and shook her head. "As long as there are men like Hawk and those who are crazy enough to follow him, there will be no peace or need for polite conversation."

July looked around and lowered her voice. "Is it possible you would give me an honest answer to a question?" she said. "What's to become of me?"

"It's not my place to say. Early on, when we were both held as prisoners, there was talk of our being sold to the Mexicans. But as you well know, my situation has changed considerably. And since the men have returned with no other white women in recent days, it isn't likely that Hawk would want to make that long journey for a single sale. Truth be told, I don't expect you would bring high dollar anyway.

"I've occasionally spoken in your behalf, telling Hawk that you are an able worker and that I consider you a friend. He has promised me that he will keep his men from bothering you."

"You consider me a friend?"

"Not really," Kate Two said. "But it's nice having someone to talk with on occasion so long as I've got to be in this hellhole. Once I'm gone—and that day will come—what happens to you is no concern of mine."

She turned and walked away laughing, her attention moving to the arrival of Hawk and his men.

She could smell the whiskey on Hawk's breath as he dismounted and approached her. Barely acknowledging him, she walked to the packhorses to examine the goods that had been received in exchange for the buffalo hides. She counted only half a dozen rifles, one small box of ammunition, several sacks of corn and beans, a single bolt of cloth, and two empty crock jugs.

Kate Two put her nose to the opening of one of the jugs, then glared at Hawk as he walked toward his teepee.

She followed, waiting until they were out of earshot of the others before she spoke. "You allowed the white trader to poison your good judgment with liquor. You did not receive fair exchange for the skins we fought so hard to acquire. You have been made a fool."

Hawk stiffened, but his piercing black eyes were unable to focus on her.

"The spirit fathers will not be happy that their war chief has failed his people," she said. "It is time for new wisdom."

Chapter 11

Taylor and Barclay reached the creek before sunup and slowly followed along its banks. Bullfrogs jumped at their approach, making widening circles as they splashed into the muddy water. Nearby an owl hooted his disapproval at their intrusion onto his hunting ground, and somewhere in the distance coyotes howled.

"Might be a smart idea to dismount and walk the horses," Barclay said. "We're gettin' close."

They traveled afoot for an hour before he signaled for Taylor to stop. "Smell that?" he said. "Mesquite burning. Somebody's gettin' the fires ready." In the first hint of daylight, they could see thin trails of white smoke rising in the distance.

Leaving their horses tethered, they silently followed the flow of the creek, careful not to emerge from the shadows of the trees. A gray dawn was approaching as they reached the top of a small rise that finally gave them a view of the Comanche camp. Below, a flurry of activity was under way.

Teepees were being dismantled, their poles stacked into neat piles. Sleds made of buffalo hides lashed to the long trunks of red oak saplings were being hitched behind horses and mules. Women and children collected items they were to carry.

"They're breaking camp," Taylor whispered as he lay prone beside Barclay. "Reckon something spooked 'em?"

"Something or somebody."

The previous evening, as Hawk and his followers sat around a council fire, Kate Two had played her role as Talks With Spirits with dramatic flair. Late in the afternoon she had announced that she had been summoned into the nearby hills to speak with the spirits and would return at nightfall to pass along their message. The ceremonial fire was already casting shadows when she rode out of the darkness into the camp. Her hair was now in braids, her cheeks were lined with yellow war paint, and in one hand she carried a lance.

She dismounted and walked to where Hawk waited, and stabbed the spear into the ground. "The almighty spirits have spoken," she said, "and you are to relay their words."

She talked slowly to allow him to translate. "The forefathers are not pleased," she began. "They say you are fighting your battles against the white man in a foolish way. You have only attacked their homes and taken things of too little value. The time has come to show new courage."

Pacing among the mesmerized warriors, she told of greater opportunities that waited on the plains south of the Red River. "If you are to be successful and grow in number, you must follow the spirit father's wishes and more boldly attack your enemy. You must raid his towns, his wagon trails, his stagecoaches. You must take more than his few horses and mules. You must take his money, for it is his true power."

Though she had no actual knowledge of such things, she said that the spirits had described to her large herds of buffalo that waited in Texas. To the south there would be no more hunger.

And then for a moment she fell silent, letting her eyes roam the nodding faces of the young warriors. Only the crackling of the fire broke the silence.

Finally she turned to face Hawk, a slight smile spreading across her painted face. "The spirits spoke of one other thing," she said. "It is their wish that I lead you on this new journey."

Hawk's jaws tightened as he glared at the white woman. He rose and quickly disappeared into the darkness. He had not translated her final words, but to those assembled the message was clear.

For some time Taylor and Barclay lay watching the activity prompted by Kate Two's grand performance.

"If one of us had a lick of good sense," Barclay said, "we woulda brung some field glasses along with us."

"Where do you think they're heading?"

"To the south, most likely. Down toward the Red River and as far away from Indian Territory as they can get."

Taylor's hand gripped Barclay's arm. With the other he pointed. "That's her," he said. Though the distance was too great to be certain, Thad was convinced that the figure he was looking at was a woman, dressed in buckskins and sitting astride a small paint. He was equally certain it was the same woman he'd long ago encountered in the Benders' way station. Across her shoulder was a rifle.

Barclay shielded his eyes and squinted. "Seems to me

she's ordering folks about," he said. "Huh. Not exactly what you'd expect of a white woman held against her will."

They watched in silence as the caravan slowly began to move southward, Kate Two riding point. In the rear, walking among the children and dogs, was another woman. Even from a distance the men could see that her shoulders were slumped, her steps a weary shuffle.

"It appears," Barclay said, "that we found those we've been looking for."

They waited until the Comanches had disappeared beyond the horizon before leaving their position and walking down to the abandoned campsite. Aside from the gray ashes of the campfires and cleared ground that had been reduced to red powder, there was little to indicate that anyone had ever been there.

Barclay looked in the direction the Indians had taken and shook his head. "Never figured on livin' long enough to see a sight like that," he said. "A bunch of savages being led off by a white woman. She must have some mighty convincin' powers."

"Could be they come to her from those dead people she claims to have conversations with."

Barclay snorted. "These Comanches might be a mean lot and the best horsemen around—and I'm includin' Union and Confederate cavalry—but ain't nobody ever claimed they're smart thinkers. What they don't seem to know is they're likely to meet up with a heap of trouble if they're going into Texas. There's bluecoats down there who can't wait to shoot 'em dead and be done with it.

"Ever since President Grant got fed up with all the broken

peace treaties and commissioned that Civil War hero Mackenzie to round up those hostiles still terrorizing settlers, a sizable number of Indians have gotten themselves killed. And from what I hear, it ain't going to be over until there's none left."

"So, how does that help us with what we're attempting to do?"

"It might be that once we find out where these people are gonna settle, we can find some help," Barclay said. "Seems it would be a wiser choice than tryin' to do it on our own and gettin' ourselves scalped. For the time being, though, all we can do is just keep following along until we figure a way to get our business done."

Taylor said nothing. The hard miles they had traveled had finally led them to their destination. Now it was again moving out of reach. He wondered if their journey would ever end. On the other hand, he had come to a new realization as he'd watched the small band take leave of its camp. When he'd seen the Bender woman, the hatred he'd nurtured rose briefly in his chest. Then it was replaced by another emotion at the sight of Jakey's mother being forced to march along behind the renegades. His thoughts returned to the young boy, scared and clad in overalls, acting far more courageous that his age required. And at that moment he realized that it was no longer Kate Two who was the reason for his quest.

As they walked toward the creek, the silence was broken by the sound of a flock of buzzards taking flight. Reaching the bank, they saw a naked body floating facedown in the shallow stream. "Looks like somebody got left behind," Barclay said.

Taylor removed his boots and waded into the water. As he dragged the body to the bank and turned it over, he could see that the dead Indian's eyes were still open, his mouth agape. Across his throat was a jagged gash.

"If I'm guessin' right as to who this might be," Barclay said, "it seems someone's done ol' Boone Stallings a great favor."

"You saying this is the man he called Hawk?"

Barclay nodded. "Used to be."

"What do you reckon we ought to do with him?"

"Seems to me the buzzards was here first."

Kate Two pulled her hat far down on her forehead as she watched from a sandbar while her new followers forded the shallow Red River. The water came only to the knees of those who shouldered the party's few belongings, carrying them into a land that the United States government had forbidden them to enter. The river formed a border between the Indian Territory and the new state of Texas—and for those who ignored the edict to stay out, dire consequences dealt by trained regiments of Indian fighters were promised.

The children waited on the opposite bank until they were lifted onto horses and ridden across. At their sides, the dogs swam the short distance. July Barstow, exhausted and lightheaded from the heat, held to the tail of one of the horses as she followed along, her tattered dress soaked by the muddy water, her bare feet burying into the sandy river bottom with each step.

That the ragtag band of renegades had so willingly agreed to follow her had come as a welcome surprise to Kate Two. Though confident in her ability to manipulate and control, she had taken a big chance when she announced that she had been chosen to replace Hawk as their leader. That his warriors—a few who understood bits of English—had embraced the notion, she felt, was a testimony to their utter stupidity and willingness to believe that she was actually in possession of mystical powers. When she explained that the spirit fathers had called Hawk on the Hill into the clouds, there to receive their wisdom before he returned, none had questioned.

If things went as she hoped, she would need to carry out the ruse only a while longer.

For many nights, while lying next to Hawk, she had plotted a way to escape the squalor of Indian life and return to the world she'd previously known. Now she had finally put the plan into motion.

The only truth she had spoken the night she stood before the council fire was that money was what empowered the white man. For her to make her escape, she would need that empowerment as well. A few successful raids, she hoped, would accomplish that goal. Then it would be time to lead her followers into the hands of the Indian fighters. The role she would then play would be that of a helpless captive in need of being saved from the heartless savages.

The caravan followed an old buffalo trail for the remainder of the day, reaching an isolated canyon just before sundown. Though fires were started, the only food available was smoked strips of horse meat and wild berries collected along the way. In a nearby stream, horses were watered as the weary travelers washed the dust and mud from their bodies.

With no time to erect the teepees before dark, buffalo skins were spread on the ground for sleeping.

At first light, Kate Two told the warriors that scouts would be sent out to locate the nearest settlement or farm with livestock that could be stolen and herded back to camp.

Chapter 12

The settlement of Dawson's Ridge was typical of the small towns that were beginning to appear on the Texas plains. A year earlier, when the wagon train had arrived, its members had surveyed the fertile grasslands, the nearby creek, which promised an adequate water supply, and the high vista, which offered a sweeping view in all directions, and called their journey to an end. With their approval, Deke Dawson, the self-appointed leader of those who had traveled from Tennessee, proclaimed it their new home. There was little argument when he suggested that the hamlet be given his name or that he be elected by a show of hands as its mayor.

A portly man with a bushy mustache and a thick mane of white hair, Dawson decades earlier had enjoyed the power of local politics before accusations of bribe-taking and various other illegal activities had forced him from office, making it necessary for him to quickly head west. To his fellow travelers he mentioned nothing of the shady dealings he'd been involved in, instead bragging that among his dearest friends back in Tennessee had been a fellow politician named Davy Crockett.

The town grew quickly as the settlers moved from tents fashioned from the covers of their wagons into sturdy cabins built from native wood and stone. Soon there was a livery and a corral, a laundry near the creek, and a tent beneath which Sunday sermons were delivered by a lay preacher who had made the trek west. Once a still was erected and fully operational, a social center where meals and whiskey were available was erected. "We'll not call it a saloon," Mayor Dawson insisted, "for there will be no women of bad character passing through its doors. The nightly playing of cards, however, will be allowed so long as the wagers are small and friendly made."

The game hunting and fishing were good, crops grew, and the spring arrival of half a dozen calves promised the beginning of a herd of cattle. And as other passersby happened onto the community, its population grew. One day soon, Dawson said, they would have need of a school and the appointment of a town marshal to see to the proper order of things. On days when he dreamed on an even grander scale, he spoke of a hotel with its own dining room and a dry goods store and grocery that would sell items regularly delivered by stagecoach and supply wagon.

It was an unusually hot afternoon when two boys, trailed by a panting dog that was not at all sure what the commotion was all about, ran toward the Dawson's Ridge Social Center. A hen and her flock of chicks scattered from their path. "Soldiers are coming," the youngsters said in unison as they waved their sun-browned arms in the direction of the creek.

Deke Dawson stood in the street, hat in hand and a wide smile on his face, as the small detail of Union soldiers approached. "Mighty proud to see you boys," he said. "Step down and tell us what it is that brings you to our fine little town."

"Just passing through on the way to rejoin Colonel Mackenzie," the leader, a stocky, bearded redhead, said, and tipped his hat. "Sergeant Patrick Murphy, D Company, Fourth Cavalry."

"A mighty long ride from home," Dawson said as a crowd gathered.

A dozen men, their blue uniforms powdered with trail dust, dismounted at Sergeant Murphy's signal. For over a year they had been away from home and families, fighting renegade bands of Indians terrorizing the Texas plains. Most of the major battles had been fought and won farther to the east in places with names like Palo Duro Canyon and Adobe Walls, leaving only isolated uprisings to be addressed. Promising that their work was nearly done, Mackenzie had divided his regiments into small companies and details, assigning them to seek out any remaining war parties. His orders had been simple. If the Indians refused to surrender and return to Fort Sill as prisoners, they were to be killed.

"To put your mind at ease," Murphy said. "We've been down south and have seen no sign of any savages, Comanche or Kiowa."

"All the same, we continue to keep a watchful eye," Dawson said. "We've got men who take their turn standing guard along the ridge every night. And we've stored away ample weaponry."

"Which I hope you never have need to use," Murphy said.

"Your words to God Almighty's ear," the lay preacher yelled out from the crowd. "Amen to that," said another.

"I'm sure the good colonel is anxious for your return," Dawson said, "but before you take leave we'd like an opportunity to show our hospitality. If you boys will join us out of the heat, the first taste of whiskey will be at my expense. And while you're washing the dust from your throats I 'spect the womenfolk would be happy to prepare you a meal far better than any you've had while on the trail."

The brief stop turned into an overnight stay for the soldiers. They drank ample amounts of Dawson's Ridge's whiskey and ate heaping bowls of venison and potato stew along with large servings of hot corn bread. Soon two fiddle players were providing music. Before nightfall several of the women arrived with cast-iron pots filled with cobbler made from wild blueberries and pecans.

Delighted by the company, the festive atmosphere, and the fascinating stories being told, the townspeople volunteered their homes to the soldiers for the night, moving into the Social Center, where they made pallets for their own evening's rest.

With the visiting company of soldiers in their midst, safety from any intruders was ensured; thus no sentries were sent to their stations.

From a safe distance the two Comanche scouts took advantage of a full moon to survey the landscape of the small settlement and listen to the faint sounds of music and laughter. A day's ride away, their new leader would be pleased to hear their news.

"It's not likely they'll be going far before they set up a new campsite," Barclay said as he unsaddled his horse. He and

Taylor had crossed into Texas and followed the travois tracks made by the Comanches until it was almost dark. "I reckon we won't be losing much ground if we get ourselves some rest."

Thad had been unusually quiet during the day, his thoughts skipping from one thing to another as they rode. Now, as they set up camp, he wondered about home and if Sister was worried for his safety and how she and young Jakey were. The milky eyes of the dead Indian he'd pulled from the creek came to mind. So did the distant images of the two women they were following after. And most of all, he pondered the strange and quiet man he was riding alongside. Tater Barclay was a mystery, equal parts kind *("If you're of a mind to make this fool's journey it occurs to me you might find some company of use. . . .")* and hard *("Seems to me the buzzards was here first. . . .")*. A lonely man, Taylor thought. As he considered such things, he also wondered if, for the first time in his life, he'd met a person he could honestly call a friend.

Barclay broke the silence with a grunt as he stretched out on his saddle blanket. "I'd greatly admire to soon see some civilization," he said. "Been so long since I was drunk, I've about forgot how it's properly done."

The following morning the two men had traveled only a few miles before the tracks of the Comanche caravan suddenly disappeared. The renegades had used branches to sweep away the marks left by the sleds and the footprints of those who followed along behind them. They had worked late into the night to erase their trail and then had turned from their southward course to travel east before arriving at the hidden canyon that would be their new home.

Urging their horses to a nearby rise, Taylor and Barclay shaded their eyes and squinted into the rising sun. They saw nothing that would indicate the whereabouts of those they'd been following. On the southern horizon, however, a faint cloud of dust came into view.

"Whoever it is," Taylor said, "they're coming instead of going. And their pace is far quicker than that the Comanches were keeping."

Barclay fixed his gaze on the dust cloud until he could see that it was being made by horsemen riding two by two, traveling in a westerly direction. When he saw that they were dressed in blue, he smiled. "Could be that we got company that's friendly," he said. "I figure we ought to catch up to 'em and say howdy."

At his rider's urging Magazine was soon in a full gallop, with Barclay's horse close behind. Taylor was waving his oversized hat as he neared the company of soldiers. Murphy signaled his troops to a halt and ordered them to raise their weapons.

"State your business," he said as Taylor and Barclay reined their horses to a stop.

"We been followin' after a band of Comanches," Barclay said.

Murphy smiled thinly. "We've been in these parts for over a week now and have seen no sign of Indians."

"They just crossed the Red River a few days back, moving their camp down this way," Taylor said.

"How many of them, not counting women and elderly?"

"Twenty, maybe a few more. Among them is a female they've kidnapped." Taylor looked at Barclay, and debated briefly whether to share his belief that they were also being led by a white woman, but decided against it. Such an observation, he knew, would immediately brand him as one crazed by too much sun.

"And what is your plan once you catch up to them?" Murphy asked.

"That part we ain't exactly figured out yet."

The residents of Dawson's Ridge were surprised to see the soldiers returning. Again, it was Deke Dawson who hurried to greet them. "Wasn't expecting a return visit quite so soon," he said.

"It appears we might have spoken too soon about the safety of your town," Sergeant Murphy said. He nodded in the direction of the two men who accompanied them and explained that they had seen Indians to the north just days earlier. "Since I've never made these fellas' acquaintance, I can't rightfully vouch for their claim. But I felt a duty to give you a warning."

As he spoke, a man tied his mule to the hitching post in front of the Social Center and hurried toward Dawson and the crowd that had again gathered. By the time he reached them, he was excited and out of breath. "Somebody took away one of the calves last night," he said.

Dawson placed a hand on his shoulder. "You sure it wasn't varmints, a pack of wolves or coyotes?"

"Not unless they've learned how to unlock a gate and leave it standing open."

A look of concern crossed Murphy's face as he listened to the exchange. "It appears while we were enjoying your gracious hospitality last evening, we let our guard down a bit too much. I believe that what these men told us is the honest truth. Most likely you were visited in the night by renegades wishing to get a lay of the land."

He motioned for two members of his detail to approach. "You will be on your way to report to Colonel Mackenzie and advise him of the reason for our delay," he said. "The rest of us will remain here to determine the seriousness of this situation."

Chapter 13

The Social Center, normally quiet and empty until much later in the day, was filled with activity after Mayor Dawson called for an immediate town meeting. Tables were moved aside, chairs aligned in rows, and the clapboard windows opened to allow whatever breeze there might be to flow through.

Dawson had invited all of the soldiers to attend, but Murphy suggested his men's time would be better spent investigating ways the town might be fortified against possible attack. Thus it was only the sergeant, Taylor, and Barclay who stood in the front of the room when the mayor called the meeting to order.

"We're here to discuss a matter of dire concern, as most of you already know," Dawson said. "It has been brought to our attention that our fine community might be in danger of attack from savages lurking nearby." He pointed to the two strangers who had recently arrived. "These two gentlemen have knowledge that a band of Comanches recently made its way across the northern border and headed in our direction. It is supposed they are now somewhere nearby and most likely considering an attack on Dawson's Ridge.

"To our good fortune," he said, wiping beads of sweat from his brow, "we have in our midst a group of men who are among the finest Indian fighters on the frontier. And being the good soldiers and brave men that they are, they have returned to help us in our time of need."

Reluctantly the mayor—clearly enjoying the opportunity to demonstrate his public speaking skills—then turned the meeting over to Murphy.

The sergeant was several inches short of six feet tall, his red hair curling around his ears. His face seemed permanently red from the Texas sun.

"As things now stand," he said, "we have only speculation that you're in harm's way. With luck, this concern will pass without need for further worry. But until we're certain of it, it's best we prepare."

He had already begun to formulate a plan. His men, he explained, were determining the locations where Dawson's Ridge might be most vulnerable. The entrances to the town would be barricaded by wagons, rain barrels, anything that would block the way of an attacker and provide shelter for armed defenders. A rotation of both soldiers and men of the community would be assigned to stand guard, night and day, along the ridge, near the creek, and toward the north. Under no circumstances would anyone be allowed to go beyond the immediate vicinity.

"If there is an attack," Murphy said, "it would likely come at night. The fact that we've currently got a full moon should give us time to prepare. Knowing Indians, particularly Comanches, they don't like to move about until it's pitch-dark."

A question came from the back of the room. "Why don't

we just attack *them*, locate their whereabouts, and get this done and over with?"

"At some point," Murphy said, "that might be an option. For now, though, the concern is for the safety of this town and the folks living here, particularly the women and children. Since we don't yet know their location, we'll stay put for a time and see if they're bold enough to try something."

"So, we're just to wait?"

"For the time being."

Mayor Dawson stepped up next to Murphy. "Thank you, Sergeant. Please know that the folks here stand ready to do whatever is necessary. There's not a man here who doesn't own a rifle or shotgun or at least a sidearm, and all know how to use them. Not with the proficiency of you and your men, of course, but we're a hearty lot and will gladly follow your command."

Murphy only nodded before making his way toward the door. "My men," he said, "will pitch tents and bivouac on the south ridge."

As the sergeant left, Dawson turned to Taylor and Barclay. "You boys are welcome to bunk down at the livery. Old man Jackson's got some spare cots he makes available to travelers. Since it was you who gave us warning, I'll see to it that there'll be no charge." He stepped back and examined the two strangers. "Could be that you might want to take advantage of our laundry as well."

Over the next several days, tension settled over Dawson's Ridge. People tried to go about their daily routines, all the while wondering if the next sound they might hear would be that of war cries and gunfire. It was like being held hostage in one's own home. Sentries manned their assigned posts and Murphy constantly rode the perimeter to make sure his men remained alert. Children, normally free to roam the town and play along the creek bank, remained close to their concerned mothers.

"I've enjoyed about all the waiting I can abide," Taylor said as he stood in front of the livery grooming Magazine. He and Barclay took their turns as lookouts at night and mingled with the townspeople during the day. They were wearing clean clothes for the first time in weeks and enjoying the coffee brewed each morning at the Social Center. Still, they found time weighing heavily. "I see no good that can come of this," he added.

The waiting ended the following night. With a waning moon low on the horizon, a small party of Comanches approached the town armed with Winchesters and bows. Blending into the shadows, they silently approached two guards on the southern ridge and quickly subdued them. After cutting the settlers' throats, they mounted their ponies and fired shots into the air and rode away.

A panic spread when the two dead men were brought to the center of town, their bodies stretched across horses and covered by military blankets. Women cried and covered the eyes of their frightened children. A dog approached one of the horses carrying the body of his master and began to whine.

"They're wanting us to follow," Sergeant Murphy said. "Most likely their plan is to lure as much of our firepower as possible away from town so they can attack in our absence."

"So, what's *our* plan?" Barclay growled. For the first time since they'd met, Taylor saw anger in his friend's eyes. The mayor stood by silently.

"We'll follow immediately and attack while the men of the town stay back to stand guard," Murphy said. "Tracking their retreat in daylight should be no problem, and I feel certain we have far more weapons than they do. It's time this is ended."

Murphy instructed the townspeople to bury the dead and continue their vigil, then led his troopers out of Dawson's Ridge.

"I don't like the looks of this," Barclay muttered, but he mounted and followed, Taylor behind him.

They had been following the Comanches' trail for a couple of hours when Barclay nudged his horse into a trot and moved up to ride next to the sergeant. "It ain't likely this'll mean anything to you," he said, "but there's one thing I neglected to tell you about these renegades we're going after. I feared you might think me plumb crazy."

Murphy looked at him without a reply.

"When we seen them breakin' camp to head this way," Barclay said, "the person leading them was a white woman."

The sergeant laughed. "Never heard of such a thing. I thought you said you boys were following after a woman who was kidnapped."

"We are. Only there're two of them. A lady bein' held against her will and the one who's now ridin' out front. It's the latter I felt obliged to warn you about." He told of finding the body of Hawk on the Hill floating in the creek and the earlier murder of Taylor's father. "My guess is she's the one responsible for both killings. What I'm sayin' is, if you've got any cause to hesitate about shooting a woman, just step aside and me and my partner will gladly tend to it."

Taylor had ridden up and was listening to the conversation when Murphy asked what the woman looked like.

"The Devil," he said.

The narrow entrance to the canyon was barely visible, hidden in a tangle of underbrush and tumbleweeds. Murphy took his field glasses from his saddlebag and carefully scanned the walls and the plateau above for signs that a trap had been set. Seeing no movement or glint from rifle barrels, he waved his men forward. His plan was one he'd used before during his search for renegade bands. He and his troops would charge the encampment with rifles raised, demanding surrender. In most cases that had worked, since those they tracked down were often too tired, hungry, and ill to offer any resistance But if the Comanches chose to defend themselves or take flight, his men were ordered to immediately shoot to kill.

They kicked their horses into a gallop and rode through the entrance in single file. They passed an empty draw on the left, then entered a small clearing fifty yards ahead. A short distance away they could see smoke rising from campfires. As they approached the circle of teepees near a steep bluff, they saw a few women milling about.

From behind them came the sound of a rifle being cocked. Taylor looked around them. They had entered a box canyon with but one way in or out.

Barclay leaned toward Taylor as he brought his rifle to his shoulder. "Don't see no horses, and I don't believe that draw we passed was empty," he said just as the first shot echoed through the canyon. The soldier in front of them slumped in his saddle, blood pouring from a hole in the back of his neck. The Indian women disappeared into the teepees.

Two dozen Comanches, wearing full war paint and screaming battle cries, approached from the same entrance through which the soldiers had traveled. Instead of hiding in the rocks above, they had waited in the draw until the soldiers had entered the canyon, then followed, blocking the only exit.

Murphy turned to see the approaching renegades. "Begin firing," he yelled. As he gave the order, his horse buckled beneath him as two arrows pierced its flank and it fell sideways, pinning the sergeant's right side to the ground. He screamed and pulled himself free. His right leg was at an unnatural angle.

He pulled his body behind the dying animal and began firing with his carbine as his men milled about and searched for cover. The smoke from the rapid exchange of gunfire clouded the floor of the canyon. Two other soldiers were shot. As their bodies pitched to the ground, their mounts were hit and fell over them. Soon the acrid scent of blood mixed with the smell of gunpowder.

"They're shootin' the horses," Barclay said. "We gotta get out of here before we're afoot and trapped."

Taylor fired his Colt at a renegade charging toward him, surprised that he hit him high in the chest. Seconds later, his pistol empty, he grabbed his Winchester and began emptying it into the crowd of oncoming Comanches. Then he saw his partner's mare go down on her front knees. More shots rang out and Barclay clutched his shoulder, his body tilting to one side as his rifle fell away.

On hands and knees, he yelled at Taylor, "Get out of here. Now!"

Taylor reined Magazine hard to the left and rode toward

where Barclay lay. He reached one hand down and helped him onto the horse's rump. "Hang on," he said, "I'm gonna try going right through them." He kicked Magazine in the ribs and snapped his reins and the horse took off directly into the Indians.

The sudden charge into them surprised the ambushers focused on the men in blue uniforms. Taylor leaned forward in the saddle, his face against Magazine's neck, and fired shots without aiming while Barclay held tightly to his waist. One of the Indians moved to cut them off. Taylor shot him and knocked him from his pony.

Magazine galloped through the Indians and jumped over fallen bodies as he made his way to the mouth of the canyon. Not a single soldier followed.

As they entered the canyon, Barclay looked up to see Kate Two standing on a bluff watching the massacre.

Magazine was quickly lathered with sweat, his breath coming in labored grunts as he raced toward the open plains. Barclay held tightly to Taylor's waist. "Ease up," he said. "They ain't gonna come after us." His voice was hoarse with pain. "They're too busy celebratin' their victory."

Taylor eased up on Magazine. He felt Barclay's grip relax and reached back to steady the big man's limp body. He reined his horse to a stop and eased Barclay to the ground. The wound to Tater's shoulder had darkened one side of his shirt with blood. As Taylor examined his partner, he saw that he had also been shot just above his left knee. Using his bowie knife, Taylor cut the pant leg away and made it into a tourniquet that he quickly applied. He pressed the remainder of the bloody cloth to the shoulder wound. While checking the horizon for Comanches who might have followed, he retrieved his canteen and splashed water on Barclay's face. His eyes fluttered, then opened.

"You've got to ride," Taylor said.

Though Barclay was conscious, his eyes were glazed, and he was unable to get to his feet without help. With great difficulty Taylor helped him onto Magazine. "Grip the saddle horn," he said as he climbed on behind and placed one arm around Barclay's waist.

"Not sure I'm gonna make it."

"You will." Taylor wondered if anyone in Dawson's Ridge's had medical knowledge as he urged the horse into a fast trot.

Barclay's head was lolling from side to side and his eyes were closed by the time they reached town. An anxious crowd gathered and helped the injured rider to the ground.

"He's hurt bad," Taylor said. "Is there anybody here who knows doctoring?"

A skinny young man wearing overalls and a straw hat pushed his way forward. "That would be me," he said. "Fetch him over to my place." He looked at Barclay's wounds. "And be quick about it."

Sloan Reynolds had spent his younger days hoping to one day go back East and study to become a doctor. However, financial hard times had killed the dream long before he and his bride had joined the wagon train that found its way to Dawson's Ridge. What he knew about medicine had been self-taught as he'd learned to care for his family's livestock and tend the small aches and pains of neighbors. He'd mended broken bones and once stitched up a man who had been in a knife fight, but had never before dealt with a gunshot wound.

Taylor placed Barclay on a bed as Reynolds's wife brought a basin of hot water and towels from her kitchen. Reynolds cleaned dried blood away from the wounds and saw that the shot to the shoulder had entered the front and exited the back. "That would be the good news," he said. "The bad news is that there's still a bullet in his leg that will need to be removed."

He looked at Taylor. "Hurry over to the Social Center and tell them we'll be needing a jug of whiskey."

Minutes later, as Reynolds's wife applied damp cloths to Barclay's forehead in an attempt to reduce his fever, Taylor held a tin cup to his lips, urging him to sip the whiskey. Tater swallowed and managed a pained grin. "That," he whispered, "is about the only good thing that's occurred all day. Aside from the fact that I didn't get myself scalped, of course." Then he removed the towel from his forehead and put a corner of it in his mouth and bit down.

Once Barclay was drunk and a knife sterilized, Reynolds removed the bullet, then began stitching the wounds with needle and thread from his wife's sewing basket. "He seems a hardy fella," he said. "If we make sure the bleeding don't start up again and keep him lying still, there's a good chance he'll be okay."

Taylor was bathed in sweat as he walked from the cabin. He could barely move. The events of the day—the gun battle, the race to get back to Dawson's Bluff, and the ordeal he'd just viewed—had left him so weak that he needed to brace himself against the railing on the front porch. Townspeople stood waiting to learn what had happened. Mayor Dawson stepped forward and placed an arm across his shoulder.

"We was ambushed," Thad said, "Made fools of. Me and Tater were the only ones to get away. I can't rightful say what the Indians are of a mind to do next. Some of them died as well. But we'll need to continue careful watch, day and night, should they choose to attack."

With that he returned to Barclay's side, where he would remain for the next two days and nights.

Despite the offer to stay at the Reynoldses' cabin while he recuperated, Barclay insisted that he be helped back to the livery where his cot awaited. Though still in pain and not yet able to walk, he had regained his senses and ill temper—a good sign, Taylor felt. Reynolds checked on him several times a day, applying fresh bandages and making sure there was no infection. Women of the town arrived with broth and loaves of warm bread.

And as the days passed, a quiet settled over the community. Though the guard posts were constantly manned and the blockades stayed in place, there was no sighting of the Comanches.

It was early evening when the mayor appeared at the livery, carrying a small jar of whiskey. "Seemed to me it was high time to drink to your good health," he said as he handed cups to Barclay and Taylor. The three men drank in silence before Dawson continued. "I've got something on my mind that I'd admire to get your opinion on," he said as he looked at Taylor. "As you're no doubt aware, folks are nervous about the possibility of the savages killing more of our people. The folks of our fine community are of good, strong stock—to be sure—but my worry is that nervousness is likely to cause some unwanted behavior. Can't say what form it might take, but it gives me cause for concern. From what I hear, there's been more drinking down at the Social Center of late and tempers have occasionally flared.

"It's that, and the fact that we're in need of leadership I'm not qualified to give that brings me here with my question."

Taylor glanced down at Barclay, who only held out his cup for a refill.

"Mr. Taylor, I find that what we're in need of is a town marshal, someone folks can look up to in this dangerous time. Is it possible that in your background is some experience as a lawman?"

Barclay responded first. "Back in Kansas," he said, "he was once officially deputized. Seen him sworn in myself. I reckon that still holds even if he's lacking a badge. You want my opinion, he'd make a right fine town marshal."

"In that case," Dawson said, "I'm officially offering you the job. Just what we might be able to pay for your services, I can't for sure say."

Taylor looked at both of them and was silent for a few moments. "I'll need some time to think on it," he said. "And if I do agree, it will be only for a brief time, until this matter with the renegades is resolved and my friend here is back in good health. We've still got matters to tend to that have nothing to do with Dawson's Ridge."

"Fair enough," the mayor said. "Sleep on it and we'll talk again in the morning." With that he raised his cup in a farewell salute and departed, leaving the half-full jar of whiskey behind.

Barclay grunted. "Well, well, well . . . I 'spect you'd better pour me another," he said, "so I can properly drink to the fact that I'm now ridin' with a man of the law."

"You know better than any that my qualifications are slim."

Barclay's expression turned serious. "Since my mind's cleared," he said, "I've been lyin' here doing a lot of thinking. First off, I ain't properly thanked you for saving my life. Not that it's worth all that much, but I do appreciate it. Second, I was wonderin' about your thoughts on what occurred up in that canyon."

"We should never have allowed ourselves to be drawn into that kind of trap."

"I'd say that was more the responsibility of Sergeant Murphy—God rest his soul—than any concern of yours. I was right proud of the way you handled yourself once all the shootin' started."

"Truth is, I was scared to death."

"Which is a natural thing," Barclay said. "What I was mostly wonderin' about was your feelings over havin' to kill somebody, even though it was only an Indian. My guess is that was your first time."

Taylor nodded.

"I'd be surprised if it's the last before we get ourselves back home," Barclay said.

In the distant canyon, the dead Comanche warriors had been wrapped in buffalo skins and buried beneath mounds of rocks. Late into the night mournful chants rang through the encampment. Kate Two called the remainder of her followers together and praised their victory, then asked for silence as she reached out to the souls of those who had lost their lives. "They are in a happy place," she said, "sitting at the sides of their fathers and preparing to follow the large herds of buffalo. You are not to worry about them. There are no white devils for as far as their eyes can see."

The ceremony came to an end when the disemboweled bodies of the soldiers were thrown into a ravine and set ablaze. Nearby, the hides of their slaughtered horses were already stretched on frames and drying.

Chapter 14

In the days following the massacre of the soldiers, the mood of Dawson's Ridge was far calmer than Thad Taylor had anticipated. The barricades at each end of town remained in place and the routine of standing guard was continued by the men while the women went about their daily chores in small groups, their children never out of sight. Still, with each passing day the threat of an attack seemed a more distant concern. The townspeople appeared to be resigned to the situation and had chosen to view it more as a short-term inconvenience that would soon be resolved.

Tater Barclay was a different story. As he slowly mended, his arm in a sling and walking with a crutch, he had begun turning away the offers of food brought by the women, complained when Sloan Reynolds would appear to redress his wounds, and hobbled about town with a constant scowl on his face. "Being stove up like this," he confided to Taylor, "makes a man of no use." He had begun spending hours in the Social Center, drinking whiskey while the rest of Dawson's Ridge went about its business.

One evening, after making his rounds to see that armed

guards were in their places and women and children were safely inside their houses, Taylor sought out his traveling partner and found him seated alone in a darkened corner of the Social Center. His head rested on a table and he was snoring loudly.

Thad put his hand on Barclay's good shoulder and shook him awake. "Time we get on over to the livery," he said.

Barclay slowly raised his head. "Well, if it ain't the marshal come to fetch the town drunk," he said, his watery eyes squinted as he looked up. "This makes me feel right to home."

The night air had helped sober him by the time they reached the livery. Barclay sat on his cot. "I apologize for not bein' much use to you of late," he said. "Never been crippled up before and I'm havin' a devil of a time dealin' with it."

"Seems you're dealing with more than being stove up," Taylor said. In the weeks they had ridden together, he had come to recognize his partner's moods. And since the nights when he'd sat beside Barclay's bed, wondering if he would survive, there was a question he'd wanted to ask. Now was as good a time as any.

"I got something to speak with you about that's likely none of my business," he said.

"Speak away. I got no secrets worth keeping."

"Back when you was fighting your fever and talking crazy in your sleep, you kept calling out to somebody name of Ray Boy. I kept thinking maybe it was kin I'd need to be in touch with if you took a turn for the worse and died on me."

Tater bent his head into his hands and didn't reply for quite some time. "He was my brother," he said. "My younger brother."

"By your speaking in the past tense, I get the strong impression he's no longer living."

Barclay shook his head and told of accompanying his brother and his family from Arkansas to stake claims in Kansas. "They found them a nice little place and after I helped 'em get settled in, I went lookin' for me a spot of my own, the one you seen when you returned my wagon.

"It wasn't no more than a couple of miles away from 'em, but it was distance enough to give us both our privacy. I'd ride over and visit on most Sundays, playin' with the young'uns and helpin' Ray Boy with whatever needed an extra hand. His wife was a fine cook and would always serve up a good meal before it was time for me to head home.

"They were about as happy as folks got a right to be."

Taylor had left his chair and stood leaning against a wall.

Barclay recalled the morning he'd seen the distant smoke rising from his brother's place and of arriving to find the entire family dead, their house and barn reduced to ashes. "Never in my life, before or since, have I felt the kind of anger I did that day. That was the cause for me to join up and become an Indian fighter for a time to see that every last one of them no-good savages died a terrible death. The sad feelings never went away—still haven't—but after a while I just got plumb weary of carryin' around all that hate. No matter what I might do, it wasn't gonna bring Ray Boy and his family back. I ain't sure I'm proud of it, but what I chose to do was give up on the idea of revenge and see if I could move on with my own life.

"Then you showed up talkin' of the killin' of your pa and the kidnapping of that boy's mama, and I understood what it was you were feeling. All of what I'd tried to put away—

losin' my only kin, my feelings for the Comanche devils—returned. Like it had been just hiding in the back of my mind, lookin' for a way to come forward again. And it has. I don't rightly know how to deal with the feelings, but they now come to me in my sleep and accompany me through my days. Like somethin' ain't been finished and needs to be."

Taylor felt a sadness sweep over him as he listened. He finally understood Barclay's willingness to travel along with him. He'd never for a minute considered it a "fool's journey." Rather, it was something he'd long waited to do.

"Maybe together," Taylor said, "we can see it done."

Barclay stretched out on his cot. "Not till I can get to where I ain't walkin' around like I'm a hunnerd years old."

"Ornery as you seem to be, I'm betting that won't be too long."

For the first time in days, Tater was smiling as Taylor left the livery to go check on those standing watch.

The following morning Barclay awoke to the sound of a bell ringing, at first thinking it was his imagination or perhaps the lingering effect of the previous evening's whiskey binge. Getting to his feet, he reached for his crutch and hobbled into the street.

A pretty young woman, her hair the gold of fresh hay, sat astride a mule, ringing a hand bell as she rode toward the middle of town. Following behind was a man dressed entirely in black, his deep-set eyes looking out from a face that was almost skeletal. He was holding a Bible against his chest.

Only after a small crowd had gathered did the bell-ringing cease. Staying in his saddle, the man tipped his hat, then spread his bony arms wide. "I am come to bring God's word of salvation, directed to your fine town by the Holy Spirit's guiding hand," he said. "I'm the Reverend Jerusalem Chadway, and traveling with me is my daughter, Joy." With a smile he added, "And you can rightfully believe me when I tell you she is most aptly named since she has accompanied me on this long and difficult mission that's taken us from town to town, buffalo camps to way stations, tawdry saloons to even the most vile of houses of ill repute."

Taylor was returning from the pasture where the cattle were being watched over and brought Magazine to a halt near Barclay. "What's all the commotion about?"

"Seems we're bein' visited by one of them saddlebag preachers," Barclay said. "I only heard a bit of what he has to say, but I'm already right certain he's crazy as a snakebit donkey. No man with a whit of good sense would bring his daughter along with him into these parts."

Even Mayor Dawson hesitated before approaching the strange-looking man. "All travelers are welcome to Dawson's Ridge," he finally said as he extended a hand. "If it's preaching you're here to do, I 'spect you're likely to find a good number of listeners."

Reverend Chadway bowed his head. "It isn't always that we're so well greeted."

Taylor made his way through the crowd for a closer look at the preacher, who was using his hat to beat the dust from his threadbare suit. "I'm wondering which way you folks came from," he said, "and if you've seen any sign of Indians about."

"Oh my, yes. Our travels have taken us onto the reservations where we've told the heathens of the Almighty's glory.

I'm not claiming that we've succeeded in enlisting a great number of followers yet, but it is our calling to try."

"I ain't speaking of reservation Indians, Reverend. I'm talking of those who roam these parts and wish harm to white folks."

Chadway nodded. "Unfortunately I hear there are those about, though it has been God's will that we have not crossed their path. There was some mention just a few days back of a stagecoach that was waylaid and robbed as it was making its way to Lone Oak. I'm told that the driver and those aboard met an unfortunate end."

As he spoke, the women were escorting his daughter toward the Social Center and urging the preacher to follow. "Let's get you folks out of the heat," the mayor's wife said as she took Joy's arm and led the way.

It was clear the ladies of Dawson's Ridge were far more excited than the men over religion coming to town. At the wives' urging, two of the unused army tents were moved to a spot near the livery, the visitors' mounts were tended, and basins of water for bathing delivered. The preacher and his daughter were invited to share the evening meal with the Reynolds family.

"How long will you be staying?" Katie Reynolds asked after Reverend Chadway blessed the meal and gave a lengthy thanks for the hospitality that had been extended.

The preacher was not a man of short answers. "Our schedule is not of our making," he said. "Rather, it is dictated by a higher power. It is my responsibility to tend the needs of those I meet along the way. Some, it seems, need more than others. If the folks here are of a mind, I'll gladly do preaching on Sunday, morning and evening, And I have no doubt my daughter can be persuaded to lead a bit of singing. She has a voice to be envied, as you'll soon learn."

And while no one asked, he was soon off on his personal history. His grandfather and father had been preachers, he said, helping build churches in small communities throughout Louisiana. "I took to the pulpit myself at age thirteen," he said. He was almost fifty when called to serve as a circuit rider, and for the past two years he had traveled through the eastern and central parts of Texas and up into Indian Territory. "My wife, a refined and genteel woman, did not embrace my new calling and simply wished me well. Last I heard, she was living somewhere near New Orleans in the company of a wealthy lumber mill owner. I pray for her soul nightly before I sleep."

He looked across the table at his daughter, who had not said a word since the meal was served. "Others better understood the nature of what I was asked to do and agreed to accompany me. Praise be to God."

Taylor had made the first of his nightly rounds of the lookout stations and was on his way to check on Barclay when he saw the preacher sitting on a stool in front of his newly pitched tent, puffing on a corncob pile.

"Mighty fine evening," the preacher said.

"So far."

"I spoke with Mr. Reynolds earlier in the evening and he told me of your concern that renegades might be planning to attack. That explains the barricades we faced as we entered town and the fact that all the menfolk are carrying guns. As you likely know, it goes against my beliefs and preachings to bear arms. Thus, aside from praying mightily for the town's safekeeping, I fear I can be of little use in this matter."

Before Taylor could respond, another voice spoke. "Mr. Reynolds also said that you've been recently picked to be the town marshal," Joy Chadway said as she stood in front of the adjacent tent, running a brush through her hair. "It was my impression that he feels much better with you now keeping watch over things."

Her voice instantly reminded Thad of his sister, and he couldn't recall when he'd seen a woman so pretty. But before he could even tip his hat in response, she disappeared into her tent.

Only as he was riding away did it occur to him that he'd failed to ask the preacher if he'd heard any mention of a woman leading the stagecoach attack he'd spoken of earlier in the day.

Chapter 15

July Barstow was exhausted, ill, and growing more despondent by the day. Though it had been just over a month since her abduction, it seemed a lifetime had passed. Any hope that she might be rescued and freed of her misery had vanished in the aftermath of the bloody victory over the soldiers. She had huddled in one of the teepees, watching over the children as the shooting and shouting were under way, praying that she would be found and taken to safety.

Finally, when the only sounds she heard were the triumphant cries of the warriors, she knew that her last bit of hope had slipped away. When she peeked from the teepee and saw the mutilation of the bodies of the dead soldiers that was under way, she drew the children near and forbade them to leave her side.

And she wondered how much longer the nightmarish routine her life had become would continue. Were it not for the chance that her son might still be anticipating her return, she would have thought seriously about taking her own life.

Once a strong and healthy woman, she had lost weight

and developed a cough that was at times so severe that it took her breath away. Her eyes, once sparkling, were lifeless, her movements the tired shuffle of an old woman.

After a long day of cleaning horse hides, her nostrils were filled with the foul smell of the task as she made her way to a teepee at the canyon's edge. It was the home of a renegade killed during the soldier attack, but she had been told she could now use it as her own. Pleased to no longer be sleeping in the open, she had just shut her eyes when a woman of the tribe appeared.

She was being summoned to the leader's lodge.

As July entered, Kate Two didn't bother to look up. In front of her, spread across a buffalo hide, were small piles of coins and paper money, a few pieces of jewelry, and several handguns. With a small fire casting shadows against the walls, she was taking stock of the items stolen during the recent stagecoach attack.

Finally she raised her head and nodded in July's direction. "There's a satchel over there that belonged to a woman passenger," she said. "She was about the same body size as you. Perhaps you would like to look through the contents and see if there is something better for you to wear."

The young woman instinctively ran her hands along the front of her filthy dress. For only a moment did she consider that she would be taking the clothes of the dead before walking over to the bag. There was a faint scent of lilac water as she opened it. Inside were three dresses, each nicer than anything she had ever owned. She selected the plainest, measuring it against her frame, then turned her back. Hurriedly she let the threadbare dress she was wearing fall to the floor and stepped into the new one. The clean cotton cloth felt soft and cool against her skin.

"Take the others as well," Kate Two said. "They are of no value to me."

July was puzzled by the act of kindness. Could it really be nothing more than the fact that this evil and ruthless woman seated before her only wished to have someone near who spoke her language? Was that the reason she had spared her life and ordered the men of the tribe to stay away from her?

"Soon you will be repaying my favors," Kate Two said. With that she began gathering the items that lay before her, putting them in the empty satchel. "Once this is full, you will learn what I mean."

As she walked into the moonlit night, July let her eyes wander across the quiet camp, mentally counting the number of teepees that were occupied. In recent days Kate Two's followers had been greatly diminished, first by the losses suffered during the gunfight with the buffalo hunters, then with the soldiers. Several young warriors had simply ridden away in the night, deserting their white leader to join other Comanches roaming the western plains. Only a dozen men remained, hardly enough to mount a major attack. None of which seemed to concern the woman who continued to speak with dead spirits, passing along words of optimism, praise, and promise that their ranks would soon grow tenfold when the long-absent Hawk on the Hill made his triumphant return.

In the meantime they were to follow her command and raid only wagon trains, stagecoaches, and small way stations, taking the white man's money.

Passing a campfire that was nothing more than glowing embers, July tossed the old dress, her last physical connection to her previous life, onto it. The fabric burst into a brief flame that was already dying by the time she disappeared into her teepee. As she tried to sleep, her mind was still filled with questions. What would become of the women and children of the tribe once all the men were gone or captured? How long would it be before their leader put her own bid for freedom into action? And, July could not help wondering, what was to become of her?

As the days passed, Taylor became increasingly doubtful that the Comanches would attempt a raid on Dawson's Ridge. He knew that the small band's numbers had been diminished during the ambush in the canyon, and it was likely their scouts had reported the number of armed defenders waiting in town. Even with the absence of the troops, the settlers far outnumbered the renegades. Still, he made no mention of his feelings, wishing to keep the men of the community prepared.

His role as town marshal had amounted to nothing more than a strong scolding of two young still-tenders who took a jug of whiskey along to their lookout post and got drunk on their watch, and seeing that none of the children strayed from the sight of their mothers.

On Sunday morning he returned from the creek, his hair still wet and combed. Barclay awoke to see his partner putting on the clean shirt that he'd retrieved from the laundry. He sat on the side of his cot, massaging his wounded leg. "Never figured you for one to go to preachin' and hymn singin'."

"Just curious. And if someone should decide to shoot the

preacher if he goes too long with his sermonizing, I 'spect the marshal might ought to be there to quiet things down."

Barclay grunted. "If I was one to be guessing, I'd reckon it's more the singin' that's attracted your interest. And should that be the case, I'd offer a bit of advice. I wouldn't be wearin' that hat that's two sizes too big. Trust me, it don't give you a handsome look. When we finally get home I'm gonna purchase you a proper one."

Taylor didn't immediately respond. When he did, it was to address Barclay's mention of returning home. "The longer we stay here," he said, "the longer it's gonna be before we see Kansas again. Those Indians ain't coming to do these folks harm." He waited for Barclay to reply and when none came, he asked, "What is it you think our plan should be?"

"I've been thinkin' on it. Most likely the renegades are still holed up in that canyon for the time being. From there they're going out to attack travelers, most likely to rob them of what money they're carryin'. There's a reason there that I ain't fully figured out. Again I'm guessing, but I 'spect they'll be lookin' to move on to the south or west sometime soon, maybe join up with another band. They do that every year, for religious reasons and courtin' and such."

"So what we should do?"

"Nothing until I'm back to where I can mount a horse. Shouldn't be too much longer. Till then, I don't want you entertainin' thoughts of giving up your marshal job to head off on your lonesome. Promise me that."

Taylor nodded. "It's a promise."

"Then I reckon you'd best be off to get some religion. Could be it might do you some good."

Reverend Chadway, still wearing his black suit, was already bathed in sweat, holding his Bible as he paced and preached. There was an almost crazed look in his eyes as he spoke. Aside from those whose turn it was to stand watch, almost everyone in town had turned out to the Social Center service. Taylor entered and took a spot against the back wall.

The preacher's booming voice echoed through the building as he railed about the damnation that awaited disbelievers ("Yea, those who do not see fit to come to the Lord and willfully follow Him are doomed to an afterlife of eternal fire. . . ."), spoke of his journey, which the Heavenly Father had blessed ("We have come far and at great risk to life and limb, but through divine guidance we've arrived here to share the promise of a great day that's coming. . . ."), and of the evils of Satan ("His reach is far and his temptations come in many forms . . . drinking and gambling, whoring and stealing and killing . . . that can drag us down to burn in the flames of hell. . . ."), and of the need to love one another ("We are judged not by our own self-worth but by how we treat those less fortunate. . . ."). No sin was left unmentioned, and every joy for those who sought redemption was mentioned. Finally, as he began to wind down after an hour-long sermon, he announced that a baptism would be held later in the afternoon down at the creek for those who wished to repent and rededicate their lives.

It was his daughter's cue to lead the assembly in "Amazing Grace." For the first verse most of the townspeople sang along as best they could before falling quiet, content to simply listen to her beautiful voice. By the time she sang "Old Rugged Cross," Taylor could not take his eyes off her.

While many of the women gathered around Reverend Chadway to compliment him on his sermon, Joy took her place behind the bar to help serve refreshments. Taylor waited until the crowd had disbursed before approaching.

Joy smiled as he neared, pouring him a glass of honey-sweetened tea. "I'm pleased to see you came to the service, Marshal Taylor."

"Call me Thad, ma'am. This marshal business is only a temporary thing. I just wanted to stop by and say I don't recall when I ever heard such wonderful singing."

"I thank you very kindly . . . Thad," she said. "Though, truth be known, you don't strike me as a man who's heard all that much gospel music. I figure you more for a fiddle and banjo kind of man."

"And you would disapprove if that's the case?"

"Hardly. I fancy fiddle playing and banjo picking myself."

Back at the livery, Barclay sat on his cot, slowly exercising his arm and leg. He was still in considerable pain but determined to toss away the crutch and sling as soon as possible.

What he'd not told Taylor was that he'd been spending a great deal of time thinking about where their journey would take them next. He already had a plan. For the near future, he believed, the Comanches would continue to stay in the canyon, venturing out only to raid targets that offered little resistance. The woman leading them was obviously interested in quickly gathering a stake. For what, he wasn't certain. Perhaps so she could finance her own getaway.

If there was to be any chance of rescuing the kidnapped woman, if she was still alive, it would have to be done soon and while the majority of the renegades were away on a raid. In their absence, he and Taylor could make a surprise visit to the encampment and try to steal her away. The plan, he knew, would likely require a great deal of patient hiding in wait. A few warriors, he guessed, would probably be left behind to guard the camp.

For the plan he had in mind to work, it was likely that more killing would be necessary.

Chapter 16

Fall arrived in Dawson's Ridge with a flourish of color and cooler days. Late gardens were being planted, and the turning leaves gave new life to the nearby hillsides. Talk of a possible Indian raid had all but gone silent, replaced by the enthusiasm for the building of a small church that Reverend Chadway had agreed to stay and oversee. His daughter had begun holding daily classes for the children in the shade of a large oak on the edge of town. Nightly card games were again being held in the Social Center. And Mayor Dawson was back to his business of assuring residents that the community was back on its progressive path.

And while Marshal Taylor insisted that a watch continue, he was considering removing the barricades from the edges of town. People were needing their wagons and rain barrels for their daily use.

Tater Barclay's wounds had healed well enough for him to borrow a horse from the livery and ride alongside Taylor on his daily rounds, though he grumbled regularly while doing so.

They were near the north ridge when they heard the children singing. Halting their horses in the shade of the sprawling tree, they listened until the chorus of voices quieted. Joy Chadway looked in their direction and smiled. "Boys and girls, say good morning to the marshal and his friend Mr. Barclay," she said.

The riders tipped their hats in response to the children's singsong greeting. "You young'uns sing mighty nice," Taylor said as their teacher approached him.

"I've promised them that if they work real hard they can sing at next Sunday's services," Joy said

Barclay reined his horse away, again tipping his hat. "Ma'am," he said, and trotted away.

"Your friend's not real social, is he?" she said.

"He just takes a bit of getting used to. You'll find him a good man if you stay here long enough to get to know him." It was his way of asking how long she and the preacher planned to remain in Dawson's Ridge.

"Fact is, I'm hoping my father chooses to stay for a bit. He's quite excited to be building another church. And, in all honesty, I'm pleased to not be traveling and sleeping under the stars."

"Seems to me this might be a nice place for settling down," Taylor said. "Once the church is built it's gonna be needing a preacher. And if you keep instructing the children, next thing you know Mayor Dawson's gonna be talking of building a schoolhouse."

"And are you contemplating making this your home?"

Taylor tipped his hat and reined his horse around. "Reckon I'd best let you get back to your teaching," he said. As he rode away, the voices of the children again filling the morning air, his thoughts flashed to the young boy waiting for his mother back in Kansas.

Barclay was standing in the doorway of the livery when he arrived. "I'm thinking it's about time we get on with our business," he said as Taylor dismounted.

Thad assured the mayor that since all had been quiet for several weeks, the likelihood that the town was in any danger was slim. What he had decided to do, he explained, was spend a few days riding the plains to see if there might still be signs of any Indians in the vicinity. Barclay would accompany him. "It'll do him good to feel of some use," Taylor said. "Meanwhile, I've made assignments for those who'll stand watch in our absence."

"And you'll be gone for how long?"

"We'll pack provisions for only a few days. Likely, we'll be back before most know we're gone. We'll leave at sunrise tomorrow."

He told the mayor their plan. A day's ride would take them close to the canyon where they'd encountered the small band of Comanches. Once near, they would wait until dark to make a final approach, coming from the bluff side of the encampment rather than the entrance. From high above they could hide and determine the movements of the renegades and how many warriors remained. "First," he said, "we've got to figure out how many of 'em there are. My guess is they're riding out on occasion to see if they can find a stagecoach or a wagon to attack and steal from. Most likely the white woman I've mentioned will lead them. I'm thinking when they're gone it'll be only the other womenfolk and little ones that remain. That's when we can get a bit closer and see if the boy's mother is still being held."

"And if they don't leave?" the mayor asked.

"We're still thinking on that."

Dawson's Ridge was still dark when they saddled their horses and left. After a short midday break, they continued until the sun touched the horizon.

They stopped when they reached a ledge that gave them a clear view of the canyon below. They tethered their horses near a small spring a couple of miles away and walked the rest of the way. It had been slow going, helped only minimally by the cloud-covered moonlight. It was near dawn when they silently made their way to a rocky area just two hundred feet above the Comanche encampment and settled in. They saw no movement below. Taylor passed a canteen to his partner. "Well?"

"I'm thinkin' that this business of getting old ain't something for the faint of heart," Barclay whispered, then gritted his teeth as he massaged his thigh. "Don't reckon you thought to bring any whiskey . . . for medicinal purposes."

Taylor made no reply and counted the number of teepees and horses hobbled in the back side of the canyon. "Even if there's a young warrior for every horse," he said, "there can't be more than a dozen, maybe a few more."

"Still ain't odds to my likin'."

The wait lasted two days as they watched the slow-moving routine of the Indian camp. The women tended fires and cooked. One, whom Barclay determined to be the band's medicine woman, occasionally disappeared into a teepee at the far corner of the canyon. The men gathered in small groups to make arrows, sharpen knives, and clean their rifles. Two of those Taylor counted appeared to be nursing wounds that had been received in the raid by the soldiers. Only after dark, when a ceremonial fire was built, did Kate Two appear from her lodge to hold court with her followers. The hostage they had come to find was nowhere to be seen.

Finally, before dawn of the third day, Kate Two emerged, dressed in buckskin and wearing her black hat. A pistol hung at her waist as she waited for one of the warriors, already wearing war paint, to bring her horse. Soon she was leading the men in a single-file exit of the canyon. Only the two injured renegades and a few old men were left behind to stand guard over the camp.

"Appears they're off to do some business," Barclay said. "Best you go fetch our horses so we can pay our visit. We'll allow 'em time to get a good distance away. Then we'll enter by the same route we took last time."

Two hours later they approached the entrance. Tater pulled his hat tight against his forehead, rested his rifle against his shoulder, and leaned to whisper to Taylor before kicking his horse into a fast trot, "Now, don't be bashful about defendin' yourself."

A rifle shot hummed past, ricocheting off the limestone ledge. Barclay quickly aimed and returned fire. The old Comanche's rifle dropped to his side as he clutched his chest and fell to his knees. As another emerged from behind a teepee, Taylor fired three quick pistol shots, the third hitting its target.

It was almost too easy. The camp had been left virtually unguarded.

While the sound of the gunfire echoed through the enclosure, the women and children ran toward the back wall of the canyon. The women fell to their knees, hands hiding their faces, while the children huddled behind them. After making sure the two warriors were dead, Barclay rode toward the gathering, pointing his rifle in their direction. "I'll keep a watch on these folks while you check the lodges," he said. "Do it quick and careful."

Taylor walked from teepee to teepee, pulling back the entrance flaps with the barrel of his rifle, finding nothing but empty pallets of buffalo hides and a human stench that caused his eyes to water. Only when he reached the one they had seen the medicine woman enter did he hear a sound. In the darkness, a low growl came from a small mongrel dog as Taylor entered. Beneath a mound of furs, he could see a human form.

Calming the dog, he approached and saw the face of a woman. Kneeling beside her, he gently lifted her head. Her hair was damp and matted by sweat, her eyes filled with fear. "Ma'am," Taylor said, "Might you be the mother of a young boy name of Jakey Barstow?"

The woman tried to focus on the man leaning over her. Through parched lips, she managed to mouth only a single word—"Jakey"—before she fell unconscious. Thad wrapped her in one of the hides and lifted her into his arms, surprised that she seemed to weigh no more than a child. He carried her from the teepee.

"We've found her," he shouted to Barclay. "But she's in mighty poor shape and in need of attention."

Barclay reined his horse in their direction. He looked down at the frail woman and shook his head. "Hand her up to me," he said, "and let's be gone."

As the frightened Indian women and children watched, the two men quickly rode away.

Once in an open space, Barclay poured water from his canteen over the woman's face and tried to get her to drink. He shielded her from the sun with his hat as Taylor and Magazine led the way.

By midmorning they had distanced themselves from the Comanche encampment and had seen no signs of other travelers. Looking behind them, Taylor noticed that the dog he'd encountered in the teepee was following them.

"Looks as if we've got company," he said.

Barclay glanced over his shoulder. "Long as he ain't got a gun, I reckon he's welcome to come along."

"You go on ahead. I'll catch up."

The dog, his tongue hanging loosely and panting, stood his ground as Taylor approached, pouring water into his hat. As the exhausted animal lapped eagerly, Thad ran a hand across his bony back, feeling the burrs and ticks embedded in its fur. "Looks like you've about run as far as you can go," he said. He lifted the dog to his shoulder and swung back into the saddle.

As they approached, Barclay glanced over at the dog resting on Taylor's saddle. "Lord A'mighty," he said, "that beats all I ever seen. Why is it you're bringin' that Indian dog along?"

"Seems he has a particular interest in the Barstow woman."

Tater snorted. "Glad to see someone does."

It was long after dark when they arrived at Dawson's Ridge. A flurry of activity began as soon as the travelers arrived at the Reynolds cabin. Barclay was directed to the back of the house, where the unconscious woman was placed on the bed.

Sloan's wife quickly alerted several neighbor women, and upon their arrival, the men were invited to leave.

Taylor walked toward the Social Center in search of food for the dog. Barclay limped behind. "I'm so badly in need of whiskey," he said, "that I'll gladly rob the place if need be."

Inside the cabin, water was heated for a bath and cool cloths were placed on the patient's forehead in an attempt to reduce her fever. On the stove, broth and tea were warming. Only when she was dressed in one of his wife's nightgowns was Sloan Reynolds allowed back into the room.

A few minutes later he walked outside to find Taylor and Barclay waiting on the porch, passing a bottle between them. "Best I can tell," he told them, "is that she's suffering with consumption and is half-starved. I judge it a miracle that you found her when you did. It's going to take some time, but with proper watching over I think we can restore her to good health."

As he spoke, the dog raced past him into the cabin. He found his way to the back room, jumped onto the bed, and took his place at the Barstow woman's feet. When one of the women tried to shoo him away, he bared his teeth and growled.

"We must get this filthy animal out of here," she said.

Taylor appeared in the doorway. "First thing tomorrow," he said, "I'll see that he's given a proper grooming. For now, though, I think it best that you let him stay where he is and do his job."

"And just what might that be?" Mrs. Reynolds asked.

"Watching over his friend."

Chapter 17

The sun was already high in the sky as Joy Chadway stepped out onto the porch of the Reynolds cabin to greet Taylor. "I see you're a late sleeper," she said. "Good thing there was no need for a marshal while you were getting your beauty rest."

Taylor's face reddened. "How's the Barstow woman?"

"July Barstow seems much better. Still got a fever and needs a great deal of rest, but she regained consciousness early this morning and even took a bit of nourishment. It's a good thing you and your friend did."

"July, you say?"

"You didn't even know the Christian name of the woman you rescued?"

Taylor shook his head. "Just her last name. Her boy's kind of a friend of mine."

She stepped toward him and touched his arm. "I must say I'm proud to know you, Marshal Taylor. And I'm sure July will be wanting to thank you personally as soon as she's feeling a bit better. In the meantime, my father is planning a special prayer service for her this evening and I hope you'll make it a plan to be present. The children will be singing."

She walked down the steps into the street, then stopped and turned. "You should also know that there's a dog inside that could use a trip down to the creek for bathing. He won't leave her bed and I understand he was another poor soul you chose to rescue. Has he got a name?"

Taylor rubbed his chin. "I reckon I could call him Dawg," he said, "unless you've got a more proper idea."

"I think Dawg would do just fine," she said.

More than a hundred miles to the southwest, Fourth Cavalry Lieutenant Charles Hudson led a company of troopers toward Dawson's Ridge.

He had never even heard of the town before a courier arrived from Fort Sill with orders from Colonel Mackenzie. Hudson and his company, which had spent months chasing and rarely catching small bands of renegade Comanches wandering the Texas plains, were to travel there immediately and check on the status of Sergeant Murphy and his men. Weeks had passed since he sent word they were investigating the possibility of Comanches in the region, and the silence had become a cause for concern. Hudson led his twenty-five men eastward with only a general idea of where the new settlement was or what they might expect once they arrived.

It did seem odd to Lieutenant Hudson, a seasoned Indian fighter, that there would be serious activity so far to the northeast, well removed from what remained of the buffalo herds and in a region so sparsely inhabited by white settlers.

On the third day of their march, they saw an ashen haze in the distance long before arriving to find the burned-out remains of a small way station. The cedar log building was gone, outlined only by its limestone foundation. The fences of a corral had been torn down and the blackened shell of a single wagon sat nearby. One dead mule lay beside it, covered by a thick coat of flies. The soldiers counted the eight bodies—travelers and the operators of the station—all scalped and skinned. Two had been tied to what remained of one of the wagon's wheels.

Old Dan, a Kiowa scout who rode with Hudson's company, walked the grounds in silence, observing the mutilated bodies, the arrows that had been shot into them, and the tracks left behind. "Comanche war party," he finally said, pointing toward a distant range of hills. "That way."

"How many?" Hudson asked.

"Maybe ten, no more."

The lieutenant had viewed such scenes before, yet each time he looked upon the savagery visited on innocent people, his anger grew stronger. As his eyes wandered over the remains of the small outpost, familiar thoughts rushed to mind. There had been little of value here for the renegades to take away. A few horses, perhaps, maybe a couple of weapons. It was unlikely that the travelers had arrived with much of worth. Once again he was reminded that the enemy he and his men had been assigned to hunt down were murderers without cause. "We will capture none of these red devils," he shouted to his men. "They will be shot dead when we find them and left for the coyotes and buzzards."

Then he ordered a detail to dig graves before they took their leave with a new quickness and purpose.

Kate Two's mood, already soured by the small bounty that had resulted from the raid on the way station, turned even darker upon her arrival back at the canyon. Greeted by somber-faced women, she and her men were told of the attack by the two men who had taken the white hostage away.

As her weary followers led the horses to the stream for water and spread the sack of stolen oats for them to eat, their leader paced the encampment, angrily kicking at one of the smoldering campfires with a booted foot. Sparks flew into the night air, reflecting in her blue eyes.

The time, she knew, had come for her getaway. "Tomorrow, when a new day dawns, I will ride onto the cliffs and summon back Hawk on the Hill," she announced. "The gods have told me that he will be followed by a hundred brave warriors who will avenge the loss of your brothers."

The voices of children drifted into the evening air, singing praise to another form of god. Aside from a couple of women who stayed to watch over July Barstow, the entire community of Dawson's Ridge had turned out for Jerusalem Chadway's prayer meeting. "It is with a joyful heart that we accept this troubled woman into our hands," he said. "You—and two brave souls in our midst—have delivered her into the care of Christian folks who will see that her health is restored and Your will is done." He lifted his Bible high into the air. "Praise the Lord."

A short distance away, Tater Barclay leaned against the doorway of the livery. He placed his hat back on his head as the prayer finally ended. "Reckon I'll drink to that," he said.

"I think I'll join you," Taylor said. A day of hearty handshakes, slaps on the back, and even delivery of a fresh-baked cake from some of the women in town had made him ill at ease.

"A right smart idea if you ask me. This business of bein'

a hero can make a man mighty thirsty. Particularly if there're others eager to do the payin'."

Lieutenant Hudson sat in the glow of a flickering lantern, holding the crude map that had been delivered by Mackenzie's courier. The trail of the Comanches continued north, toward the Red River. The community of Dawson's Ridge, however, was in a more southerly direction. Since his orders were to go there, he reluctantly opted to discontinue pursuit of the Indians and first learn the whereabouts of his fellow soldiers.

"We'll obey our command," he told his top sergeant, holding the lantern. "But neither will we forget the savages. See that the men are ready to head out by six. No bugle calls."

As the sergeant walked away, a trooper, still in his teens, brought the lieutenant a hot cup of coffee. He had delivered the orders and map and been instructed to remain with the company and serve as an aide to the lieutenant until their return to Fort Sill.

Hudson took the cup, warming his hands against its rim. He invited the trooper to take a seat. "You're going to have to remind me of your name."

The young man was briefly speechless, aware that enlisted men rarely spoke directly to officers. "Benjamin Lee, sir. Everybody calls me Ben."

Lieutenant Hudson looked across at the young man, trying to recall himself at that age, a newly enlisted cavalryman. "So, how are you taking to life on the plains?"

"I 'spect it's something that takes a bit of gettin' used to."

"That it does. When I signed up to soldier, no older than you, it never occurred to me my duty would one day be to chase renegade Indians all over a godforsaken place called Texas."

"Would you mind my asking a question, sir?"

"What might that be?"

"Does there come a time when you get to where you can put things like we seen back at that way station out of mind?"

Hudson sipped at his coffee. "The honest truth is the kind of evil you were exposed to today is likely gonna haunt you for a lifetime."

The young soldier nodded. "That's what I feared."

Chapter 18

Kate Two wished for a mirror, not to admire her beauty but to make certain that she looked the part of a woman who had long been held against her will. Late into the night she sat in her teepee, cutting away her long black hair, then rubbing sand into her scalp and against her face. She pulled the stolen rings from her fingers and placed them in the small chest along with the money and other pieces of jewelry taken during the recent raids. Gazing into the box, she knew it was far less than she had hoped for, but it would have to do. She removed her buckskins and slipped into a plain cotton dress sewn by some now-dead settler's wife.

Talks With Spirits, once so proud, self-assured, and commanding, was no more. In her place would be a ravaged and helpless woman lucky to be alive. When the camp was silent and the fires had burned down, she would take a mount from the corral at the end of the canyon and disappear. If anyone noticed, she would explain that her leave-taking was to go into the nearby hills to summon Hawk back to his role as leader of the remaining warriors. In truth, she planned to hide the treasure box away in a cave she'd located, then travel west. With luck she would eventually encounter someone who would believe her story of being abducted and held by the renegade band of Comanches, listen in amazement as she told of her escape, and recognize her desperate need for help.

Her plan was vague and might undergo change, but it was the only one she had been able to come up with. Somehow she hoped to eventually make it to Mexico, there to begin a new life, free from pursuit of the law and away from the Indians she had come to so despise. They were filthy and stupid. Even she was amazed at their acceptance of the notion that she had mystical powers and the ability to communicate with their ancestors. They were savages in every sense of the word. It had not been their willingness to roam and live like animals or even the cruel desecration of bodies of their victims that caused her to count the days before she could flee. When she first saw the renegades eagerly drink the warm blood and eat the stomach contents from a freshly killed buffalo, she had determined they were inhuman.

The only thing that masked her disgust was the recurring dream she had of being in a cantina, dancing and laughing as men looked at her with adoration. They bought her drinks and paid her money for brief moments of privacy and pleasure. In her imagination Kate Two was without a history, young, free, and happy again.

Lieutenant Hudson rode point, his men following behind in columns of twos. There was a welcome cool in the early-morning air, a signal that the oppressive heat of the Texas summer had finally come to an end. Soon, he knew, the weather would bring another kind of discomfort, cold winds that would feel like icy pinpricks against the face and sudden snowstorms that would make travel increasingly difficult. Having ridden the plains long enough to see the seasons change, he dreaded what was to come and longed for the comforts of his home and family.

"By late in the day," he said to his sergeant, "we should arrive at Dawson's Ridge. With good fortune we'll not only meet up with our comrades but also find that the settlement has proper food and drink."

No sooner had the words left his mouth than he caught a glimpse of a lone rider far ahead, moving slowly along a rise. He peered through his field glasses. It was a woman.

As the soldiers approached, she seemed not to even notice them. Her head was down, nodding gently with the plodding pace of her horse. She rode bareback and wore no hat.

"Ma'am, can we be of help?" Lieutenant Hudson asked as he rode up beside her. He needed only to see her physical condition for an answer. She was dirty, seemingly exhausted, and near faint as he helped her down from her horse. "Where is it you've come from?"

Her voice was a hoarse whisper. "Indians . . . They killed my family and took me away. I've been their prisoner for so long . . . don't know where I am . . . Help me, please."

While a soldier sheltered her with his hat, Hudson put a canteen to her lips and watched as she drank greedily. Then her knees buckled.

"Place her in the supply wagon," the lieutenant ordered, "and have Corporal Braun—isn't he the one who does some doctoring?—ride with her and see to her comfort. We'll continue on to our destination and hope we can find her additional help there."

As the wagon swayed, following along behind the soldiers, Kate Two lay beneath a blanket, her head propped against a sack of flour. She kept her eyes closed and said nothing.

Up ahead, Lieutenant Hudson was quiet for a while. Then he turned to Ben Lee. "Even being aware that this is a hard land," he said, "it seems there is always some new encounter that causes one to wonder at the infinite amount of suffering and pain it has to offer. God only knows the torment that poor woman's been put through. I'm eager to learn how she came to escape those who took her from her family and have no doubt treated her most unkindly."

It was nearing dust when the company crested a hill and could look down on the small settlement. Hudson scanned the village with his field glasses, looking for bluecoats, and felt his heart sink when he saw none. In the distance he could hear the voices of two young boys as they ran toward the center of the town. "More soldiers coming," they shouted. "They's more soldiers coming. . . ."

Taylor walked out to meet the visitors as townspeople gathered in the street.

"This is Dawson's Ridge," Lieutenant Hudson said. "Would that be correct?"

"It is."

"We're here in search of a detail of soldiers last seen in these parts."

Taylor pointed in the direction of the Social Center. "Best we go inside so we can discuss the matter. There're tents already set up where your men can settle and tend their horses."

"I take it the news you have for me is not good."

"'Fraid not," Taylor said.

Mayor Dawson and Tater Barclay were already inside when the lieutenant entered to hear the story of the brutal canyon ambush. He listened in silence as Taylor described what had occurred.

"How many Indians are there? And we'll need a map to the campsite of the renegades." Hudson slammed his fist onto the table. "A few days back we happened onto a way station that had been raided. It seems likely that it was the same bunch of savages who did the killings there. It was our plan to go in search of them once we learned the fate of our fellow soldiers. Now, it seems, there is an even greater urgency."

Barclay spoke. "Unless they've been recently joined by others," he said, "there ain't that many of 'em. Not more'n a dozen or so braves. You and your men should have no difficulty overpowerin' 'em—if you handle it right. Murphy, bless his soul, didn't. And we'll gladly lead you to where they're camped . . . if you'll make me one promise."

"And what might that be?"

"That every last one of 'em will be left dead."

Hudson nodded. "We will leave at daybreak."

As he left to join his men, Barclay and Taylor walked onto the porch of the Social Center. Thad called out to the lieutenant as he wearily made his way down the street, "We're sorry for the loss of your fellow soldiers," he said.

Hudson, lost in thought, gave no response.

A half-moon was peeking over the ridge, and the night air had cooled. "For all the good they're doing," Taylor said, "it seems to me these Indian fighters have been assigned a mighty undesirable task. I reckon there are times when they wonder if it will ever end and they can go back to living normal lives."

Barclay grunted. "Without them doin' what it is they do, this frontier ain't never gonna be worth the time it takes to get here. I say God bless 'em and give 'em all the ammunition they need. As far as livin' a normal life goes, I could use a bit of it myself."

They headed toward the livery. They would go to bed early, though neither anticipated getting much sleep.

When they talked with Hudson, there had been no mention of the rescued woman. Members of the community, however, had quickly been made aware of the civilian traveler. As the soldiers settled into their bivouac, the women of Dawson's Ridge were showering her with attention.

"An army tent is hardly a proper place for her to rest," Sloan Reynolds suggested to the medical officer. "She will come to our cabin where she can get cleaned up a bit, have some food, and begin regaining her strength. You can look in on her as often as you feel necessary. In fact, I'd appreciate it if you could pay a visit to another survivor of an Indian kidnapping who is already being cared for. Her condition, I'm afraid, was far more serious when she came to us."

Reynolds smiled as he looked at Kate Two, who sat resting beneath the tree where just hours earlier the town's children had gathered for their singing. "You'll be welcome to our home. My wife and her friends will watch over you with great care. I'll take my leave and spend a few nights down by the livery with Brother Jerusalem so you ladies can enjoy your nighttime privacy."

Kate Two, still feigning exhaustion and bewilderment, had briefly stiffened at the mention of another woman who was being cared for. She moved a hand to her inner thigh, making sure the knife she'd strapped there was still in place beneath her dress.

Reynolds's wife insisted that she take their bed, then bathed her face with a cool rag while others were warming broth and biscuits in the kitchen. When it was suggested that she might like to change into a nightgown, Kate Two begged off, insisting that she was too tired and only wished to sleep.

"You mentioned that another woman is being cared for," she said.

"She was rescued from the Comanches several days ago by our town marshal and Mr. Barclay. It was quite heroic, from the story I've heard. The poor thing is suffering from a threatening cough and is still quite weak. She sleeps most of the time, but my husband says she's showing improvement. Perhaps tomorrow you will meet her."

"Only if she's feeling up to it."

It was late into the night, after all lamps had been doused and everyone else was sleeping, when Kate Two quietly made her way along the hallway and into the cabin's other bedroom. She bent close to the bed and saw by the moonlight that it was, in fact, the woman who had been taken from her camp.

Placing her lips close to the pillow, she whispered, "Wake up, my friend. I've come to see you."

July Barstow opened her eyes and felt the cold blade of a

knife pressed against her throat. Was this another of her fevered dreams? She began to shiver uncontrollably.

"If you say one word that might indicate you know me," Kate Two said, "I will cut out your eyes."

At the foot of the bed, Dawg growled and bared his teeth as the intruder slipped out of the room.

Chapter 19

Lieutenant Hudson raised his arm, signaling his men to halt. They had been riding for much of the day. According to Barclay and Taylor, they were nearing the canyon where the Comanches were camped.

"If they have lookouts," Taylor said, "they'll likely be on the forward rim near the entrance. You might send a few men around to the back side to determine the situation, then signal down if the opening is clear to travel through."

Hudson had already waved for his Kiowa scout to join the discussion. The lieutenant studied the crude map of the encampment that Taylor had drawn from memory, providing the location of teepees and the corral. "If your recollection is correct," he said, "there should be no more than a dozen mounts. Their number should tell us if there are members of the party elsewhere, hiding in wait. Our scout will take half a dozen men to the back cliff and determine if the corral is full. If so, they'll use their rifles to do away with the horses, leaving our adversary on foot as we attack. Their shots from above will be our signal to charge."

Tater, trying to rub away the leg pain that the long day's ride had caused, nodded. The attack would be swift and efficient. He reined his horse away from the discussion to seek a position near the front of the company of waiting soldiers. *If I were a praying man, I'd be asking that the first renegade in the sight of my Winchester's the one who's caused me to hobble about like an old man.*

As he rode away he heard the lieutenant's final words. "We'll take the lives of no women or children. They'll be captured and escorted to Fort Sill, as we've been ordered."

An hour later a shot from the rim of the canyon rang out, and the first of the Indian ponies fell to its knees.

The assault lasted only a few minutes as the soldiers burst through the canyon entrance, firing at the small group of Comanche warriors who had gathered in the center of the encampment. Two fell dead before they could raise their weapons and another was knocked to his knees by an oncoming horse. The others quickly tossed aside their weapons and raised their hands. Clearly, they had been surprised and unprepared.

Behind a nearby teepee, women huddled with the children, their moans and screams echoing through the canyon.

"Bind the savages immediately," Hudson said. "They've made it far too easy on themselves. By their cowardly surrender they have made more work for us. It will be a long, hard road to Sill."

He ordered that all weapons be collected and each teepee be searched and then burned.

The scout, arriving from the canyon rim, rode to where the women and children huddled. He began explaining that their lives were no longer in danger and that they were now prisoners of the U.S. Army. A youngster, no more than ten, spat in his direction.

"Such a pathetic lot," Hudson said as he let his eyes roam the aftermath. "I find it hard to believe this small band, dirty and sickly and hungry, could have caused so much death and suffering. And where are their leaders?"

Barclay approached the lieutenant. He and Taylor had just come from the teepee that had once been the home of the Indians' leader. "Appears we missed one," Tater said. "The big lodge is empty. Looks like someone took their leave quickly and well before we arrived. Guns, clothing, and blankets were left behind."

Hudson paid the observation little mind as he focused on the activity of his men and the days that lay ahead. "I'll send a few men back to Dawson's Ridge to fetch our supply wagon," he said. "Our going north will be slow, so they should have no trouble catching up."

Taylor shook his head. "You're gonna walk these people all the way to Fort Sill?"

"We've got no other choice, what with their horses dead. It's a tactical decision I will no doubt live to regret in the days to come."

"You could've kept the promise I asked of you," Barclay said, "and left 'em all dead."

Hudson cast his eyes skyward, squinting into the bright and cloudless day. Then he straightened in his saddle. "Mr. Barclay, sir," he said, "it is they who are the savages, not us. I appreciate your help, but you're free to return home now. I hope you'll be so kind as to thank the people of your fine community for their warm hospitality and assure them that there is no longer any danger of an Indian raid. At least not from this sorry lot. And if you'll ask them to care for the woman we brought with us, it would be greatly appreciated."

Taylor's heart jumped. "Woman?"

"I suppose I failed to mention her last night as we were discussing more vital matters. We encountered a woman on the trail who had escaped captivity, perhaps from this very group of renegades. At any rate, she's now being tended by your womenfolk."

The two men were well on their way back to Dawson's Ridge before they stopped at a spring to allow their horses to drink and rest. "Why," Taylor said, "did we never bother mentioning that the leader of those Indians back in the canyon was most likely a white woman?"

"Unless that lieutenant's more a fool than I think, he'd not have believed us."

"And are you now thinking what I am about this woman they're tending to back in town?"

"I'm thinkin' the whole notion sounds crazier than an outhouse rat. But it just might be that the woman who killed your pa is right this minute enjoyin' herself some hot soup and the Christian care of the Dawson's Ridge ladies."

Magazine's gait was steady, his head held high, as they made their way south. It was as if the territory was familiar and he knew the way, anxious to reach his destination and in need of no direction from his rider.

"I miss my horse," Tater said. They were the first words he'd said for several miles. It was, in fact, the first mention he had made of that moment in the canyon weeks earlier when his mount had been shot from beneath him. While the horse loaned him by the livery keeper was a strong and reliable animal, it was not his, not the one his late brother had given him when it was a just-weaned colt.

"What was it you called him?"

Barclay sighed. "Sad to say, I never got around to givin' him a proper name. Should have, I suppose, but I never could come up with something that fit."

Chapter 20

Brother Jerusalem had spent much of the morning overseeing construction of the small church, offering endless suggestions and talking excitedly of the "glorious day when it would be completed and its doors swung open by the very hand of God." The men who had volunteered to raise the building were relieved when he finally bade them good day and walked off in the direction of the Reynolds cabin.

He was surprised to see that the blue-eyed woman who had been brought to town by the soldiers was sitting on the porch. Her hair was still wet from the washing the women had given it, and she was wearing a clean dress. Her face was sunburned and her lips were cracked; still, she was striking.

"It delights me to see you feeling well enough to be outdoors enjoying this fine morning," the preacher said as he approached. "I feared you might be bedridden for a time, like the poor Barstow woman. I take it you are feeling better." He removed his hat and shifted his Bible from one hand to the other. "I'm Brother Jerusalem."

"It's kind of you to ask," Kate Two said. "Restless dreams

aside, I slept well, thank you, and the ladies have done so much to see to my comfort that it embarrasses me."

"You'll find, as I have, that this is a community of good Christian folks."

"I take it you've been looking in on the other woman who escaped from the Comanches."

The preacher brushed dust from his coat and nodded. "She was near death when our marshal and his friend rescued her. I view her survival as a miracle."

"Have you had an opportunity to speak with her about her experiences with the Indians?"

"She's spoken little since her arrival. Thus far she's remained bedridden, waking only now and then to take small amounts of nourishment. Wasn't even able to attend the prayer vigil we held for her. Still, I make it a point to stop by regularly to learn of her progress. I'm told that her strength is returning ever so slowly."

Kate Two smiled at the preacher and rose to her feet. "That's mighty nice of you. And I appreciate your inquiring as to my own well-being."

"Would it benefit you to talk of the ordeal you've experienced? You'll find I'm a good listener."

"Strange as it might seem," she said, "I seem to have no recollection of the time prior to meeting up with the soldiers yesterday. I'm sure things will come back to me once I've rested, but for now everything is a blank. It's as if part of my life has been taken from me."

"It could be that things you've experienced are best locked away, the manner in which God is offering you His protection."

She smiled again. "You seem a good man, Brother Jerusalem. There's coffee brewing inside. If your time permits, perhaps you would like to have a seat and I'll fetch you a cup. It's such a pleasure having someone to talk with.

"Last night," she said as she returned, "I believe I heard talk of the soldiers planning to make an attack on some nearby Indian camp."

He took the cup of coffee and sat beside her. "They left before daylight," he said. "My understanding is that it's the camp where the Barstow woman was being held. The marshal and Mr. Barclay rode along to point the way."

"I'm sure you've said a proper prayer for their safe return."

"Yes, ma'am. Several, in fact."

"And I will do so as well. How soon can we expect their return? It occurred to me in the wee hours of the night that I've not properly thanked those who found me."

"It's my guess that it will be tomorrow morning before they're back."

She rose to return inside the cabin and said, "As unchristian as it might sound, I hope they'll not bother to return with any captives."

It was late in the day when the preacher saw her again. "Would it be considered improper for a lady to ask a preacher if he'd mind joining her for a brief walk about town?" She had found him in front of his tent, Bible open in his lap, as he was preparing the sermon he planned to deliver on Sunday.

He closed his Bible and stood. "I'm pleased to see you up and about."

"I just felt a bit of exercise and fresh air might do me good." She nodded in the direction of the Reynolds cabin. "The women back there have been making such a fuss over me that I thought I might give them some rest by getting away." There was a chill in the late-afternoon air and she pulled a borrowed shawl tightly around her shoulders.

"I'm afraid there's little of interest to see," he said, "but I'd be most pleased to keep you company as you stretch your legs."

They walked slowly, past the livery and the Social Center, by tents and cabins as a few curious passersby nodded and a couple of children waved. Soon they were on the edge of town, where the church was being built. Leaning against a pile of split logs that would soon become the front wall, he pulled his pipe from his pocket and filled it. "This," he said, "is going to be the place that draws this community together as one. Without a church, a town is nothing but small parts moving in wasted motion, blind to God's master plan. It will be here that neighbors are joined and learn to love one another."

"I'm sure it will be a fine church. I expect you're quite proud."

Moving on, they reached the shade of the oak where his daughter led the youngsters in singing. The preacher asked Kate Two if she would like to rest a bit. "My daughter, Joy, calls this 'her tree,'" he said. "She says the best part of her day is when she gathers the young'uns under its branches and hears their voices lift up in song."

"I heard them while I was sitting on the porch this morning," Kate Two said. "It reminded me of my childhood churchgoing, back when I sang in our choir."

"I take it you're a woman of faith?"

"Oh my, yes," she said, gently placing her hand on his arm.

The preacher smiled. "I suspect that's what allowed you to make it through the ordeal you've recently experienced."

By the time they returned to the preacher's tent, the lanterns were on in the Social Center and the mingling of voices could be heard inside as people gathered to await the soldiers' return. The tent adjacent to Reverend Chadway's was dark, his daughter at the Reynolds cabin helping prepare an evening meal for July Barstow.

"It was a pleasure spending time with you," the preacher said.

"Could I ask one additional favor?" Kate Two said. "I'd like to check to see that my horse is being cared for, and it appears no one is currently at the livery. I would appreciate it if you would accompany me."

"I'd be happy to."

Inside the shadowy building the only sounds came from a couple of horses and a mule pawing at the hay-strewn floors of their stalls. Near the doorway, Kate Two reached into a feed barrel where she'd hidden the Army Colt she'd stolen from the Reynolds cabin.

Jerusalem dropped his Bible when he felt the gun's barrel shoved against his rib cage.

The pleasant lilt had disappeared from Kate Two's voice as she pushed the preacher forward. "Saddle two horses," she said. "And be quick about it."

Chapter 21

When Taylor and Barclay arrived back at Dawson's Ridge near midnight—they had decided to ride straight through instead of camp for the night—they were surprised to find a number of people milling about in front of the Social Center. Their interest in what might have transpired at the Comanche encampment had been displaced by a more immediate concern.

"The preacher's disappeared," Mayor Dawson said as Taylor dismounted. "Along with two horses. And the woman the soldiers brought along with them is missing as well."

Taylor scanned the crowd, looking for Reverend Chadway's daughter. He saw her standing alone near her tent, arms folded, her head down. She had obviously been crying.

"Something bad's occurred, I know it," she said as he approached. "I've got this terrible feeling." Tears again came to her eyes.

"How long since you seen him?"

"After working with the children in the morning," she said, "I spent most of the day over at the Reynolds place, helping tend the Barstow woman. I'm told that some people saw my father walking with the other rescued woman early in the evening."

As they talked, Sloan Reynolds approached. "Marshal, it appears the two horses weren't the only things taken. When I went to fetch my pistol, it was gone, along with a pouch of ammunition. What do you think might be going on?"

Tater Barclay said, "If I was guessin', I'd say that woman has taken him away at gunpoint with no good intentions."

Joy Chadway fainted into Taylor's arms.

The men carried her to the Reynolds cabin, where she was placed in the same bed Kate Two had occupied. Then they gathered on the front porch.

Mayor Dawson paced nervously. "We didn't even know her name."

"Kate Bender," Taylor said through gritted teeth. "She's the reason Tater and I come this way. We've been tracking her. She was a killer back in Kansas and continued her murdering ways when she joined up with that renegade band of Comanches."

As he spoke, Reynolds's wife appeared in the doorway. "Marshal Taylor," she said, "if you have a moment, July Barstow would like a word with you."

Her voice was weak, but some color had returned to her cheeks. There was a brightness to her eyes he had not seen when he took her from the Comanche camp. "You know who she is, don't you?" she said as she looked up at Taylor.

He nodded, reaching down to pet Dawg, who lay at the foot of her bed.

July grabbed his arm. "She has no soul, you understand. She knows only evil and lies. I overheard the ladies talking of her leaving with someone."

"The traveling preacher."

"His life is in danger, you know. She will use him for whatever purpose she has in mind. Then when she has no further need for him, she will leave him dead." Her voice was growing weak, and Taylor leaned forward to hear her. "If you go after her, your life will also be at risk. And I wish for your safety. You have saved my life with your brave efforts, and for that I thank you ever so kindly. Because of you and your friend I now have hope that one day I will again see my son."

"Ma'am, Jakey's being well cared for, by my sister back home. He'll be happy to see you when we return. But first, you have to regain your strength. And I have a bit more traveling to do."

Tears slid down her cheeks. "I will pray that you return soon."

Thad smiled as he turned to leave. He took a couple of steps toward the doorway, then turned back toward the bed. "I was wondering if I might ask a question of a personal nature."

"What might that be?"

"How is it you came by the unusual name of July?"

For the first time in longer than she could remember, she attempted to laugh. "As the story was told to me," she said, "I was supposed to be born in the month of June and that would be my name. Same if I'd been a boy. But apparently I was a bit stubborn and late arriving. My mama had no other name selected. So it was decided that July would have to suffice."

"I think it's a fine name," Taylor said, "and I'm pleased to finally meet you properly."

Barclay was waiting on the porch. "Seems to me you're attractin' quite a large number of lady admirers," he said.

Taylor ignored him. "We'll allow the horses a night's rest, then be on our way in the morning."

"And which way is it you figure on us headin'?"

"I reckon we'll need to sleep on that."

It was still an hour before dawn when Kate Two used one of the matches she'd taken from the Reynolds cabin and lit a torch to illuminate the cave. She and the preacher had ridden through the night at a steady pace, their horses lucky to avoid roaming rattlesnakes and the prairie dog holes that pock-marked the region.

Jerusalem Chadway watched as she located the small chest and began moving its contents into saddlebags. "What is it you want of me?"

"For the moment, you can turn your head while I change from this dreadful dress," she said.

He turned to face the rock wall until she again spoke. "As we travel," she said after changing into pants, boots, and a flannel shirt, "you are to be my escort. If anyone asks, you are a kindhearted preacher taking a young woman to reunite with her mother and father. Exactly where, I've not yet figured out. Our aim for now is to distance ourselves from those who might be looking for us. And in exchange for your agreement to help, I will allow you to live to preach another of your sermons."

There was a coldness in her voice that caused the preacher to shiver. The gun she'd earlier pointed at him was now in a holster that hung against her hip. She was wearing her brother's hat. Kate Two, once again in control and filled with confidence, was back, a menacing smile on her face.

"I warn you against any attempt to escape. I'm a far better rider than you and can catch you with ease if need be. And, of course, I have the gun."

The frightened preacher's only response was to nod.

Part Two

Chapter 22

The two men sat on the front porch of the hotel, watching as a young man rode a bicycle along the main street of Waco. Neither had ever seen such a contraption before, much less a town of such size. At the far end of the street, a shrill whistle and billowing smoke signaled a steam engine's arrival at the depot. People hurried about in all directions, visiting the mercantile, post office, bank, doctor's office, courthouse, eateries, and buildings on the square where cotton traders headquartered. "I hadn't figured on there being this many folks in the whole state of Texas," Barclay said.

Since they had crossed the newly built bridge that spanned the Brazos River and ridden into town, Taylor and Barclay felt like out-of-place drifters. Waco, with its location on a spur of the Chisholm Trail and its railroad stop, had become a destination for those driving cattle to market. Too, thousands of bales of cotton were harvested by farmers in the region and transported to the town's mills.

There were churches for Baptists and Methodists, and in a section of town favored by the less godly, dozens of bawdy saloons and gambling houses lined a side street.

"I reckon this is what the future of the so-called frontier's gonna look like," Taylor said.

For days they had traveled with no real destination in mind. They agreed odds were good that Kate Two and the preacher had headed south, so they had simply set out in that direction, hoping to pick up the trail along the way. Only the faint recollection by a family days earlier had given them any cause for optimism. The settlers recalled a pretty woman accompanied by a skinny older man briefly stopping at their cabin to inquire about buying biscuits and coffee.

"Wasn't no names exchanged," the farmer had said. "They made their purchase and rode on. Heading south."

Trail-weary and discouraged, Taylor and Barclay had determined that their dwindling poke would allow a small spurge. They had paid fifty cents each for tubs of hot water and bathed away the grime of their travels, then eaten venison steaks in the hotel dining room.

It was as they sat on the porch at sunset that an elderly man, white-haired and limping more noticeably than Barclay, approached.

"You boys gonna be staying with us?" he asked. "Name's Eli Stampley. I'm the proprietor of this fine establishment. You ask anyone and they'll tell you the Captain's Place is the best in town."

"Just passing through," Taylor said. "We've already availed ourselves of a bath and a fine meal. That stretched our budget about all it can stand."

Stampley smiled. "I was going inside to have myself a cup of coffee. If you boys are of a mind to join me, it'll be on the house."

The purpose of the invitation became quickly apparent. Eli Stampley loved to talk, particularly about himself.

A native of Tennessee, he told of coming to Texas and serving as a Texas Ranger under Captain Jack Hays. Without a single question from his visitors, he recalled battles fought with Indians, bank robbers he'd helped apprehend, and bloody border wars fought with Mexican cattle rustlers. He wasn't sure how many men he'd killed during the course of his lengthy career. "All I can say is it was a substantial number, even if you don't count the Indians and Mexicans. When I got this leg shot up," he said, "I had to retire. That's when I moved here and bought this hotel."

Barclay wanted to ask how he'd been able to afford such a purchase on a Ranger's salary but remained silent.

"So that's my life story, such as it is. What is it that brings you gentlemen to these parts?"

Taylor saw no reason to keep their purpose secret. "We're hoping to find a couple of people who are on the run."

"Bad people, I'm guessing."

"One's a killer. The other's being held against his will."

When he went on to explain that he was talking about a woman and a preacher, Stampley shook his head. "In all my years as a lawman," he said, "I never heard tell of a combination like that. You think they might be here in Waco?"

"We've got no idea."

"Back in the days when we were searching for somebody, it was often as not that we'd find him hiding in plain sight. Big as this town has become, it's mighty easy to get yourself lost in the crowd. And, sad to say, we've got a growing number of folks here who ain't exactly law-abiding. For the right incentive, they'd be quick to help a body hide away. I got no badge anymore, but I'm still on a friendly basis with most who do." He smiled again. "And I know a few ne'er-do-wells down in the part of town we call Six-Shooter City who'll sometimes confide in me."

Barclay spoke up. "Way things been going, we'd be obliged for any help, large or small." He recognized an excitement in Stampley's voice as he offered his suggestion. The old Ranger was a man clearly yearning to reclaim, even briefly, the thrills of his past.

Stampley said, "Here's my suggestion—you fellas take a room for one night here at the Captain, give your horses a rest, and enjoy the hospitality of Waco. Meanwhile, I'll see what I might be able to find out."

Taylor shrugged. "I reckon sleeping in comfort for a night would do no harm."

"And a taste of the local whiskey might also be in order," Barclay said.

Stampley doffed his hat as he limped away. "I'll be in touch."

Taylor watched the old Ranger disappear into the crowded street. "I wish I had some of his lawman experience. Maybe if I did I'd have a better notion of what it is we're up against. I keep asking myself what I'd be thinking if I was Kate Bender, where I'd be heading and what I planned to do with that poor ol' preacher. Then it occurs to me that I've got no way of figuring out a woman's thinking."

"You're trouble's not understandin' women," Barclay said. "It's just that you ain't yet grown mean enough to have thoughts like a bandit. Jerusalem Chadway is likely already gone to whatever reward awaits a crazy circuit preacher. If the Bender woman's made it this far, she's got no further need of him."

Taylor shuddered. "You thinking she might be here?"

"Could be, but not likely for long. Any outlaw headed south most likely has Mexico in mind. If he can get across the Rio Grande, everything changes for the better. Course, if it was me, I'd be jumpin' on one of those trains that's headed west and ride it to the last stop. But I'm guessing Miss Bender has her mind set on some other plan."

On the other side of town, Kole Guinn was already drunk, though it was only midday. Also a former Texas Ranger, he had retired shortly before Stampley and purchased a small ranch and a herd of longhorns. He'd been married twice, but after his first wife died and his second caused him so much grief that he sent her away, his only real passion had been adding to his fortune. Over the years his spread had grown into one of the largest in central Texas. He was tall and broad-shouldered, his slicked-down hair and neatly trimmed beard still as black as they'd been in his younger days. He too liked to brag of his days as a Ranger, fighting Indians—a black patch, covering an eye socket gouged out by a Comanche, evidence of his past valor. His greatest pleasure, however, came from the knowledge that he had become a powerful and wealthy man, intimidating to all and feared by many.

The interior of the Roost was dark except for the hint of daylight that came through the open door. Aside from Guinn, who sat at a back table, a half-full bottle of whiskey at arm's reach, the only other patrons were two men who earned their wages as wranglers and bodyguards for the rancher. It would be their responsibility to see that their boss got back to the ranch safely once his bottle was empty.

"What causes you to come interrupting my privacy?" Guinn said as he saw Eli Stampley limp into the saloon. Then he laughed. "Come and sit, you ol' rascal."

The two usually fell into sharing tales of their Rangers days, but not this time. "I've come to make you aware of a situation," Stampley said.

Guinn put down his glass and leaned forward. "And what might that situation be?"

"You told me a few days back about a woman who rode up on your ranch, telling of how she'd been abandoned by her family."

"A pretty thing. Pretty as a flower. She wasn't abandoned, though. Her folks fell ill and died when they were traveling this way from Kansas. She told me she's trying to get to some little town down south where she's got kin. Can't help feeling sorry for her."

"She still at your place?"

Guinn nodded, the smile returning to his face. "I've invited her to stay for a while. My housekeeper came into town yesterday to purchase some clothes for her. I'm thinking one of these evenings soon I might bring her in to the Captain for a nice dinner."

"I don't think that would be wise. There're two men there at this very moment, saying they're tracking a woman and a man."

The rancher shrugged. "Can't be Kate they're looking for. She rode in alone."

Guinn was calling for another bottle as Eli Stampley left, wishing he'd never spoken to the two strangers back at the hotel. This, he told himself, was an involvement he didn't need. Fearful of the drunken rancher yet closely bound to him, he would have to play the role of Guinn's protector.

It was something he'd been doing for longer than he wished to remember.

They had come to Texas as restless young men, friends who had known each other since boyhood. They had planned to join the Confederate army, but the Civil War ended shortly before they arrived. Learning of the newly formed Texas Rangers, they applied and were accepted. And for a time the thrill of being a part of a respected group of law enforcers and Indian fighters had more than sufficed. Stampley had found his life's calling. In time, however, Guinn began to aspire to something more than public adulation and the adrenaline flow that came with each chase, each gun battle and capture.

He complained that a Ranger's salary would never allow one the stake necessary to purchase a sizable parcel of land on which to plant cotton or start a herd of cattle. Greed began to drive Guinn as surely as it did the cattle rustlers and hijackers he had sworn to apprehend.

Stampley had first become aware of the length to which his partner and friend was willing to go to improve his financial state after their patrol had encountered a small band of Indians in the process of raiding a farmhouse near the Rio Grande. The renegades had been surrounded and killed in short order, but not before the settlers had died at the hands of their attackers.

While searching the adobe house for survivors, Guinn discovered a small leather pouch hidden behind a loose fireplace stone. He pulled its drawstring open to find that it contained coins and a small gold wedding band. Stampley was the only

Ranger to see him shove the pouch into the pocket of his coat.

Stampley's friend had become a thief. When he'd tried to confront him about his wrongdoing, Guinn's casual response had surprised him. "Them being dead," he said, "they got no use for it. Besides, I'm owed for the eye I sacrificed."

In time, such behavior became commonplace.

When thieves were apprehended, Guinn made it a habit to take part of the money they'd stolen for himself. Increasingly, it was he who did the robbing, blaming it on phantom outlaws. By the time he'd accumulated enough money to make a down payment on a small ranch outside Waco, he was making deals with rustlers to drive some of the stock they'd stolen to his place in exchange for allowing them a head start toward freedom. Word spread through the outlaw community that Ranger Guinn was a lawman who would ignore their trespasses for a price.

And as his fortune grew, so did the size of his ranch. Owners of adjacent properties became frequent targets of raiders and rustlers. Once their herds were diminished and their wills gone, they agreed to sell out to Guinn. Most of those now working for him were men he should have arrested while wearing a badge.

Stampley knew what his friend was doing but said nothing. Throughout their relationship, Kole Guinn had always been the leader, Eli Stampley the follower. To ensure Stampley's silence, Guinn had promised to one day set him up in a business of his own.

It was after he'd been shot in the leg, very nearly losing it when an infection had set in, that he'd retired and purchased the Captain's Place. The money had been loaned to him by Guinn.

In time, both men flourished. Stampley found that he was well suited to run a hotel, turning it into one of Waco's showplaces. And while Guinn rarely appeared on its streets, he became one of the town's most powerful men. Bankers eagerly agreed to his every whim, officials accepted his bribes, and in the dead of night, stolen cattle continued to arrive in his pastures.

Each spring an annual barbecue and dance was held on Guinn's Ranger Hill Ranch. The elite of Waco was invited. For many it was more summons than social event, yet all came, none wishing to risk the ill will that might result from not attending. Eli Stampley hadn't missed the celebration in years.

The morning sun was still on the horizon as Kate Two stood on the front porch of the massive ranch house, still in the first store-bought nightgown she'd ever worn. As she brushed her hair—it was slowly growing back to its original length—she surveyed the landscape of Ranger Hill. Pastures extended as far as she could see, the barbed wire fences seemingly endless. Longhorns grazed in every direction. Across the way hired hands were already at work, applying a new coat of paint to a barn. From inside there was the smell of coffee brewing.

"I hope the morning finds you feeling well," Guinn said as he appeared in the doorway.

"I'm fine, thank you. And yourself?"

"Unfortunately I imbibed a bit too much while in town yesterday. Until I've had an ample amount of Juanita's awful coffee, the drums in my head aren't likely to stop their beatin'."

As if on cue, the housekeeper arrived on the porch, steam rising from the two cups she was holding.

For a moment, Kate Two silently watched as a cow led her calf to a watering trough, then turned to the rancher. "You have a beautiful place here, Mr. Guinn. I expect you're quite proud of it."

"That I am." He cleared his throat. "I had an interesting talk with a friend while visiting in Waco. According to him, there're a couple of men in town looking for some folks. A woman and a man—outlaws, I suppose—they've tracked this way. Since it isn't too often that a lady comes riding into these parts . . ."

"It can't be me they're looking for," she said, a clipped tone in her voice. "They'd have no reason. I've done nothing wrong. And, besides, I'm traveling alone."

Guinn took a seat in a nearby rocking chair. "I understand. I was just passing the story along to make conversation. What those fellas are up to is of no matter to me. Nor should it be to you. You're safe here and welcome to stay as long as you like."

Kate Two's only response was to lean toward him and gently place a kiss on his forehead.

Guinn smiled and looked up at her. "I'd appreciate it if you'd take to calling me Kole."

Miles away, a tired and riderless horse, its saddle hanging to one side, slowly made its way down the main street of Dawson's Ridge.

Chapter 23

"I don't think he's bein' truthful," Barclay said as he brushed crumbs of corn bread from his beard and pushed back from the table. Eli Stampley had just walked out of the dining room.

"And why is that?" Taylor had sensed Stampley's discomfort but had felt no reason to question what he'd said.

"It's one of those things that comes with gettin' up in years—and being around liars for much of your life. You learn to pick up on things. That man was so nervous he was near soilin' his britches. And you noticed he wasn't as glad to see us as he was yesterday. Kept lookin' away when he spoke. And nobody who properly runs a hotel suggests that paying customers ought to think about movin' on."

Stampley had told them that he'd spoken with the town marshal, who knew nothing of the whereabouts of the travelers they had mentioned, nor had he received communication from any other agency looking for a man and woman who might be on the run. "Fact is," Stampley told them, "the marshal seemed more interested in who you folks are and what your future plans might be. I tried to assure him you were law-abiding gentlemen, of course."

He'd also visited Six-Shooter City, asking if any new faces had been seen lately, particularly a woman. "No luck there neither. It's my opinion that you boys are wasting your time looking in the wrong place. Much as I'd like to continue renting you that room and taking your meal requests, I'd suggest you be on your way before those you're tracking get too many more miles ahead of you."

Guinn sat at the large desk in his office, eating a bowl of chili with extra jalapeños, his traditional cure for a hangover. "Juanita," he called out, "where's Ruben and Buck? They get lost?"

The housekeeper peeked through the doorway. "One of the men just left to go get them from the back pasture. I'm sure they'll be here soon. You want more chili?"

"My taste buds are done paralyzed."

There was the sound of horses outside, and moments later, the two men who had seen him home from the saloon appeared in the doorway.

Buck Lee and Ruben de la Rosa had been small-time cattle rustlers along the Mexican border before they'd become acquainted with Guinn and gone to work for him. They were both broad-shouldered and brawny. Buck, in his thirties, wore a reddish brown beard. Ruben was smooth-shaven and younger. They stood stiffly in front of their boss's desk as he outlined what he wished them to do.

"Word is there're a couple of men in town, looking to find some folks, a woman and a man traveling together. Find out more about who they are and what it is they're up to. Old man Stampley can fill you in on what details he's learned since they've been staying at the Captain."

They nodded. "Is it possible she's who they're looking for?" Buck asked, pointing toward the guest room at the top of the stairs.

Guinn looked at both men for a moment. "They're not to know she's here. Is that clear?"

Again both nodded.

"What would simplify this matter," Guinn said, "would be to make sure these gentlemen, whoever they are, have good reason to get out of town and take their business elsewhere."

"Be okay if we clean up a bit before we head out?"

"Absolutely. I wouldn't want you arriving in town looking like a pair of outlaws," Guinn said. "And here—enjoy yourselves a bit afterward." Her tossed several silver dollars at the table.

Buck grinned. "That's what we was thinking to do."

Listening from behind his office door, Kate Two smiled.

A chilling wind blew and the day was clabber gray as Taylor and Barclay left the Captain's Place and walked down the main street. "I hate giving him the feeling he's running us out of town," Taylor said.

"Maybe that ain't to be the case. Seeing's how we got no other plan to pursue, I'm of a mind that we spend a little more time here before we move on. What I'm thinkin' is we fetch our horses and give the appearance of taking our leave—but for only a short distance. We can find ourselves a campsite somewhere along the Brazos and wait a bit. Come nightfall when this place called Six-Shooter City gets busy, we might pay it a visit and ask some questions ourselves. If anyone's to know of folks on the run or hidin' out, it'll likely be those who ain't exactly the best of this town's society."

"Takes one to know one, you're saying?"

Barclay smiled. "Someone lies to you, he's hidin' something he don't want you knowin' or gettin' too close to."

Taylor found his friend's upbeat mood puzzling. He had made no mention of it, but he was becoming discouraged to the point of suggesting that it was time they turned back. He had no good reason to believe they were any closer to finding Kate Two than they were when they left Dawson's Ridge. Winter was coming, no time to be on the trail. And he felt a growing guilt that he'd lured Tater into a pursuit in which he had no real stake. He'd already been shot and was now gimp-legged because of him. Most likely Reverend Chadway was dead or soon would be, another event Taylor considered his doing.

As they reached a corner where people were hurrying in and out of a mercantile, they saw an old man sitting on a blanket, leaning against the wall, his head down and eyes closed. Neatly spread in front of him were his wares.

"Hope he ain't dead," Taylor said as he looked down on the frail figure.

"No, still alive," the man said, lifting his head and smiling as he looked up at the men through watery eyes. He was Indian. "I am Huaco Joe."

For years he had been a fixture in Waco, a descendant of the tribe after which the city was named. When the treaties with the United States government had been agreed to, the few remaining members of the Huacos tribe had dutifully made the trek north to an Indian Territory reservation. All but Huaco Joe, who had chosen to stay behind, living what remained of his life in freedom. For years he had roamed the Waco streets, judged by most to be crazy but harmless. He slept in alleyways, ate little more than what a benevolent café owner offered him from his back door, and sold his handmade relics.

On his blanket were a dozen small circular reeds, draped with beads and feathers, all held together by a spidery weave of strings.

"What are these?" Taylor nodded toward the display.

"Man With Big Hat does not know magic of the dream catcher?"

"Reckon not."

In broken English, the old Indian explained the spiritual legend attached to his crafts, telling how for centuries the dream catcher had offered protection to its owner, warding off evil spirits and capturing nightmares, all manner of danger and bad ideas. Trapped in its web, all negative things disappeared. "Dream catcher promises future safe and happy," Huaco Joe said.

Barclay bent down and held one in his hand. "Might be a good idea I get me one of these," he said as he pulled coins from his pocket.

"It would be wise to share with Man With Big Hat," the Indian said as he leaned back against the wall and closed his eyes.

"Now, don't that beat all! I never figgered on gettin' friendly advice from no Indian," Barclay said as they walked away.

Before noon they rode west along the Brazos River, a few miles out of town. They made camp beneath a limestone outcropping on the riverbank, lit a fire, and waited for the remainder of the day to pass. It was dusk when they saddled their horses to begin the short trip to the part of town called Six-Shooter City. Barclay hung his dream catcher on his saddle horn. "Can't never be too careful," he said. A fog had settled over the Brazos and a light mist was adding to the chill in the air. From across the river, an owl hooted.

Six-Shooter City was nothing more than one long dirt street on the southern edge of town with a dimly lit string of clapboard buildings. Most had hand-painted signs above their doors with names like the Watering Hole, Trail's End, and the Roost. Those with less imagination simply advertised their establishments as a saloon. Close by were a few smaller buildings without names, their purpose easy to determine by women standing in their doorways, flashing tired smiles to passersby.

Despite the foul weather, horses were tethered at every rail and the noise of laughter and loud talk could be heard up and down the street. Somewhere in the distance a woman's off-key voice was singing a plaintive song about the pain of a man whose son had died.

Taylor pulled his hat farther down on his forehead to ward off what had turned into a gentle rain. "Aside from getting drunk, what's our plan?"

"A sip or two sounds nice," Barclay said, "but there'll be no gettin' drunk. Don't want nobody finding us lyin' dead in the street come morning. And I'd strongly advise stayin' clear of them whorehouses if you don't want to get knocked in the head and robbed of what little money you got."

"Any idea where we might start?"

"First one we come to. I'm not expectin' we'll walk in and find the Bender woman and the preacher standing at a bar, having theirselves a high old time, but maybe if we can strike up a conversation or two, somebody might know something useful to us."

Neither noticed the two men who followed behind them

as they made their way through the door of the Watering Hole.

Several hours later, they stood at the bar of a nondescript saloon. From one place to another they had surveyed the clientele—wranglers and farmhands mostly, drifters and sad old men begging for drinks. Occasionally a few of the whores would parade through, flaunting their worn-out bodies. None whom Taylor and Barclay spoke with had heard anything about a pretty woman and a preacher passing through. "Fact is," one man said, "we don't never get no *pretty* women down in this part of town, unless of course you're too drunk to know the difference. And I'm bettin' no preacher's *ever* bothered coming here attempting to save somebody's soul."

It was late and the rain had turned to tiny pellets of ice when they decided to leave. "For all the good we done," Barclay said, "we just as well had got drunk."

As they reached their horses, they heard a raspy voice call out, "You boys lookin' for somebody, I hear."

As Taylor turned, a fist slammed into the side of his face and his hat fell away. On his knees and trying to shake off the sudden dizziness, he didn't see another man swiftly appear and send Barclay sprawling into the muddy street with a blow to the back of his head. As Taylor tried to get to his feet, a boot crashed against his rib cage.

A couple of men, their arms around two laughing whores, staggered past, showing no interest in what was taking place.

The attackers dragged Taylor and Barclay into a darkened alleyway, where the beating continued. Thad tasted blood and screamed as his hand was stomped on. Barclay shielded his face with his arms, allowing the other man to deliver a series of sharp blows to his midsection. "We don't want 'em dead," the older assailant said. "They need talkin' to before we finish our business."

They lifted their near-unconscious victims into sitting positions against the wall of the saloon. "You boys been asking about things that are none of your business," Buck said. "Ain't nobody here that's of interest to you. Understand what I'm saying?"

Neither Taylor nor Barclay could acknowledge.

"We're gonna leave your horses tied in front as a friendly gesture. When you're feeling up to it, best you mount up and get moving out of here, fast as you can. Don't be looking back or coming back, lest we have to show how bad things can really get."

The two men walked away in the direction of one of the whorehouses. Taylor lay unconscious. Barclay groaned, vomited, and passed out next to him.

When they came to, a shadowy figure stood over them, arms folded to keep a blanket tight against his skinny body. It was Barclay who first recognized him.

"I'll be wantin' my money back," he said, his mouth so swollen that his words were little more than a mumble. "That dream catcher thing don't seem to work."

"Because you are fool," Huaco Joe said. "You make white man boss angry. He send men to bring message."

"White man boss?"

"He who owns much land and many cattle. He who is evil and feared. Guinn."

Taylor woke and tried to focus. Putting a swollen hand to

his head, he winced. "Seems I done lost my hat again," he said.

Barclay and Taylor staggered to their horses and made their way out of Six-Shooter City, the drunken laughter of the late-night revelers echoing behind them. Once back on the riverbank, they were too weak to even build a fire, instead wrapping themselves in blankets to ward off the sleet and cold.

After two days mostly spent sleeping, Taylor built a fire beneath the overhang. "I'm gonna ride into town for supplies," he said. "I'm not sure how much I can chew with this jaw I fear might be broke, but ain't no use us lying around starving to death."

Barclay attempted to get up, but a sharp pain in his rib cage made it too difficult. "I reckon I'll wait here so long as you promise not to go lookin' for more trouble," he said.

Taylor tightened a wool scarf over his head and ears. "Don't worry. I'm 'bout troubled out."

Huaco Joe sat on the same corner where Thad had first seen him, his wares spread on the wooden sidewalk. Again he seemed to be sleeping, an oversized hat pulled down to hide his face.

"Fine-looking hat you got there," Taylor said as he nudged a boot against the Indian's leg.

Huaco Joe raised his head and opened his eyes. "Belonged to a man I believed would now be dead."

"Not quite."

"You feel better?" He smiled as he lifted the hat from his head and handed it to Thad. "And your big friend?"

"We're gonna live. Truth is, I've lost fights worse'n that before. My partner too, I expect."

The town was virtually empty because of the sudden blast of winter weather. Thin sheets of ice formed over the puddles in the street, and a cold north wind blew beneath dark clouds.

Taylor noticed the old man shivering beneath his threadbare blanket. "I come into town for some supplies. Got coffee and biscuits and some dried beef to take back to our camp. Seems to me your business ain't all that good today, so why don't you ride back with me? We've got us a good fire going."

By the time Magazine approached, Barclay had managed to get on his feet and was adding more wood to the fire. He shook his head as he saw the Indian riding behind Taylor. "Seems you're mighty fond of pickin' up strays."

"I owed him a favor. He found my lucky hat."

At the word *lucky*, Tater let out a laugh that quickly ended when sharp pains shot through his ribs. "I don't reckon your friend might also be a medicine man, is he?"

The three men sat silently around the campfire. To avoid the pain of chewing, Taylor soaked his biscuits in his coffee. Barclay ate little. Huaco Joe, meanwhile, ate ravenously as he nudged so close to the warmth of the fire the others worried he might burst into flame.

"You must not go back to that place," he said. "Leave and ride far away."

"Can't do that till we settle our business with those fellas who jumped us," Barclay said.

"Your enemy is not them."

In the many years he'd lived in Waco, Huaco Joe had blended so well into the background that to most he was all but invisible, a feebleminded ghost. People passed him without notice or nod, spoke freely when he was nearby as if believing he was deaf or did not know their language. As a result the Indian saw and heard many things. It amused him that the secrets of Waco were not kept from him.

"It is rancher who is to be feared. He is like Great Spirit who gets all he seeks. And he wishes you to go away."

"Why's that?" Taylor said.

"I know not. Only that you have angered him."

Huaco Joe did his best to explain the power Kole Guinn held over the community, and told them of the ranch where he lived. "It reaches for many miles with cattle as far as the eye can see. His grasslands reach high as your waist and the waters run freely."

"You seen this place?" Barclay said.

"Many years ago, as a boy, when buffalo herds made the land their home. Since white man come and kill them and built long fences, I have not. But I have heard stories."

Barclay shifted to ease his pain. "Any concernin' a woman and her travelin' companion who might have arrived there recently?"

Huaco Joe shook his head slowly and reached for another biscuit. "Only woman I know came to town a few days past. She who works for rancher Guinn buy new clothes. But I hear her say they are not for her."

Taylor looked across the campfire at Barclay. "Sounds like maybe the Bender woman's got herself a new friend."

Buck Lee was surprised to find the smiling woman seated at the dining room table across from Guinn. Days earlier he'd reported on the encounter with the two strangers, certain they had provided them ample reason to leave town. It puzzled him that Guinn had wanted to talk more.

"It seems," Guinn said, "that you boys didn't make yourselves clear enough when you spoke to them. If Eli Stampley is correct, they've not yet departed."

Buck frowned and stroked his chin whiskers. "You sure he ain't mistaken?"

"He was told that one of them appeared in town yesterday, buying supplies and talking with that crazy ol' Indian. Word he got was that Huaco Joe rode away with him."

"For what purpose?"

"That I can't say. Refresh my memory on what it is they were asking about the other night when you followed 'em."

Buck glanced over at Kate Two.

"Her hearing what you've got to say is no problem," Guinn said.

"Like I done told you, all we heard was that they were lookin' for some folks—a woman and a preacher—who they thought might have come this way. I never got no explanation of why. Neither did Ruben. They was near dead when we left 'em."

Juanita appeared and refilled the cups of Guinn and the woman but didn't bother asking Buck if he would like coffee.

When the housekeeper was gone, Kate Two spoke. "Perhaps 'near dead' wasn't how you should have left them."

Guinn stared at her, then at the men. "Me and Kate, we had a long and honest discussion on the matter last evening. She made me aware of her embarrassment about not fully explaining the troubles she's having, when she first arrived."

Buck's eyes traveled back and forth between the two.

"See," Guinn said, "she's fleeing from a husband who

talked harshly to her and beat her on more occasions than she can recall. Fearing that she might one day wind up dead at his hand, she finally gathered courage to take her problems to her preacher. He advised that the only option he could see was for her to run away and reunite with her folks down South. He agreed to help her with her escape and they've been followed ever since by her husband and his old man."

Buck nodded. "And what's become of the preacher?"

A soft, almost fragile tone returned to Kate Two's voice. "At my urging, he turned back," she said. "While I was most appreciative of his help in getting me away—we left in the dead of night, telling no one of our plan—I felt badly that he was leaving his church and congregation behind. It wasn't right for me to deprive him of his calling. A day or so before I arrived here, I finally convinced him that I could make it the reminder of the way on my own. Unlike my husband and his hateful father, he was as nice a man as—"

Guinn said, "So Kate's worry is not only for her own well-being, but that of the preacher. I've assured her we can keep her safe here, but it is her concern that should those two return home and find him back to his preaching, his life will also be in great danger."

Buck again looked at the woman, then his boss.

"Find 'em," Guinn said, "and put this matter to rest."

As the two hands walked out, Kate Two reached across the table and gently placed her hand on his arm.

Chapter 24

"Seems I ain't got much left that ain't busted or broke," Barclay said as he struggled to get aboard his horse. Though Huaco Joe had helped him tightly bind his ribs with a strip of cloth cut from the Indian's blanket, they still pained him. The cold had increased the dull ache in his leg.

"Least your face is still pretty," Taylor said. He attempted to smile despite the fact that his jaw was still swollen. The vision in his right eye remained blurred.

It was not yet dawn and the last of the stars that shone promised that a clear blue sky awaited sunup.

Huaco Joe had drawn them a map that he said would take them in the direction of the ranch. He had no idea of its actual size or boundaries or where the ranch house might be located. "You will know when you see it," he told them. "I have been told it is like the place where the Great Spirits reside."

Now that they were convinced they knew the whereabouts of Kate Two Bender, their plan was simply to locate Guinn's ranch. "Let's see if we can learn what it is we're up against," Barclay said. "If we can get us a look at where she's stayin' and not be seen while doin' it, I reckon we'll have accomplished our first goal. What our second goal might be, I got no idea."

Huaco Joe would be pleased to await their return, keeping the fire going and eating what remained of the biscuits.

They rode along the riverbank, beneath a canopy of cypress and weeping willows, before reaching the open flatlands that seemed to stretch as far as the eye could see. In one direction was Waco, in another cotton fields that waited for new seed once winter had passed. To the south was a sea of grasslands, the color of straw. They passed groves of pecan trees where squirrels played games of chase and jackrabbits perched, ears held high to determine what danger might be headed their way. Tangles of blackberry bushes had lost their leaves, their bare branches tangled and fruitless. Even in its off-season slumber, it was a beautiful land.

They had been riding for only a few hours when they reached a strange-looking fence. Tautly stretched between each post were three strands of wire with pointed barbs. Beyond it they could see hundreds of cattle grazing. "This must be where we was heading," Taylor said.

Barclay gazed toward the horizon. "Looks like somebody's intent was to fence off the whole state." He turned toward a grove of trees. "We don't wanna call notice to ourselves, so best we take cover over there till it gets nearer dark. Once we've determined that no one 'cept cows are moving about, we'll follow the fence line and see where it takes us."

Taylor was also looking at the endless line of cedar posts. "Could be we're in for a long ride."

"Wish we'd brung along some of them biscuits," Barclay said.

As the day dragged on, all they saw were two Mexican ranch hands who appeared to briefly ride among the herd and along a short stretch of fence line before leaving. Still, they waited until sundown before continuing their journey.

It was late into the night when they climbed a gentle rise that afforded them their first look at what they'd come to see. In the distance below, lantern lights twinkled from the windows of a huge ranch house, two stories high, a porch completely surrounding its exterior. From their vantage point it looked larger than Eli Stampley's Waco hotel. Nearby was a large barn and behind it was a corral that contained a dozen or so horses. Two bunkhouses sat next to the corral. At the far end of the compound was plowed ground that would be a garden when warm weather returned. An orchard, its trees bare, lay beyond.

The place was quiet and peaceful, so orderly and manicured that it seemed to have been built yesterday.

"It appears this fella Guinn has done quite well for hisself," said Taylor.

Barclay's reply was a grumble as he peered through the field glasses given him by a sergeant back in Dawson's Ridge. "My guess is that inside those bunkhouses he's got ample manpower to care for his needs. We'd be foolish to ride into that kind of trap."

"You're saying we come upon a hopeless situation?"

"Not exactly," Barclay said. "But for now we've seen what we needed to."

They turned their horses toward their campsite. By the time they reached the Brazos, the eastern horizon was a lighter gray.

* * *

There was no fire burning when they reached the overhang. "Reckon our visitor's left?" Barclay said as they approached.

Huaco Joe's body lay across the smoldering coals of the campfire. His dream catchers were strewn about, broken. Taylor kneeled beside the old man. There was a bullet hole in the middle of his forehead. The blood had frozen on his face, and his lips had no color.

Barclay reached down and lifted one of the Indian's arms. "Somebody stomped his hands and broke his fingers. He was tortured."

Taylor's thoughts flashed back to the night in the Six-Shooter City alley. "For what reason?"

"Tryin' to get him to tell our whereabouts would be my guess." Barclay held his shotgun up and looked out into the gray dawn. "Best we get away from here quickly."

"Not before we give him a proper burying."

They used broken tree branches to dig into the sandy river bottom soil. Neither spoke as they wrapped the Indian in his blanket and lowered him into the shallow grave. Taylor gathered the pieces of the dream catchers and placed them atop Huaco Joe's body. Then they covered it with soil and a few heavy stones.

A knot formed in Taylor's stomach as he stood over the mound of damp dirt. He was surprised that it was not fear he was feeling. Rather, it was the dark and troubling knowledge that yet another victim of his mad journey would haunt his conscience.

They were again riding toward Waco. "Somebody's been alertin' folks to our movements," Barclay said, "and I've got a suspicion who it might be. I told you I believed that crippled old fella who runs the hotel was a bit too sneaky for my likin'. I figure we need to have us a talk with him."

It was early enough in the morning that there was no one to see them as they made their way to the narrow alley behind the Captain's Place. As they tethered their horses in the small stall where hotel patrons were allowed to board their mounts, Taylor reached for his rifle.

Barclay shook his head. "Your pistol and my shotgun ought to be enough."

They walked toward the back entrance that led into the kitchen.

Eli Stampley was a man who slept little, a pattern that had begun during his Ranger days. None of his small staff had yet reported to begin their duties, so he had prepared coffee himself and sat alone in the dining room, sipping from an oversized cup.

"I see you too are an early riser," Barclay said as he stepped through the kitchen door.

Stampley looked up at him with raised eyebrows, then leaned back in his chair. "I thought you boys was long gone," he said.

"We got some talkin' we need to do." Barclay gripped one of Stampley's arms and jerked him to his feet. "Somewhere with a bit more privacy."

Stampley limped toward the kitchen, the barrel of Barclay's shotgun in his back, and took a seat on a small stool. Fear began to dance in his eyes. "You fellas figuring to rob me, you're gonna be sorely disappointed," he said.

"More'n likely, I'm gonna kill you," Barclay said.

"Pray tell why?"

"Payback for gettin' us beat by your friend's hired thugs and the death of that poor ol' Indian who harmed no one."

"I got no idea what you're talking about."

Taylor unholstered his Colt and moved closer. "You ain't all that good at lyin', are you?" He pointed his gun at the hotel owner. "I'd consider breakin' one of your fingers for every lie you told, 'cept you ain't got enough of 'em on your hands."

Stampley was breathing rapidly as he shook his head. "I don't know what you're talking about. You're making yourselves a big mistake. When I tell the marshal—"

Barclay swung the butt of his shotgun at the side of the man's head and slammed him to the floor. Taylor took the coffeepot from the nearby stove and approached. "As you've likely determined, my friend here is not a patient man, especially early of a morning. Unless you want hot coffee poured over your head, I'd suggest you begin acting a bit more friendly."

"Tell us about your friend, this man named Guinn," Barclay said.

"He'll see the both of you dead," Stampley said. His words came in a weak stutter. "What is it you want to know?"

Barclay pushed the shotgun barrel deeper into the innkeeper's side. "Why is it we've become such an annoyance? And why'd you see it necessary to run and tell your friend of our reason for bein' here?"

"He's got a fancy for the woman you're searching for. He wants to protect her."

Taylor shook his head. "And your job is to keep him aware of our intent?"

"I didn't intend for any harm to come of it. You'll do yourselves no favor if you intend to confront Kole Guinn. He's a man who expects to get what he wants. And what he wants at present is for the two of you to be dead and gone."

"But he has others do his dirty chores for him," Barclay said.

"The two who approached you over in Six-Shooter City—Ruben de la Rosa and Buck Lee—tend to most of his unsavory business. They're mean and loyal." He rubbed his head. "It was Ruben who long ago fired a shot into this leg. He was a cattle rustler down on the Rio Grande back then, and me and Guinn came up on him and were in the process of making an arrest. Before we could disarm him, Ruben pulled his pistol and shot me from not six feet away. I was lying there, bleeding like I was gonna die, and Guinn, he had a conversation with Ruben and then jes' let him ride away. Kole rode me to a doctor to get patched up, but only after I swore never to tell the true facts of what happened. That was the last time I seen de la Rosa until he showed up working on Kole's ranch."

His voice took on a mixture of fear and anger as he spoke of his relationship with Guinn. He'd agreed to be his ex-partner's eyes and ears in Waco in exchange for the money to purchase the Captain's Place. It had also bought his silence about the activities conducted on the ranch. "He's gotten more crazed with each passing year," Stampley said. "And I don't mind telling you that I worry on what he might do to me if he was to learn that I'm telling you his business."

Barclay said, "Why don't we just shoot him dead and be done with it?"

"Don't think I ain't thought on it," Taylor said.

"You'll not face a fair fight with Kole Guinn," Stampley said. "He's got at least a dozen hands working at the ranch. Then there are those who occasionally visit, driving stolen cattle to be released into his herd. They're all armed and willing to do anything Kole asks of 'em."

"And what of your town's marshal?" Taylor said.

"He ain't about to get himself crossways with that bunch. It was Guinn who made sure he got his badge in the first place. The marshal and those who serve as his deputies are as rotten as those working for Guinn. They'll only be trouble if you approach them."

Barclay held a coffee cup toward Taylor. "Don't sound like a fella's odds are too good in these parts unless he's friendly with the right folks," he said as Thad poured. He returned his attention to Stampley. "Truthfully it's too early in the morning for me to be shootin' folks, so we're gonna leave you be. That is, if you agree that we were never here and don't go runnin' to anybody to share what we've spoke about."

Stampley nodded and rubbed the side of his head again. Long after the two men disappeared through the back door, he sat there trying to think of the excuse he would provide the soon-to-come breakfast crowd for the swelling.

The day was clear, the sun a red ball as it peeked over the horizon. Two horses were saddled and waiting at the barn as Kole Guinn and Kate Two approached. Juanita had been up early, preparing a picnic lunch they would carry along as they toured the ranch.

"I hope you slept well and are rested," Guinn said. "We've got a lengthy ride ahead of us if you're to see everything.

Aside from a couple of spreads down on the south part of the state, this is the largest ranch you'll likely see."

"Just how large is it?"

Guinn smiled. "I don't rightly know, exactly."

They rode out into the tall grass that brushed gently against the bellies of their mounts. In almost every direction Kate Two saw large herds of cattle. Guinn noticed a puzzled look on her face as she observed the line of fence they were nearing.

"Time was," he said, "all this was open range. No spread, regardless of size, was fenced. It was a more honorable time. But as the rustlers came and greedy folks began stealing from neighbors, folks found a need to put a border to what was theirs."

He pointed to the strands of wire strung between each fence post. "Barbed wire," he said. "It's a new invention by some fella up North. When I learned of it, I put in an order and had it shipped here. It took four wagons to deliver it from the train station."

"You must be a very rich man," Kate Two said.

Guinn smiled. "Gettin' there."

They rode along streams sheltered by live oaks and pecan trees and stopped to watch a family of deer drink daintily from its cold waters. Wild turkeys peeked from the tangles of a stand of blackberry bushes.

It was midday when they stopped near a spring-fed pond and ate the sandwiches and drank the buttermilk Juanita had prepared. The warm breeze and blue sky suggested that winter might still have some time to wait.

Guinn watched their horses as they grazed nearby. "I know times have been hard for you," he said. "You're welcome to stay on the ranch for as long as you want. I'd be lying if I said I don't enjoy your company. I'm thinking you might find some comfort here, at least for a while."

She seemed to blush. "It's a very kind offer," she said as she rose to retrieve her horse. "And I'll give it serious thought." Walking away, her back to the rancher, she smiled.

No longer was Mexico in her plans. She had found the perfect hiding place.

In Dawson's Ridge there were women feeling far less confident about their futures.

Daily, after leading the children's singing, Joy Chadway walked alone to the highest point above the town and stood, letting her eyes roam in every direction, hoping that her prayers might be answered. She often imagined the approach of a horse called Magazine, bearing two men—her father and Thad Taylor, safely returning to her. But with each passing day her hope grew more faint.

Meanwhile, July Barclay's strength was returning, allowing her to walk among the townspeople, who tried with little success to lift her spirits. She constantly thought of her son, far away in Kansas, and wondered if she would ever again see him. She too prayed for the return of Taylor and his friend. They were her only hope. And like that of her new friend Joy, it was fading.

Chapter 25

"Do you trust him not to go running to this fella Guinn and tell him of our conversation?" Taylor asked. They were riding west, following the tracks the train took every afternoon as it departed Waco.

"I trust him 'bout as far as I can throw that horse you're ridin'," Barclay said. "It's for that reason I suggested we get out of town and find us a new place to hide out till we make up our minds what it is we should do. Seems the woman we've been lookin' for has found herself a place to her liking and won't be goin' no farther. If what the old man back at the hotel says is fact, she's charmed herself a rich fella and is likely to settle down with him. I 'spect her traveling's done for the time being." He went silent for a moment. "And I gotta say I'm mighty pleased by it. This trip's about wore me out."

Taylor saw the weary expression in his companion's eyes. He had taken note of the occasional winces when his horse's gait caused pain to his ribs, and though Barclay never mentioned it, he was aware that his still-mending leg continued to bother him.

"Being honest," Taylor said, "I wish we'd never left Kansas."

"A bit late for that," Barclay said.

A short time later they saw smoke, lazily drifting from the chimney of a cabin in the distance. Near the railroad tracks was a water tower mounted on log stilts. There was a small barn nearby. A man in a wagon filled with wooden barrels urged a team of mules in the direction of a small lake.

The middle-aged man in the wagon didn't see the two riders until they were alongside him. Tipping a straw hat back, he smiled. "Howdy. You fellas ain't outlaws here to rob the train, are you?"

Taylor smiled back at him. "No, sir, we ain't. Just traveling through. What is this place?"

"A watering stop. It's here that the train stops to take on water before he continues on. You'll be hearing the engine's whistle soon enough. It's my job to see that water's ready when it arrives. Name's Donovan. Jeb Donovan. This ain't exactly a town—just me, my wife, and the two boys—but we've given it a name. Make yourselves welcome to Patricia."

With that he popped the reins and urged his mules on toward the bank of the lake. "If you boys would be willing to lend a hand," he said, "I reckon there might be coffee and biscuits up to the house when we're finished."

Taylor dismounted. "My partner's a bit stove up," he said, "but I reckon I'm able-bodied enough."

As they dipped buckets tied to the end of ropes into the lake and began to fill the barrels, Donovan continued to talk. "The property's owned by the Missouri-Kansas-Texas Railroad. Back in my younger days, I was a gandy dancer, helping lay rails. 'Fore that I worked for the Waco Bridge Company, which built that fine structure that crosses the Brazos. But I finally got a bit weary of the labor, so when I was asked if I'd consider manning this here watering station, I seen it as a new opportunity.

"The train conductor sees to it that our supplies are delivered regularly from Waco. This time of the year the engineer sees to it that a good amount of coal is left off for our heating needs. Got about everything we need right here, including our privacy."

"You ain't worried about Indians?"

"Nothing here they'd likely be interested in 'cept them two mules and to watch a cabin burn. Fact is, we've not seen renegades in these parts since the treaty."

An hour later they were seated in the kitchen. Barclay and Taylor were introduced to Donovan's wife as she poured coffee and brought a plate of biscuits and corn bread from the stove. Outside, the children were unhooking the mules.

"So," Donovan said as he drained the last sip from his cup, "what is it that brings you fellas this way?"

Taylor glanced in Barclay's direction before he replied.

Tater nodded. "Might as well tell 'em what our business is," he said.

"I'm the marshal of Dawson's Ridge up in the northern part of the state," Taylor said. "We've been on the trail of some folks that have broke the law. A few days back we got ourselves into a confrontation that didn't turn out in the manner we would have liked. My partner here has some ribs that are paining him and I ain't feeling all that spry myself. For a time I feared my jaw was broke."

"I see no badge," Donovan said.

"Dawson's Ridge ain't much bigger'n your watering station," Taylor said. "It couldn't afford to provide me one."

Barclay said, "We got a bit of money in our pockets.

We're wonderin' if we might pay you to allow us to make camp down by your lake for a few days. We'd also like to purchase feed for our horses if you can spare it. You can trust that we'll be no bother."

Donovan looked toward the stove where his wife was standing. "It's a bit of an unusual request," he said. "If you wouldn't mind stepping outside and seeing that them boys are tending the mules proper, my wife and I will discuss your proposition."

A few minutes later he joined them on the front porch. "My wife don't take too kindly to the sidearms you're wearing but says you seem honest and in need of our help. She says she's got salve you're welcome to apply to your ailments. And she'll provide meals during your stay, long as it's only for a short while. You can board your horses in the barn, and being as how nights are getting cold, you can bunk there if it suits you. Does two dollars each seem fair payment?"

"Indeed it does," Taylor said.

It was the most carefree time they had spent since leaving Kansas. For three days they rested, watched the train as it stopped each afternoon for water, fished in the lake with the Donovan youngsters, and later enjoyed meals of fried catfish and cornmeal. Mrs. Donovan's salve sped their healing process. In time, Barclay was feeling well enough to help with filling the water barrels and even spent a few moments skipping rocks across the lake's smooth surface.

Sitting near the barn on a bench made of worn railroad ties as the cold night air approached, they could see their breath as they talked. The cloudless sky was filled with stars, and the moon was so bright that it cast shadows.

"Seems these folks have made themselves a pretty nice life," Taylor said. "Can't say I've ever been in a more peaceful place."

"It ain't a place that gives a man peace. It's family," Barclay said. "Not that I'm no expert on the subject, but seems to me if you've got a wife and young'uns and everybody loves everybody, life can be spent with a good amount of pleasure."

"I reckon that's how it once was for your brother and his family, before . . ."

Barclay took his time before he replied, "There was as much love there as you could ever hope to find. It was a joy for me just to witness it. And then it was suddenly taken by those devil Indians who never knew for a day of their lives what such feelings were all about."

Taylor had never seen Barclay in such a somber mood.

"Ain't my business to be tellin' another how to tend his business," Tater said, "but I'm of an age where I can speak my piece whenever I want. Seems to me once we get ourselves back home it would be a proper time for you to consider settlin' down. Maybe find yourself a wife and begin raisin' a family. You could do a lot worse than that pretty preacher's daughter back in Dawson's Ridge. She's clearly got an interest in you, though I don't for the life of me rightly know why."

Barclay rose and limped toward the barn. "What it is I'm tryin' to say is you don't want to end up like me."

The following morning, Barclay's familiar gruff demeanor had returned. He glowered and muttered to himself until midmorning.

"Good to see you in such fine spirits," Taylor said as he sat beside him in back of Donovan's wagon.

"Here's what I'm thinkin'," Tater said, using a branch to draw a map in the dirt. "The only chance we got to get near the Bender woman is to create some manner of distraction that will cause Guinn's men to be away from the house for a time."

Taylor studied the fence line that Barclay had drawn from memory and the X that indicated the location of the house.

"What I've been thinkin' on ain't the perfect plan, and if you can come up with something better, I'd admire to hear it. But, for now, this is what I propose. In the barn, Donovan's got some shears he uses for cuttin' metal. I figure we'll borrow 'em without botherin' to ask and speak to him about sellin' us some of his coal oil."

"For what purpose?"

"One of the things I was waiting on was for the weather to clear and the grassland on the back side of Guinn's place to dry out. That and the moon to disappear. If we can get to the ranch and cut away some of the wire fencing in the night, then set a few grass fires, I figure the cattle will stampede. Might need to fire a few shots to get 'em movin'. The commotion should cause Guinn and his ranch hands to come see what the ruckus is about."

"What are our chances of getting caught?"

"That's something we'd best not think too hard on right now. As soon as we set the fires and get the cattle movin', we ride far enough to be out of sight and see how fast we can get to the main house and pay our visit."

Taylor thought on it a while. "I think it's a good plan," he said. "Risky, but good. I say let's do it."

"We done overstayed our welcome, so after we help Mr. Donovan tote the water, we should be on our way."

* * *

As they filled the barrels, Donovan's boys sat astride the mules watching. Having been told that the visitors would soon be leaving, they wanted to spend as much time in their company as possible.

Taylor's thoughts were not so much on the plan his partner had outlined as they were on what he'd not mentioned. If they were successful in luring the ranch hands away and finding Kate Two, what was to happen next? Since their travels began it had been mentioned only once. He recalled Barclay's observation when he'd first told him of his desire to find her and Jakey's mother. *"I take it you're plannin' to save one and kill the other,"* Tater had said.

During their months on the trail, the bloodlust that had once driven him had faded. Or at least had changed to something else. Perhaps his feelings about justice had taken on a new definition. While he still strongly believed that the world would be better off without the presence of Kate Two Bender, he pondered the manner in which it should be done. The murder of his father was not her only crime. There were others who had lost family; others who had suffered mightily because of her evil deeds.

He found himself daydreaming of a scenario in which he and Barclay would rush into the house, take her hostage, and deliver her back to Thayer, leaving her final punishment to Marshal Thorntree.

It was a consideration he would not share with Barclay. "We'll just see what comes," he muttered to himself as the last barrel was filled.

* * *

"You boys have been right good company," Donovan said as they prepared to leave. "We enjoyed your stay and hope you'll come again if your travels bring you back this way." He lifted two jars of coal oil up to Taylor. "There'll be no charge," he said, "nor will I ask what it is you intend doing with it. I'll only wish that you take care and keep yourselves safe."

His wife stepped onto the front porch and handed one of the children a bandanna filled with biscuits she'd just taken from the stove. He hurried toward Barclay and lifted it up to him. Tater put it in his saddlebag alongside the shears he'd taken from the barn.

Dawg's tail wagged as he followed July Barstow toward the Dawson's Ridge Social Center. A shawl draped over her shoulders to ward off the cold, she felt invigorated by the crispness in the air. There was a new spring in her steps. For reasons she could not fully understand, her spirits had improved as her health returned. Her cough had all but disappeared, and she'd grown strong enough to involve herself in the daily activities of the community. On occasion, she had even gathered the children to teach them simple arithmetic and spelling.

"That ol' friend of yours seems to have a need to know your whereabouts every minute," Mayor Dawson said, pointing to the dog as he greeted her.

"I hope he's causing no trouble," July said.

"No trouble a'tall. It's good to see you feeling better." He tipped his hat.

The mayor, like all the residents, had made her feel welcome. The compassion they had shown when she first arrived had gradually evolved into friendship as she recovered and was able to move about. None asked that she recount her days being held captive by the Comanches, nor was there ever mention of her son.

She entered the Social Center to join the women gathering to make pies for the upcoming Thanksgiving celebration. She smiled when she found Joy Chadway seated at a table, shelling pecans. The preacher's daughter had become her best friend.

"It's nice to see a smile on your face," Joy said.

"I'm not able to fully explain it," July said, "but the truth is, I am feeling quite good. I had the most wonderful dream last night."

"Tell me about it."

"You'll likely think it strange," July said before launching into her story.

It was late in the afternoon, the setting sun casting long shadows, as she walked alone by the creek. She was wearing her best dress, and a soft wind blew through her freshly washed hair. She felt a strange sense that her body was weightless as she walked along the creek's edge, as if she could step out onto the water without so much as getting wet. She was humming a hymn Joy had been teaching the children, feeling a peace she thought was lost forever.

Across the water she saw a blurred image of men on horseback. Then she heard someone calling her name. "We're back," she heard, "and we've brought a surprise." Staring toward the voice, she saw that it was Thad Taylor who first came into focus. He was smiling as his horse pranced toward the creek to drink. Next to him stood Mr. Barclay wearing the first smile she could remember seeing on his face. He was nodding, as if to tell her all was well.

From behind a nearby bush appeared a third form, smaller than the men but also smiling. "It's me, Ma. Jakey."

As if weightless, she floated across the creek, over the water, hurrying to welcome them.

"What it means, I can't say," July said, "but I choose to view it as a sign that good things are to come."

"As I think you should," Joy said as she stood and hugged her friend. "Perhaps it is the Almighty whispering in your sleep to tell you that you can cease your worry, that He has a plan for a happy ending to all your troubles."

July nodded, suddenly embarrassed by the enthusiasm with which she'd shared her fantasy. "Best we get to baking," she said.

It was later in the day, after the pies were cooked and lined on tables to cool, when Joy called her away from the other women. "In your dream," she asked, "was there no sign of my father?"

To avoid being seen in Waco, Barclay and Taylor chose a slow, looping route that took them across the Brazos and onto flat farmland where cotton would soon be planted. They saw a few cabins and farmhouses in the distance but quickly passed them by until they had reached the bend in the river where they'd earlier camped.

"I think we can best get our bearings if we start out from here," Barclay said.

Taylor looked across the water toward the overhang where

they'd hidden out, where they'd found Huaco Joe dead. "Fine with me," he said, "but I'd prefer not to return to our old campsite."

"Nor would I," Barclay grunted. "We'll find us a place to pass some time. Then after nightfall we'll head toward the ranch. We'll wait till daybreak to set the fires. That way Guinn's men will be able to see the smoke and we can make our escape without our mounts steppin' into a prairie dog hole or runnin' into one of them wire fences."

Soon the horses were taking drinks from the river while their riders sat beneath a willow, sharing the biscuits Mrs. Donovan had prepared. Barclay's ribs no long pained him as he drew deep breaths, and Taylor was pleased that the swelling in his jaw was gone. "I'm proud to say I can almost chew right again," he said.

"And I consider bein' able to breathe properly my latest blessing," Barclay said.

There was nothing more than small talk left to share as both men contemplated the dangers of what lay ahead.

Chapter 26

Kole Guinn moved from his chair to place another log in the fireplace, a portion of his drink spilling onto the rug. He was pleasantly drunk. Seated nearby was Kate Two, watching silently as sparks flew up the chimney. She twisted one of the stolen rings on her finger while she compared the massive room to the dirt floor of her Comanche teepee. As she considered her new situation, she smiled.

"It'll be Thanksgiving soon," Guinn said. "I hope you'll still be here to share it with us." That Kate had given no hint of how long she would stay before continuing her journey to reunite with her family had frustrated the rancher. "I generally invite some folks out for the day and Juanita cooks up a big meal. Turkey, dressing, bread pudding. It's always a good time."

When she failed to respond he continued. "Down in that thicket by the creek," he said, "there're turkeys so big they ought to be branded. I always ride down there and shoot a few for Juanita. Sometimes I bring back a deer as well. Maybe you'd like to accompany me."

"I'm afraid I know very little about guns and shooting," she said.

"I'd be pleased to teach you." He reached for the whiskey bottle that sat on the floor next to him.

She had no intention of leaving. Men were searching for her; she needed the safety and protection she could depend on Guinn and his ranch hands to provide. Too, the luxury of living on the ranch was something she'd never dreamed of. Though she didn't particularly like the drunken old man seated across from her, he had been gentlemanly and generous. Beneath all the fascination he clearly had for her, however, was a ruthless man to whom the comfort of wealth was his only true love. That was the part of Kole Guinn she admired.

"I'd be pleased to spend Thanksgiving here if you like," she said. "Winter traveling isn't something I'd really care to do."

More whiskey sloshed from Guinn's glass as he raised it in a salute. "We'll need to buy you a new dress for the occasion."

"That would be nice," she said. "Perhaps Juanita can find one on her next trip into town."

"You wouldn't prefer shopping for one yourself?"

"No, I'd rather stay here. Now I think I'll retire if you don't mind." She left Guinn staring into the fireplace, still smiling long after she had made her way up the stairs.

So taut was the barbed wire strung that with each cut it gave off a pinging sound as it recoiled away from each post. As he walked along the fence, Taylor cut the strands while Barclay remained on horseback, shotgun across his saddle, keeping watch. Once there was a sizable hole in the fence, they would move on to create another opening through which the cattle could escape. Thad cut wires until his hands ached and the shears grew dull.

It occurred to Barclay that Kole Guinn must be a man of great arrogance, so sure that none would dare steal his stock that he didn't even bother to have his pastures watched over at night.

"We've got to set the fires on the back side of the herd since it ain't likely even cows are stupid enough to go runnin' straight into the flames," Barclay said as they rode onto the ranch. While they waited on the river he had fashioned torches from short limbs and dried moss, soaking them in the coal oil.

In the darkness the riders could make out only silhouettes of hundreds of longhorns. In some areas the brittle grass was still so high that only the horns of the steers were visible. A curious few slowly rose as the horses passed, but most chose to ignore the predawn trespassers.

"They got no idea how excitin' things are gonna get here in a few minutes," Barclay said. He handed a torch and a jar of coal oil to Taylor and pointed in the direction of another group of cattle. "Once you get behind that bunch, light your fires—spread 'em out at a good distance—then hightail it toward that opening you cut up the way. With luck we can be gone and hid before anybody gets here."

As the flames reached into the darkness, the cattle stirred, listlessly at first, and then they began to move about aimlessly, snorting and pawing. Only when Barclay fired several pistol shots into the air did they began to move more swiftly, headed toward the fences. Soon a stampede was under way, the longhorns escaping through the openings, some even trampling fence that hadn't been cut.

Barclay saw Taylor riding in his direction, torch still in hand. "Time we take our leave," he yelled.

The shots had wakened the bunkhouses, and the hired hands, still in their long johns, rushed out into the cold night air. On the southern horizon, in the direction from which the shots had come, was an orange glow.

"We got ourselves a fire," Buck Lee yelled. "Everybody get your britches on and mount up."

Ruben de la Rosa ran toward the house to alert Guinn. He found him sleeping in his chair, the bottle perched on his chest empty and the fireplace faded to embers. He shook the rancher awake, he said, "Boss, we got troubles. There's a fire burning down in the south pasture."

Guinn wiped his hands across his face. He'd been dreaming of a turkey hunt, and for a second he didn't understand why his foreman was standing next to him.

"Fire, boss," de la Rosa said, raising his voice as if addressing someone hard of hearing. "And there were gunshots."

"Rustlers?" Guinn asked, awake and sobering.

"Most likely."

By the time he had his boots pulled on, Guinn was alert and in command. "You're sending the men to check it out?"

Ruben nodded.

"I'll ride with them. Have a couple of the boys stay back and load water onto a wagon, then hurry along." As Guinn spoke he glanced toward the staircase. Kate, awakened by the commotion, was standing at the balcony. Wearing a white cotton nightgown, her hands to her face, she looked frightened. Then Juanita appeared from her room adjacent to the kitchen.

Guinn hurried toward the doorway and reached for his coat and rifle, Ruben at his side. "I'll lead the men," he said as he put a hand to his foreman's chest. "I want you to stay here to watch over the women."

"But, sir . . ." De la Rosa's argument faded into the night as Guinn bounded down the porch steps. One of the hands had already saddled his horse and held the reins out to him.

Barclay and Taylor quickly distanced themselves from the pasture and were hiding in a grove of trees when the wranglers appeared, whipping their mounts through the tall grass until they reached the fast-spreading fires. In the glow of the flames, only a few bewildered and bawling calves could be seen, the straggling remains of the herd.

"They might bc chasin' those cattle all the way to Mexico," Barclay said as he watched the frantic activity through his field glasses. "First, though, they got to figger out what to do about puttin' out the fire 'fore it takes the whole pasture."

Taylor had already turned Magazine and was moving farther into the shadows of the tree line. Barclay followed. As the rode they could hear the clattering of the water wagon hurrying to join the others.

While his men pounded the burning grass with dampened burlap sacks, Guinn found a spot where the fire had burned down and forced his horse through the lingering heat and smoke, following the escape route of his cattle. When he reached the fence, he dismounted and carefully examined several of the smoldering cedar posts. He swore loudly when he found the cut wire.

The sky was turning early-morning gray as Barclay and Taylor reached a small rise from which they could see the dim outline of the ranch house.

"I wish we could have gotten here while it was still dark," Barclay said.

Somewhere in the distance a rooster crowed.

"We riding in or approaching on foot?"

"Depends," Barclay said as he pointed toward the stone entrance to the ranch. "A man who ain't got sense enough to keep watch over his cattle might not feel any need for a lock on his gate. If we can pass through, I say we ride. That'll allow us to make our exit quicker."

"By what we seen back in the pasture, it appears everyone's gone."

"Not everyone, I hope."

Kate Two had dressed quickly after Guinn left and was pacing the kitchen as Ruben sat at the table, drinking coffee. He was still angry at being ordered to stay behind.

"What's wrong?" Kate said.

Ruben didn't bother to look up. "I never hired on to stand guard over no women," he said.

"What's happening out in the back pasture? Indians? Rustlers? What?" Something, she felt, was not right. Why set a fire if stealing cattle was your intent? She knew it was not the Comanche way, and doubted even the most simpleminded of thieves would risk calling such attention to themselves.

She looked at de la Rosa with contempt. "I imagine," she said, "that your boss would be most disappointed to learn that you're carrying out the duty you're assigned by sitting here drinking coffee, with not even a firearm within reach."

In his haste to alert Guinn, Ruben had quickly pulled on his pants and boots before rushing to the house. His pistol was still back in the bunkhouse.

"I'm gonna go fetch it right now," he said.

"If you see an extra rifle," Kate Two said, "I'd appreciate your bringing it to me."

Ruben laughed. "You'll find plenty of guns back in the boss's office. He collects 'em. Just be careful you don't go shooting yourself."

As they slowly approached, Barclay held up a hand, signaling Taylor to stop. They watched as a figure left the house and walked in the direction of the bunkhouse. "Don't look like the Bender woman," Barclay said. "It appears there're more folks here than we expected." For a few moments he pulled at his beard. "Guess we'll need to split up and take our chances. I'll check out the bunkhouse and you go to the house. Remember the advice I gave you when we rode into that Indian camp a while back?"

"To not be bashful about defending myself," Thad said.

"That applies in this case as well."

Moving quietly, Taylor looped Magazine's reins around the hitching post and made his way up the steps. The only light he could see came from the kitchen. He looked through a window and saw a Mexican woman standing in front of the stove.

As he entered he pointed his Colt toward the woman with one hand and placed a finger over his lips with the other. She burst into tears. Thad rushed to her and placed a hand over her mouth. "Lady, I ain't gonna hurt you," he whispered. "I'll remove my hand if you promise to be quiet. Who else is here?"

Her whole body was shaking. *"Lo siento . . . No hablo inglés."*

Taylor guided the woman to a chair. "Sit," he said. *"Por*

favor." He looked around the room for something he could use to tie her up with. There was no need. Her chin was already dipping toward her chest. She had fainted.

He slowly made his way into the main part of the house, squinting into the darkness as he went. In the dining room he let his free hand run across the smoothness of the large table, then moved through another door toward the faint glow of the fireplace. He was careful to avoid the empty bottle lying on the floor. After every few steps he stopped and listened but heard only the rhythmic ticking that came from a grandfather clock located against a far wall. There was a faint odor of stale cigar smoke and whiskey mixed with the aroma of the coffee that wafted from the kitchen.

Taylor moved along walls filled with paintings of majestic longhorns and mounted heads of deer. He stopped for a moment to look at a huge portrait of a young Texas Ranger wearing a white hat, a gold star pinned to his chest. There was a proud, almost boastful, smile on the subject's face.

As he climbed the stairway the house grew even darker. He could barely make out the row of doors along the upper hallway, each one closed. As he gently turned the knobs and entered each bedroom, he felt a combination of relief and disappointment when he found them empty and unused.

Opening the final door, his Colt pointed into the darkness, he was unaware of any movement. As his eyes adjusted, he could see that it was smaller than the other rooms. It had only a bed and a small chest. A quilt was rumpled into a heap and on the floor lay a discarded nightgown. The drawers of the chest hung open. Atop it in a small silver dish were several women's rings. The faint scent of lilac lingered.

From downstairs came the crashing sound of breaking glass.

"She's here," Taylor whispered.

He made no effort to muffle the sound of his boots against the polished wooden stairway as he rushed down the stairs and into the main room. Looking about, he saw an open door to a room he'd not checked. In Guinn's office he found things strewn about, the drawers of his massive desk open. The glass front of a gun case had been smashed, shards sprinkled on the floor. Taylor didn't bother to determine what might be missing from the collection of firearms. He knew that Kate Two was now armed and aware of his presence.

He returned to the kitchen. The Mexican woman lay on the floor, blood smeared across her forehead. She was barely conscious. She raised herself on one elbow and, with a shaking hand, pointed.

Taylor ran to the door. Across the way was the barn.

Kate Two had instinctively known from the moment Ruben had arrived to alert Guinn of the fires in the pasture that a danger far greater than burning grassland and stampeded cattle was nearby. She was certain it had something to do with her and the men who had been tracking her.

She knew it was time to leave.

After Ruben left to retrieve his sidearm, she had entered Guinn's office and frantically searched for the key to his gun case. Unable to find it, she hurled a chair into the glass and chose a rifle that was so polished and well oiled that it looked as if it had never been fired. There was a box of shells in a drawer at the bottom of the shattered showcase.

In the kitchen, Juanita had regained consciousness and was slowly getting to her feet. Without a word, Kate Two swung the butt of the rifle against the housekeeper's face and she fell to the floor. Kate Two ran to the barn to saddle her horse. With everyone distracted, she hoped to distance herself far from the ranch before anyone knew she was gone.

She retrieved a saddle from the tack room and began to search the stalls for her horse. Then she stopped. Though time was short, it occurred to her that the old housekeeper and Ruben, both blindly loyal to their boss, could not be left as witnesses to her departure.

She turned toward the house.

Barclay cursed the growing light of day as he kneeled behind a watering trough, watching for signs of movement in the bunkhouse. His bad leg throbbed and the foul smell of smoke and coal oil lingered in his nostrils as he aimed his shotgun at the doorway. His plan was simple. As soon as anyone came into view, he would shoot.

Inside, de la Rosa, alerted to activity up at the house by Juanita's scream, peered from a darkened window to see a man crouched and moving toward the bunkhouse. He appeared to be carrying a shotgun. If he was to carry out his boss's wishes, he needed to be at the house. But his path was blocked by an unknown enemy.

His choices were few. He could remain in the bunkhouse until it was light enough to clearly see his target and hope that his aim was good. Or he could take advantage of the night that remained and escape through the back door, which opened onto a path leading to the privy. Even if he did that, the open space to the ranch house would make him an easy target. Sweat began to bead across his forehead.

Then he saw another figure carefully moving in the direction of the barn, gun in hand. Ruben was unable to make out his face but immediately knew who the man was when he saw the hat was far too large for his head.

"I told Buck we should have left 'em dead," he said to the empty room.

By the time Taylor reached the barn, his heart was racing. Daylight was fast arriving. He could see his partner in the distance, gesturing toward the bunkhouse. Inside the barn, it was still dark as a cave. He pressed himself against the side of the building and listened. The only sound was made by the stirring of the horses. Thad took a deep breath and called out, "I know you're in there, and I'll not be leaving until you come out and show yourself."

The response was a rifle shot that buried itself into the wall above him, sending splinters of wood flying. Taylor ducked and raced through the doorway, reaching the cover of a stack of hay bales before a second shot came from the darkness.

"Who are you?" a woman's voice called out.

As she spoke, Ruben burst out of the back of the bunkhouse and ran toward the house. Barclay stood and raised his shotgun to his shoulder. De la Rosa stopped and fired his pistol. At the same time Barclay squeezed the trigger of his weapon.

Both men fell to their knees. From his hiding place, Taylor heard a second shot from Barclay's shotgun. Then silence. "You okay out there?" There was no reply.

"You don't remember me?" he yelled into the darkness of the barn. "We met up back in Kansas where you once lived with your crazy family. I've come a far distance to make you pay for what you done."

Kate Two lay prone in one of the dark stalls. She had no

idea who her adversary might be. She responded with another shot that buried itself into one of the hay bales just to Taylor's side. She knew she had the advantage of invisibility. The gray light that had begun to filter through the doorway of the barn gave her an advantage. She could occasionally see the tip of the man's hat. She would need to be patient.

"If you'll toss aside your rifle and show yourself," Taylor said, "I might decide not to kill you." He fired a flurry of pistol shots into the darkness and heard the high-pitched sound of an animal in pain. A saddle horn brushed against Kate Two's leg as the wounded horse fell beside her.

"I don't know you." She fired another shot that hit his shoulder. When she heard him cry out, Kate Two jumped to her feet and ran in his direction.

The pain felt as if a hot branding iron had been pressed against his back, momentarily knocking his breath from him. His vision blurred and nausea overwhelmed him. He looked up to see the woman pointing a rifle at him. Blood began to soak his shirt.

Kate Two looked down at the man, trying to recall having seen him before. After a moment she nodded. "It was you who came looking for your father, the simple old doctor who wished to reach out to his dead wife."

"And for that you killed him?" Taylor slowly got to his feet, showing no concern for the rifle pointed at him.

She laughed. "It was more the fact that he had money we wished to relieve him of, as I recall."

"He would have given it to you without your killing him."

"But that would have taken the fun from it."

"And what of Brother Jerusalem?"

She sighed. "Such a tiring fool. I wearied of his company

quickly, listening to him praying for my soul and quoting scripture. For my own peace of mind I shot him while he slept, and I delighted in burning his Bible." She aimed the rifle. "Speaking of which, it might be a good time for you to say a short prayer."

Taylor lifted his gun with an unsteady hand. He was pointing the Colt, hoping to squeeze the trigger before she fired, when a thundering blast came from the doorway.

Kate Two's face suddenly turned raw and bloody. Torn flesh embedded in her hair, and bits of teeth spewed from where her mouth had once been. Her body convulsed. She was still gripping the rifle when she sank to the dirt floor.

Thad turned to look at Barclay. Whiffs of smoke still rose from the barrel of his shotgun. The front of his shirt was stained with blood. Taylor ran toward him. He said, "You shot bad?"

"Reckon I am," Tater said, his voice weak, the words labored. "Not as bad as that other fella, though. I give him what was coming after the beatin' we was given." He attempted a smile as his eyes rolled upward. "Best I get off my feet." His knees buckled.

Taylor sat beside him, cradling his head in his lap, stroking his hair, as Tater Barclay died.

When he walked back to the ranch house, he took a seat at the kitchen table and let Juanita care for his wound. Kate Two's shot had entered the back of his shoulder and exited just below his collarbone. After applying salve and bandages, she moved to her ironing board and handed him one of Guinn's shirts.

"Vamos," she said. *"Ándale."*

Taylor nodded. "*Gracias.*"

He led Barclay's horse to the barn where he'd wrapped his friend's body in a blanket he found in the tack room. Somehow he managed to lift him across the saddle, tied him down with rope, and stuffed his hat into a saddlebag.

"Time we headed home," Taylor said.

As he rode away, Barclay and his horse following, the distant glow of the fires had turned to faint pillars of white smoke rising into a cloudless new day.

Chapter 27

By the time he reached the Brazos and located a shallow place for crossing, Taylor felt feverish, and his shoulder throbbed. The long night had seemed endless, a nightmare he could only fully believe after repeated glances back at Barclay's body. He was relieved to finally see the water tower of the Patricia settlement ahead.

Jeb Donovan, straddling one of his mules, rode to meet him. "Didn't expect seeing you boys back so . . ." He reined his mount in when he saw the body draped across the horse.

"I'm in need of some help," Taylor said. "You might want to ride ahead and tell your wife and the boys to remain inside the house until I can get us into your barn." He watched as Donovan rode ahead and ordered the boys from the yard, then hurried toward the barn to swing open its door. Once he'd joined him, Taylor slowly dismounted.

"I must say, you look a bit worse every time you arrive," Donovan said as he noticed the large red stain on the rider's shirt. "Best let my wife take a look."

Taylor shook his head. "I appreciate the offer, but I'll be needing to get on my way as quickly as I can."

"What is it I can do for you? You being followed?"

"I recollect you've got a good amount of coal left by the train," Taylor said, "and I'd appreciate the loan of some of it. And maybe some salt if your wife's got it. As you can see, my friend here's dead and I plan on taking him home for burying. What I need to do is pack his body proper so the wolves and coyotes don't pay him undue attention along the way."

Donovan considered the situation. "You'll be needing a wagon as well. That, or maybe we can fashion a sled of some kind that can be pulled along behind your horse."

"I'll not take your wagon," Thad said, "but the other idea seems a good one."

"You go on up to the house and get yourself tended to. I'll see to things here." He placed a hand on Taylor's good shoulder. "Don't worry about frightening the boys. Just be forthright and tell 'em what you feel's right about what happened. They're grown enough to understand."

Patricia Donovan was already waiting on the porch as Taylor slowly made his way toward her. She helped him into the cabin, then directed him to sit at the kitchen table and remove his shirt. She cleaned the wound and examined the holes where the bullet had entered and exited. "What we'll now need to do is going to be a bit painful," she said, "but necessary if you're to avoid infection."

She placed her sewing basket on the table and began to thread a needle. Then she handed Taylor a wooden spoon. "You'll want to bite down on this."

The boys watched in silence as she stitched the wounds shut with small, steady hands. When she finished, she gently rubbed salve over her handiwork and found a clean cloth that she tore into bandages.

Taylor looked across the room at the two youngsters. "We met up with the folks we've been seeking," he said, "and a good deal of shooting took place."

"Where's your friend?" the oldest asked.

"I'm sorry to say that he's dead."

After a long silence the other finally asked, "Were the bad people killed as well?"

Taylor nodded.

Except for the time he spent tending the trains, Donovan busied himself in the barn. He removed Barclay's body from the horse and laid it on a sheet of canvas on which he'd spread a thick layer of coal. He shoveled more coal atop the body until it was covered. He went into the house only long enough to get a small sack of salt from the kitchen and poured its contents over the coal. Finally he wrapped the body tightly with rope.

Inside, Taylor had forced himself to drink a cup of tea Patricia had prepared before falling into a deep sleep on the Donovans' bed.

By the light of a lantern Donovan worked late into the night. With small trunks cut from saplings, he fashioned a sled on which to lay the body, lashing the poles with strips of leather and greasing each knot to ensure that they would not work loose. He cut rope the proper length to allow it to be connected to the saddle. Then he gently rolled Barclay's body onto the cradle-looking bed and bound it tightly.

"Mr. Barclay," Donovan said, "it was a pleasure knowing you. I believed you're now ready to continue your travels."

The Donovans were on the front porch the next morning when Taylor appeared in the doorway. The sun was barely peeking over the horizon. Jeb, tired from his long night, nodded and said, "I hope you're feeling better."

Thad forced a smile. "I appreciate all you folks have done. My friend would as well."

The two men walked toward the barn, where Magazine was already saddled and the sled attached. "Want me to saddle the other horse, or will you allow him the comfort of traveling bareback?" Donovan asked.

His sons had followed, and the stood in the doorway. Taylor looked back at them. "These young'uns can't be riding mules all their lives," he said. "This here's a fine animal, strong but gentle, and I think my friend would be pleased for them to have him. The saddle as well."

They ran toward where Barclay's horse was tethered. Donovan smiled at Taylor. "You're sure on that?"

"I know they'll give him good care."

From the end of the barn, the eldest called out, "What's his name?"

"Odd as it might seem, he ain't got one. But I'd offer a suggestion."

"What's that?"

"You might think on calling him Tater."

Chapter 28

Kole Guinn paced the bunkhouse, his muddy boots pounding the floor with every step. Around him were gathered several of his hands, tired and dirty from firefighting and fence mending. The others had been sent to round up the escaped cattle.

"Nobody . . . does this . . . to me," he said, his voice rising with each word.

He and his men had returned to the ranch house near sunset. They rode up on Ruben's body, which lay on its back, a gaping hole torn in the chest. His eyes were open, he still clutched his pistol, and his boots lay nearby. "Blowed him plumb outta his boots," one of the hired hands whispered.

Another of the men found Kate Two and summoned his boss to the barn. Guinn waved him away and stood silently for some time, looking down on her, trying to summon some memory of what her beautiful face had once looked like. Only after he'd regained control of his emotions did he walk into the yard and summon Buck.

"First thing in the morning I want you to hitch up a wagon and ride into town," Guinn said. "We'll be needing two caskets. Send a couple of the boys down to that grove by the creek and have them begin digging graves for a proper burial. And see about locating a preacher who can say a few words."

Buck was already walking away when his boss added, "And stop at the hotel and bring the old man back with you. I want to speak with him."

Eli Stampley sat between Buck Lee and an elderly priest as the wagon made its way toward the ranch. None of the men had spoken since leaving Waco. The hotel owner's hands trembled as he gripped his cane, and he wondered about the purpose of the two wooden caskets behind him.

Guinn was standing on the front porch when they arrived. He waved Buck and the priest away to tend to preparations. "Come and sit, Eli," he said. "I've got a burying to attend shortly, but first we've got some talking to do."

The two men sat, and Guinn described the events that had taken place. "This was done by those two men you told me about and I intend to see that they pay for it. In your speaking with them at the hotel, you didn't make mention of the woman who was visiting, did you?"

Stampley shook his head. "I told them nothing, Kole. Not a word about you or your business. God's truth."

The fear in Stampley's eyes told Guinn that his old Ranger comrade was lying. But he would deal with that later. "Did they make any mention of where they'd come from?"

"Nothing of a specific nature. Seems one of 'em might have spoke of Kansas, but I ain't sure. All I recollect is that they rode here from someplace up north, looking for folks, a man and a woman. I told you soon as I learned of it."

"That you did," Guinn said as he patted Stampley's bad

knee. "And I take it you never seen or heard of them again after they took leave of the Captain's Place?"

"There was some talk that they was beat up pretty bad," Stampley said. "On your orders, I 'spect. It was my guess that they left town as soon as they was able to get on their horses."

Guinn stared at the old man. "Apparently that wasn't the case." He rose and stood by the porch railing. "Long as you're here," he said, "you might as well stay on for the funeral."

"Who is it that passed?"

"Ruben and the lady they were in search of. Both shot."

Stampley felt a dryness in his throat as Juanita appeared on the porch with coffee. Guinn gently draped an arm over her shoulder. "Those men even laid hands on this poor woman," he said, calling attention to the bruise on her forehead. "They're clearly bad people in need of killing for what they done."

Coffee spilled from Stampley's cup as he attempted to lift it to his mouth.

Thad Taylor leaned forward, his head down, as he rode into a cold north wind. The going had been slow since he left the Donovan place, Magazine snorting his displeasure at having to pull the heavy load across the uneven terrain.

There was a smell of oncoming snow in the air.

Thad's grief was like nothing he'd ever experienced. Occasionally he talked to his dead friend.

"I ain't shying from no blame for what's happened," he said, "but if you'd been less eager to accompany me on this trip, things might have turned out better. Course I'd likely be dead too, long ago, without you being along." His words disappeared into the wind and he tugged his hat tighter onto his head. "All I'm saying is I'm sorry for all the bad that took place. Looking on it now, I ain't certain it even makes much sense."

And he repeatedly replayed the scene in the barn, realizing that he had felt no real satisfaction in the fact that Kate Two was dead. When he had finally come face-to-face with her, pointing his Colt at her breast as she aimed her rifle at him, could he have pulled the trigger? Could he have killed a woman, even one so evil and with no hint of remorse? Barclay, in his own dying moments, had put the question to rest by tending to the chore himself, a final favor.

Though he was anxious to reach Dawson's Ridge, the shortened days made it necessary to make camp early. Nightly seeking shelter beneath outcroppings that would break the wind. He gathered branches and made a fire, not only for his own warmth but to keep curious predators away. He slept little, his rifle always across his lap as he served as protector of his friend.

So haunted was he by the past, he gave little thought to the possibility of encountering hostile Indians or roaming bandits. The thought that the man whose ranch they had set fire to might seek revenge barely crossed his mind.

It was on the fourth day when he heard the children singing. Even from a distance he recognized the hymn. As he approached the community, dreading the news he would soon have to deliver, pellets of sleet danced against the brim of his hat. He stopped atop the ridge and looked toward the large tree near the creek, now bare of leaves, and realized that the children had abandoned their outdoor lessons and were inside the Social Center. There were no people moving about.

For a time he sat astride Magazine, listening to the young voices.

At the Guinn Ranch, Buck Lee and two other hands were in the barn, saddling their horses, as the boss stood nearby. The rancher's glowing anger had not subsided. Even during the brief funeral he had constantly ground his teeth and dug at the ground with his boot. Eli Stampley had stood nearby, head bowed in an effort to avoid eye contact with his old friend.

"Seeing as how there was blood from more than one here in the barn," Guinn said, "there's a good chance that one of 'em was shot. That being the case, I'm guessing that they'll be traveling slowly." He had thought of little else but the two nameless men since his return to find Kate Two and Ruben dead. He was certain they would not risk going into Waco, where people kept watch for him. "Likely they've headed north.

"What trail they might be taking, I can't say, but you're not to return until you find them."

He approached Buck and handed him the rifle that had lain beside Kate Two's body. "When you do catch up to 'em," he said, "see to it you use this."

The sled trailing Magazine left two long tracks in the sleet that had begun to cover Dawson's Ridge's lone street. No one rushed into the foul weather to greet him.

His legs stiff from the long ride, he stood in the doorway of the Social Center for some time before one of the children noticed him and called out, "The marshal's back." Joy Chadway quickly turned toward him, her expression like that of someone seeing a ghost. Then she smiled.

The look on his face answered her question even before she reached him. "We thought we might never see you again," she said. There were giggles from the youngsters as she reached out and touched his shoulder.

She said, "Where's your friend?"

Taylor removed his hat, small pellets of ice falling to the floor. During his ride he had tried to think of how he might break the news but had come up with no satisfactory plan. "Barclay's dead," he said. "And I'm sorry to say so's your father."

Joy burst into tears as the room fell silent. Taylor stood awkwardly before her, searching for words of comfort that didn't come.

Soon the Social Center was filled with people, smiling as they welcomed Taylor back, then somber as they heard the news. Several of the women began preparing a large pot of stew while others gathered around Joy in an effort to console her. Taylor drank coffee while someone volunteered to take Magazine and Barclay's body to the livery.

Mayor Dawson arrived and shook Taylor's hand. "I'm sorry that you lost your friend and that Brother Jerusalem is gone. But I'm mighty pleased to see you back safe. How is it you became involved in such tragic events?"

Thad knew the mayor would persist until he had answers. "The woman the soldiers rescued and brought here," he said, "was who me and Tater were looking for. She was responsible for a number of killings, including that of my father back in Kansas. We found her hiding out down near Waco. Before she died for her sins, she told of shooting the preacher somewhere along the trail. She never said where it occurred, so it's unlikely we'll ever be able to locate his remains."

"Was it she who murdered your friend?"

"No," Taylor said, "it was a man who was trying to protect her. She was about to shoot me when Tater killed her and saved my life."

Mayor Dawson shook his head and placed a hand on Taylor's shoulder. "I'll not ask you to tell me more," he said. "I can see these events have been painful for you."

Thad could only nod.

The wind was howling by the time he walked to the livery where Magazine had been fed and groomed. A fire was burning in the potbellied stove, and against the wall Barclay's sled had been covered in blankets. Taylor realized he was exhausted.

On the bunk lay two saddlebags, his and Barclay's. He pulled off his boots and reached toward the one that contained Tater's belongings. Unbuckling the strap, he reached inside and removed the eyeglass, Jeb Donovan's shears, several loose shotgun shells, a pouch that contained a few coins, and a small wooden frame. In it was a faded photograph of a smiling young woman, pretty and posed in a frilly dress. Though he'd never seen it before, Thad knew immediately who she was.

Spreading the opening of the saddleback to look inside, he saw that all that remained inside was a folded piece of paper.

He moved closer to the lantern to see the words written on it.

For Thad Taylor, to reed win I have gone to meet my maker.

First off I want to say this is the only letter I ever rote.

Next I want to say it has been my honor to have got to no you. You are a good man. I wisht I could say as much for myself.

I got no way to know what took place to cause you to be reading this but I want you to know I figgered it might happen. It's a nuther of them things I told you about that folks jes come to know when they git older.

If I am still in one peece and it aint too much of a bother, Id admire to be berryed back in Kansas, along side of my brother and his family. Don't go doing nothing extry like a head stone, Jes lay me out next to my kin. Theyre restin under a big tree on the place they used to call home before the injuns came. I tole you about it so it won't be to hard to find.

I got little to leve behind. Theres a few dollars in this bag. If someone aint done stole it you can have it. You might think on spending a bit of it on a taist of whiskey for ol times sake.

My place back home aint much but the house and barn are sturdy. The water well is deep and the land is purty good. You might ax the Barstow lady if she would like to have it as a place to settle on. I spect she an her boy won't be wantin to go back to where her husband got kilt by those injuns.

Tell miz Chadway for me that Im sorry we dint save her pa. Seems to me he was plum crazy but he dint disurve to get kilt. If there really is a heven hes likely up there talking away and happy like he had good since. I sur hope so.

Lastly, I got my regrets though its a bit late to worry on that. Jes figgered Id make mention of em.

May be if that lady Id hoped to marry hadn't turned me away and maybe if I hadnt drunk so much or shot so many folks I would of turned out a better man. All I can do now is leeve that up to your doing.

Your frend, Tater Barclay

Taylor was still staring at the letter when he heard a woman's voice. "Marshal, it's Joy and July Barstow. Are you decent?"

"Decent as I'll ever be," he said as he quickly pulled on his boots and tried to smooth his tangled hair.

Joy's eyes were red, but there was a faint smile on her face. July cradled a pan of corn muffins in her arms. "If you're too weary and wish to sleep, we can come back tomorrow," July said. "I was with the children, trying to teach them to add and subtract, when you arrived. I just heard that you were back."

"It's good to see you up and about," Taylor said. "I take it you're feeling better than the last time I seen you."

"Much better, thank you. In many ways I'm feeling my old self. And for that I'm forever indebted to you and your friend." She glanced toward where Barclay's body lay. "I've come to tell you how sorry I am that he's dead."

Taylor nodded. "Too much of that's been occurring of late." He handed Barclay's letter to July. "Something here you might want to think on."

As July read, Joy moved toward the bunk and sat next to him. She took his hand. "I'm afraid I didn't conduct myself as properly as I should have earlier. In my sadness over the news of my father, I didn't make clear the fact that I'm glad you're back and safe." She bent toward him and kissed him lightly on the cheek. "You've been in my thoughts a great deal. I prayed daily for your return."

"I just wish we could have . . ."

Joy put a finger to his lips. "He lived a good life, for which I'm sure he's now being rewarded. And he'll be remembered." She smiled. "While you were gone, the church was finished. Mayor Dawson announced that it would be called Jerusalem's House. My daddy would have liked that."

"I 'spect he would."

July Barstow handed the letter back to Taylor, tears running down her cheeks.

Taylor folded the piece of paper and placed it back in the saddlebag. "Is his proposal of interest to you?"

"I can be ready to leave whenever you are."

"It will be a hard trip."

"It's one I've nightly dreamed of making," she said.

"I'll arrange to borrow a horse and we'll ride out come morning."

Before leaving, July walked over to the quilt-covered sled. She placed a hand on it and said softly, "Thank you kindly, Mr. Barclay."

Taylor and Joy sat silently for some time. "It's a fine and Christian thing you're doing," she finally said.

"What future plans have you considered?"

"Though I loved my father dearly," she said, "I long ago wearied of his constant travel. I like it here in Dawson's Ridge. The people have become friends, and the children have brought sunshine into my life. I've been trying to do the Sunday services, preaching Daddy's sermons as best I can remember them. I lack his forceful delivery, but I figure I'll get better at is as time goes on."

Thad nodded. "I think it's a good plan."

"Maybe one day after you've tended the responsibilities you've taken on, you'll think about returning," she said. Smiling, she added, "You are the town's marshal, as I recall."

Taylor returned her smile. "It's something to think on."

Buck Lee and the two young ranch hands spent the day cursing the task they'd been given. With no idea what route the men they were seeking might be taking, they had decided to travel an old buffalo trail that wagons and stagecoaches favored. To reach it required them to first ride in a westward direction.

A feathery snow was falling as they neared the railroad water station. When they got closer to the tower, they saw two youngsters riding bareback, yelling their delight in the first full blast of winter weather.

"That horse yonder looks familiar," Buck said as he kicked his into a trot. It was one that had been tethered to the rail in front of the saloon when he and Ruben encountered the two men.

"Howdy, fellas," he said as he approached. "Seems you're having yourselves a fine time playing out in this snowfall."

The boys looked at the three riders but made no reply.

"We're on the way to meet up with a couple of friends," Buck said, "and was wondering if they might have come this way."

It was the younger brother who spoke. "There was two men here for a time, but they've gone."

"Did they say where it was they were headed?"

"No, sir, they just left out, going that way." He raised an arm and pointed to the north.

Buck tipped his hat and smiled. "Much obliged. I reckon we'll catch up to 'em soon enough."

"One of 'em was dead," the youngster said.

As they rode away, Buck laughed. "Could be," he said, "that our job's already half-done."

Chapter 29

As Taylor and July Barstow left Texas behind, crossing the Red River into Indian Territory, the landscape turned harsh. Once green and gently waving, the grass lay dormant and straw colored. Mesquites aside, the trees were bare and a cold gray fog blanketed the landscape.

They had left Dawson's Ridge at daybreak, the whole town turning out to bid them farewell. One by one the children came forward to hug July. Mayor Dawson shook Taylor's hand. "I hope we'll be seeing you again one day soon," he said. Joy Chadway stood away from the crowd, arms folded across her chest, Dawg sitting at her feet. Only when Thad turned to look in her direction as he rode away did she wave good-bye as Dawg stood and barked.

They rode at a slow pace with little conversation. As they reached every rise Taylor would stop and scan the horizon with the field glasses he'd taken from Barclay's saddlebag.

"You're expecting us to be followed?" July said.

He had not spoken to her of the events at the ranch except to explain how Barclay had been killed. "Just being careful," he said. "With good luck our route is unknown to anyone.

Anyway, the bluecoats have cleared the region of renegade Indians. Aside from this unfit weather, we should have no problems."

July tugged a blanket closer around her shoulders and looked at him from beneath her bonnet. "She was an evil woman, you know." It was her first mention of the person she'd only known as Talks With Spirits. "I never in my life experienced pleasure in learning that someone was dead before. But, Lord forgive me, I felt no sadness when you told me your friend had killed her. She had no soul, nor did she have any kind feelings for anyone but herself."

Taylor only nodded as he put away the glasses. Kate Two Bender was not someone he wished to think of. "If I recollect," he said, "there are small caves in the hillsides up the way. They should provide us some shelter against the cold tonight."

During the first days of their trip, they saw few other travelers. They encountered only a lone wagon, a family making its way south. "How much farther to Texas?" the driver called out as his wife and three children peered from beneath the canvas stretched across its bed.

"Couple more days before you reach the Red River," Taylor said. "You folks picked a mighty hard time to be traveling."

"That we did," the driver said. "But we had little choice. The owner of the land I was working on the halves up and sold out and then invited us to leave. We've got relations down the way we're gonna move in with."

Taylor noticed that the eyes of the children were fixed on the sled behind Magazine. One seemed about to inquire before his mother put her hand to his mouth.

"We wish you a safe trip," July said.

The only other people they saw that day were some distance to the west. A small band of Indians, no more than six or eight, were slowly headed in the direction of a reservation Thad knew to be near. They appeared old and defeated. Their horses appeared malnourished, and they showed no interest in the white travelers.

Fog had thickened, turning the evening air damp, as Thad unhitched the sled and removed the saddles from the horses. He led them to a nearby spring before gathering wood for a fire.

July reached into the flour sack she'd filled with provisions and her few belongings and handed him a small pot. "If you'll fill this with water I'll brew coffee," she said. "Unfortunately that'll be the extent of my cooking." She had only dried venison and what remained of the bread cooked by the women before their departure.

"The squirrels and rabbits have the good sense not to be out in this weather," Taylor said, "so I hope you understand that I'll not be doing any hunting for our supper."

July smiled. "We'll make do. But just so you know, I plan on fixing you a meal unlike any you've ever had once we reach our destination."

Taylor added logs to the branches that were ablaze. "I reckon a fella can't ask for a more proper incentive than that."

When July woke the following morning, she found Taylor standing at the mouth of their shelter. His hat was pulled far down on his head and his hands were buried in his pockets as he looked out on a howling snowstorm that had arrived during the night. Tracks he'd just made while searching for firewood were a foot deep and being quickly filled.

"We won't be doing any traveling today," he said as she moved to stand next to the fire.

Half a day's ride away, Buck Lee and the two young hands that Guinn had sent with him—Dwayne Coats and Billy Sommers—had no protection from the sudden storm. They camped in open range and woke in the middle of the night to the wind and snow coming down so hard they could barely see their hands in front of their faces. With only their hats, long coats, and saddle blankets for cover, they huddled by a fire, shivering and sharing the bottle of whiskey Lee had brought along.

"If old man Guinn hadn't been so all-fired anxious for us to get on the trail," Sommers said, "maybe we might have had us time to put together some provisions."

"Blankets sure woulda been welcome," said Coats. "And something to eat."

Buck said nothing. He resented the fact that they had been ordered to accompany him instead of more qualified men. Those his boss had chosen to ride with him were weak and stupid, sent along because they were viewed as expendable. By dawn they were drunk.

"I'm near froze, I'm hungry, and I'm thinking this ain't something I hired on to do," Sommers said.

"I'm a cowhand, not no manhunter," said Coats. "Soon as this storm's passed I'm gonna head back." He looked over at Sommers. "You'd be wise to do the same thing."

Buck drank the last of the whiskey and threw the empty bottle into the snow. "And just what kind of reception is it you expect you'll get when Guinn sees you ride up?"

"I'm not figgering on going back to the ranch to work for

that crazy old man. He can have my back pay. I'll take his horse in exchange for what he owes me and find me another ranch to work on somewheres else."

Sommers nodded in agreement. "I'm with you, Dwayne."

Lee said, "Listen, you two, we was chosen to find those who set fire to the pasture and stampeded the cattle. It's proper to make them pay for that, not to mention that they killed Ruben."

"De la Rosa was your friend, not mine," Sommers said. "Far's I'm concerned, he ain't no great loss. He was a mean and spiteful Meskin who was far too proud of hisself. I got no good reason to be seeking revenge for his killing."

Buck brushed snow from his beard as he got to his feet. Kole Guinn had treated him well since he and Ruben were young men first hired to rustle cattle for him. He'd paid them well, provided them food, shelter, and good horses. When they'd been thrown in jail after altercations in Waco saloons, it was always their boss who spoke with the marshal and saw that they were set free. More than once Guinn had paid whores from his own pocket to tend to their private needs. In every way, Lee believed, his boss had earned his loyalty.

"What I'm saying is, if a man's paying your wages and tells you something needs doing," he said, "you should do it."

Dwayne laughed. "Not if it don't make good sense and might get you killed." Billy nodded his agreement.

Lee staggered through the snow to his horse and pulled his rifle from its scabbard. He stumbled briefly as he turned and pointed it in their direction.

"You're plumb crazy as he is," Sommers said.

Buck shot him first, levered another round into the chamber, and aimed at Coats. "All you boys have done is give me misery and slow me down," he said as he pulled the trigger a second time. He moved closer and looked down as the snow around the dead men turned red.

He added more wood to the fire, then sat silently for the remainder of the night, wishing there was more whiskey. He thought of his dead friend Ruben and whores and the warmth of the bunkhouse back at the ranch. And as the cold air began to clear his head, he recalled the conversation he'd had with the family they'd passed the day before. *"All I can rightfully recall was that the man wore a hat that seemed too big for his head. That and the fact that his horse was pulling some kind of load,"* the man in the wagon had said.

Lee knew he was getting close.

When the snowstorm started, Taylor had found a nearby draw that offered some shelter for the horses. He brushed snow from their backs, only to see more collect even before he could finish. Near the entrance to the cave, Barclay's makeshift carriage had already disappeared beneath a white mound.

July, wrapped in a blanket, looked up as he returned with more wood for the fire. "How long do you expect we'll be here?"

"Could be a while. No way of knowing how long this storm will last. Or how soon we can travel once it clears."

Soon a bright blaze was again burning, embers dancing above the flames before being swept out into the storm. Outside there was an eerie silence. No birds called out and nothing moved.

"Tell me about Mr. Barclay's place," July said, breaking a long silence.

"I was only there a couple of times and then just briefly. But from what I seen, it's a fine place. You read what he described in his letter. When we left to come this way, he spoke with a neighbor about watching over it in his absence, so I 'spect it's been taken care of."

"Is it a place Jakey would like?"

"I'd think so. Most likely, he'd like any place where his mama is."

"I'm so anxious to see him. Likely he's grown a foot. He had his ninth birthday not long ago, you know."

The day passed slowly, July trying to urge Thad into conversation. "I realize you're not much of a talker," she said, "but it's one of the things in life that gives me great pleasure. Most women are like that, I suppose. When I was with the Indians, the only one who even spoke English was that horrid woman. At times, though, even hearing words from her foul mouth were welcome. Then, when I arrived in Dawson's Ridge, it was the conversations with the women there that helped me heal. Folks talking to each other is a good thing, Mr. Taylor."

"I just never had much that was worth saying."

"Oh, I doubt that. From what I saw, Miss Chadway was most interested in speaking with you. And, if I'm not mistaken, you with her." July smiled as Thad blushed and rose to his feet.

"Reckon I'll fetch some more firewood," he said.

On the morning of the third day, the skies cleared to a blue so bright it caused Taylor to squint as he stepped from the mouth of the cave. The wind had stilled and the sun was a welcome ball of orange on the horizon.

"If it stays cold," he said, "the ground will remain frozen, allowing us to move on."

"I'll make you some coffee," July said, "and then we can be on our way."

Buck Lee's horse moved through the snow in a slow, prancing motion, its legs disappearing beneath the frozen crust with each step. Through the early part of the day the cold felt good, clearing his head. Despite the freezing temperature, he broke into a sweat as the whiskey left his body. The only remorse he'd felt as he left the bloodied campsite was leaving the brothers' horses behind. Bringing them along would slow him, he decided. He'd left the brothers' frozen bodies where they lay, a gift to scavenging wolves and coyotes who would soon find them.

It was dusk when he arrived at the cave. The tracks in the frozen snow and the remains of a campfire assured him he was on the right trail. "Won't be long now," he said.

Five miles ahead, Taylor scanned the horizon through his field glasses. The endless blanket of snow gave off a glare as the sun began to set. "To our good fortune," he said to Magazine as he stroked the horse's neck, "it appears we're the only ones who lack good sense and are attempting to travel."

He turned to July. "Though we've only made it a short distance today, we need to make camp. These conditions are exhausting for the horses, and we can't afford to wear them out."

"If I have learned anything in recent days," July said, "it is patience."

Chapter 30

Taylor had decided that they should travel along the main northward trail as much as possible. He had no intention of going near the Cookson Hills again, where there might be a chance of encountering members of Big Boone Stallings's strange clan. While there was always the possibility of bandits, he doubted they would leave the warmth of their hideouts for the small gain he and his traveling companion might offer. And, as he'd assured the Barstow woman, it appeared the region was now free of renegade Indians. That the family they'd passed a few days earlier had experienced no problems along the way was cause for optimism.

He was beginning to feel that they would soon reach Kansas without incident when he noticed a dark speck on the southern horizon. Wiping the glasses clean, he watched as it grew larger. For the next mile or so he would frequently stop and look through the glasses. Soon he could tell that it was a lone man on horseback.

"It appears we're being followed," he told July. "He'll catch up to us soon."

"Who is it?"

"Most likely someone from the ranch sent to even a score." He fell silent for a while. "There's still plenty of daylight. I want you to ride on ahead. Stay on the trail. Once you've gone as far as you can, look for shelter. I'll catch up to you soon."

"You're going to take this man on?"

Taylor slapped the flank of her horse. "Go," he said. "Now."

As she rode away he still had no clear idea of how to deal with the oncoming danger.

Buck Lee hated the cold, and though he'd not admitted it to those he'd left dead, he too resented this mission. Shivering and hungry, he cursed Kole Guinn. He knew that it was not the burned pastures, or the stampeding of his cattle, not even the death of de la Rosa, that sent his boss into such a rage. It was the death of that woman who had suddenly appeared at the ranch and caught his boss's fancy. It was because of her that he had ridden through a blizzard, farther into an untamed and ugly region he hoped to never see again, and killed two men. He cursed her as well.

Thad remained atop the small hill, watching as the rider slowly advanced. When the man got close enough that he might be able to see that he was being watched, Taylor rode Magazine down the hill and onto a flat, open space. He unhitched the sled and brushed the remaining snow from the canvas covering Barclay's body, then found a branch, which he stuck into the ground behind it. He placed his hat atop it.

That done, he sent his horse over the hill and moved quickly to a snowbank fifty yards away, using another branch to brush away his tracks. He began digging with the butt of his rifle. Soon he had a hole deep enough to lie in with his rifle at his side.

Lee recognized that the tracks he'd been following for the last mile or so were freshly made. He pushed all the troubling thoughts from his mind and was suddenly alert and focused. He readied his rifle and rested it against the edge of his saddle. When he crested a small rise and saw what appeared to be a bundle of canvas lying in the snow ahead, he stopped and dismounted. Crouching, he moved close enough to see that the top of a hat peeked from behind it. He used his horse as cover and moved into a nearby stand of bushes, then crawled to position himself behind the fallen trunk of a large tree.

"I'll not be ambushed," he called out. "Just as well you show yourself so we can get this over with." He fired a shot that hit the canvas with a dull thud. A second shot hit the hat, sending it flying. "If you're able, stand and we'll talk."

Taylor lay motionless in his hiding place. It would now be a game of patience. As he breathed, small flakes of snow scattered in front of his face. His legs were already stiff and he could barely feel his finger on the trigger of his rifle.

Across the way, Lee didn't take his eyes off the canvas, looking for any sign of movement. "You dead?" he yelled.

Thirty minutes passed in silence. Finally Lee rose from behind the tree trunk, his rifle aimed and ready. Though convinced that the man he'd been tracking was likely dead or seriously wounded, he still moved carefully.

A puzzled look spread across his face as he reached the

canvas mound and saw only the empty hat lying in the snow behind it. As he let his rifle drop to his side, he didn't see the snow-covered form nearby as it rose and rushed toward him.

Taylor raised his rifle and pulled the trigger. Lee grabbed at his neck, his hand quickly filling with blood. "What the . . ." He dropped to his knees. His body convulsed and he fell face forward. His legs continued to move, making strange patterns in the snow. Taylor walked over, pulled his Colt, and fired a second shot that caused the body to go still.

Taylor shivered as he brushed the snow and ice from himself. His hands were shaking so badly that it took several attempts before he could pick up his hat. For a moment he stared down at the bullet hole in its crown. Then he leaned forward and retched.

He used his boots and the butt of his rifle to cover the body with snow, then went in search of Buck Lee's horse. He was tethered in the brush, showing no sign that the gunfire had spooked him.

Taylor brushed his hand against its mane. "I won't leave you here," he said. "I've got a job for you to do."

An hour later, when he caught up to July, Magazine was no longer dragging the sled. It was attached to Lee's horse.

July looked carefully at Taylor in an effort to make sure he was not injured. She inhaled deeply when she noticed the bullet hole in his hat, but she asked no questions.

"We've still got some daylight," Taylor said, "so let's go on a bit farther until we make camp."

They rode side by side in silence.

It was not until they huddled in front of a blazing fire that

July spoke. "I'm pleased that you are unharmed," she said, reaching over to place a hand on Thad's arm. "And I'm grateful for your efforts to keep me safe."

Taylor continued to stare into the flames.

She said, "Killing's not in your nature, is it?"

"Didn't used to be," he said.

As they crossed the border and into Kansas, the landscape became increasingly familiar to July Barstow. Her spirits soared, and Taylor felt a sense of relief sweep over him. The danger and brutal weather were behind them. Two days later, under a cloudless sky, the steeple of Brother Winfrey's church appeared in the distance.

"I remember this little town well," July said. "My husband brought Jakey and me along with him once when he when he came here to buy seed. We had such a pleasurable day."

They rode past the church, then the livery and general store, before arriving in front of the marshal's office. Despite the cold, Brantley Thorntree sat dozing in his chair on the board walkway. He lifted his head and opened his eyes only when he heard the squeak of saddle leather as Taylor dismounted.

The marshal looked at Taylor, then the woman, and finally the weather-beaten sled. "Appears you've returned with good news and bad," he said.

"This here's July Barstow," Taylor said. "She once lived in these parts till their place got raided by Indians."

"I remember," the marshal said as he rose and tipped his hat.

"Tater Barclay was shot dead," Taylor said. "It was his wish that he be buried on his brother's old place, so we've brung him home."

"Being honest, I thought it would be him hauling your body back. It never occurred to me that Tater, mean and stubborn as he was, might get hisself killed. I figgered he'd outlive us all. What of the Bender woman?"

"Tater killed her. And in doing so saved my life."

"Was it her who put that hole in your hat?"

Taylor shook his head. "That's another story."

"Which I'll be wanting to hear once we've got you folks settled."

Thorntree called out to a young boy playing nearby, "Run down to the smitty and have him come up here," he said, "then go fetch Brother Winfrey and tell him I need to see him." He turned to July. "If you'll accompany me, we'll go down to the house so you can meet my wife. She'll see to it that you get fed a proper meal and some rest."

July shook her head. "I can't bother—"

"She'll welcome the company and having someone to talk to instead of me. Mr. Taylor, he can bunk over at the livery. He knows it well. I'll see to it that he's taken care of once we get you settled."

As he spoke, the blacksmith and the preacher were hurrying toward them.

"We'll be having a funeral tomorrow," Thorntree said. "A casket needs building and a bit of preaching will be called for."

As the blacksmith took the reins of Buck Lee's horse, he looked at Taylor. "Seems you're about my best customer," he said.

"It does appear that way."

Brother Winfrey watched the sled as it moved down the street. "Tater Barclay?"

"I'm afraid so."

"A far better man than most gave him credit for being."

Taylor's throat tightened. "I can rightly agree with that. I never knew a finer man," he said.

By nightfall, several women had gathered at the Thorntree house. When she woke from a brief sleep, July could smell food cooking. Water had been heated and poured into a tub so she could bathe. A nightgown was neatly folded at the end of the bed.

"You'll be sleeping here tonight," Mrs. Thorntree said. "I've instructed my husband that he can stay down at the jail."

At the livery, the marshal arrived with a bottle of whiskey. "Talking comes easier when a man's got something to lubricate his tongue."

Late into the night, Taylor described the journey he and Barclay had taken. He'd never talked so much. As if needing to purge himself of the memories of the past months, he described the encounters with Comanches, the adventures in the Cookson Hills, the beating he and Barclay had suffered at the hands of men hired by a vengeful rancher, and, finally, the events that led to the death of Kate Two Bender. He talked of an old Indian named Huaco Joe, of a dog, and of a place called Dawson's Ridge.

Thorntree listened without interrupting. Only when it seemed Taylor's story was ended did he clear his throat and speak. "Seems you've told everything 'cept how you got the bullet hole in that awful-looking hat. But that can wait for another time. What you've done told me sounds like one of them stories you read in books," he said. His knees creaked as he rose from the hay bale where he'd been sitting. "So now you've got a happy ending ahead, reuniting the Barstow woman with her boy back at your place."

"That's my plan."

"And a fine one it is." Thorntree raised the bottle in a salute. "Get some rest and tomorrow we'll put Tater to rest."

"One other thing before you go," Taylor said as he reached into his saddlebag and retrieved Barclay's letter.

Thorntree moved near a lantern and silently mouthed the words as he read. "I think this makes it official that his place now belongs to Mrs. Barstow should she wish to have it," he said. He folded the letter and handed it back. "It's things like this—and the stories you been telling me—that Brother Winfrey spoke of. Tater was a good-hearted man." He swallowed hard, wiped his eyes, and turned away.

By morning the blacksmith had built a wooden casket and loaded it onto a wagon. He unstrapped Barclay's body and was preparing to lift it when Taylor arrived. "Let me give you a hand," he said. "Tater wasn't no small fella."

While the smitty went to get a hammer to nail the lid shut, Thad took the small photograph he'd found in Barclay's belongings and placed it in the casket.

"I had a bit of extra time," the blacksmith said as he returned. In his arms was a wooden cross. "I figgered a marker might be needed in the event someone wants to pay him a visit later on."

Given directions by the marshal, the Weatherby brothers had ridden ahead to dig the grave. When they'd learned of the death of the man they'd occasionally ridden with as deputies, they were eager to help.

Taylor had one more stop to make before leaving for Barclay's burial. He walked down the still-deserted street to the church. Reaching its steps, he called out, "Brother Winfrey, you up?"

The preacher appeared at the doorway. "I was just doing some thinking on what I might say about our friend," he said.

As he spoke, Taylor unbuckled his gun belt. He carefully wrapped it around the holster that held the old Army Colt that Winfrey had given him. "I'll not be needing this anymore," he said.

"Are you certain?"

"That," said Thad, "is the one thing I'm sure of."

"It was a very nice funeral," July said as they rode back toward Thayer. "I think Mr. Barclay would have been very pleased. All your hardships of returning him home to his friends and family were worthwhile—don't you think?"

The day was warm and sunny and the service short. After Taylor and the Weatherby brothers placed the coffin in the ground, Brother Winfrey spoke for a few minutes, calling Tater a fine person who he hoped the Almighty would welcome to his heavenly home. After Marshal Thorntree put the cross in place, July laid a wreath on it that the women had helped her make from strips of cloth and ribbon the night before.

"I guess each of us thinks from time to time about our final days and what our resting place will be like," July said. "It's my hope to spend my eternity in a setting as lovely as that of Mr. Barclay and his kin. Even as the preacher spoke, the birds were singing and you could hear the sound of the water rushing past in the creek. Come spring, the trees will leaf out and provide him comforting shade. The wildflowers will bloom and the grass will green and it will be even more beautiful."

Thad did not tell her of the violence that had once played out there, changing Barclay's life forever. "I'd prefer he was still living," he said. "I'm gonna miss him."

Chapter 31

Taylor offered Buck Lee's horse and saddle to the blacksmith as payment for building the casket. He refused. "It was an honor to be asked to help," he said as he shook Thad's hand. "There'll be no charge."

"In that case, if Miz Barstow's in agreement, her boy will be receiving a mighty nice surprise for his Christmas. He's of an age where he should be having his own horse."

They planned to leave at first light the following morning. If they kept a good pace, Taylor assured July, they could reach Independence by nightfall. She was so excited that it was difficult to sleep.

One of the women had given her a dress to wear at the funeral and urged her to keep it for the remainder of her journey. "You'll want to be looking nice when your boy first sees you," she said.

"I'd have given you one of mine," Mrs. Thorntree added, "but since I'm a few pounds over your dainty size you'd look like you were wearing a tent." As they prepared to leave, she lifted a sack filled with food up to July.

Her husband stood nearby, looking toward town. He

smiled when he saw two riders approaching. "Finally," he said as Jason and Mason Weatherby arrived.

"My so-called deputies will be riding along with you and see you safely home," the marshal said. "They've been properly sworn in and if they don't get lost or shoot themselves in the foot, maybe they'll be of some use."

"I appreciate the thought," Taylor said, "but there's no need."

"It's something they asked to do," Thorntree whispered.

The four riders moved at a steady pace, stopping only briefly to eat the fried chicken and corn bread and share the jar of apple cider Mrs. Thorntree had sent along.

The hand-painted sign pointing the direction to the HOME OF THE BLOODY BENDERS was still in place, but Taylor saw no curious visitors as he glanced down the road. Instinctively, Magazine quickened his gait.

As they reached the area near where July and her family had once lived, Taylor noticed that July's lips were pursed and she held her reins tightly.

"It was my intent to take you out to the Barclay place before we left Thayer," he said in an attempt to interrupt whatever dark thoughts she was having. "But those ladies was making such a fuss and all, there just wasn't time. And I figgered you'd be more anxious to see Jakey."

"You *figgered* right," she said.

It was moonless dark when they reached the gate to Dr. Taylor's ranch. In the distance was the outline of the house. "I reckon since we got you this far without needing to fire off a single shot," Jason Weatherby said, "you can safely make it the rest of the way on your own. We'll be on our way."

Taylor said, "Stay till tomorrow. "You don't want to be traveling at night."

"We'll head on in to town. The marshal gave us a few dollars he said was for lodging, and a short visit to one of your finer saloons." His brother laughed. "Without telling him, we brung a little money of our own along."

"You might think on spending it at a place called Stubby's," Taylor said. "It was once a favorite of mine."

Sister stood on the front porch, squinting into the darkness. She was barefoot and hadn't taken time to put on a coat. "Who's out there and what's your business?"

"It's your long-lost brother," Thad called out, "and I've got a lady with me. We was wondering if we're too late for supper."

Sister let out a joyful scream, jumped from the porch, and ran toward the familiar voice. Magazine turned his head in an effort to see who it was that was frantically trying to climb onto his back. "It's really you," Sister said as tears welled in her eyes. "It's really you!"

Taylor had not even completely dismounted before she was hugging him tightly. "It's really you," she said.

"Yep, it *really* is. And I'd like you to meet this lady who's come with me. Her name's July Barstow."

Sister turned to the woman. She looked exactly as Jakey had so often described her. For a moment Sister was speechless, and more tears ran down her cheeks. Then she regained her composure and turned back toward the house. "Jakey," she yelled, "get yourself out here. And hurry. Somebody's come to see you."

July was already off her horse and running toward the porch before her son appeared in the doorway. A wide smile on his face, he raced into his mother's arms.

Later, they sat in the parlor, arms around each other. Several times July looked across the room to thank Sister for taking care of Jakey in her absence.

"He's a fine young man and a pleasure to be around." She and Thad were standing side by side in front of the fireplace.

"Before it gets too late I'd best go out to the barn and bed down the horses," he said.

There, amid the smell of cedar wood and hay and saddle soap, he was surprised how comforting the familiar surroundings were, how nice it felt to finally be in a safe place. It was good to be home.

He poured oats for each of the horses and was brushing Magazine's mane when Sister entered.

"I felt a need to allow them some privacy," she said. "I've got no idea what you had to do to accomplish it, but you've made a mother and son very happy. And me too. I have to tell you, there were times when I wondered if I'd ever see you again. I'm so glad you're back." She hesitated. "Do you want to talk about it?"

"Not right now, I don't think. I missed you," he said, "and I'm sorry if I caused you worry."

She watched as he tended the horses and was delighted when he pointed out that one would soon be a gift to Jakey.

"Will you be staying?" she finally asked.

He explained to her that July Barstow had been offered a place near Thayer and that he expected she would be inclined to settle there. "I'd like to travel back with her and the boy to see that they get there safely."

"You know they'd be welcome to remain here."

"July strikes me as an independent woman. She'd likely prefer to make a new start on her own. There're good people over that way who'll look after her if need be. And it's not so far away that you couldn't visit on occasion."

"And have you given any thoughts to what your plans might be beyond helping her to get settled?"

Taylor shrugged. "I'm thinking I might travel back down to Dawson's Ridge. I picked me up a good dog along the way and had to leave him there."

Sister smiled. "I'm not sure I'd believe any man would travel all the way to Texas just for a dog. A lady friend, maybe."

Her brother blushed. "Her name's Joy, and she's the daughter of a man who was once a preacher before he was killed."

Sister moved toward him and placed a kiss on his cheek. "It's nearing Christmas," she said. "In fact, Jakey and I were going to go into the pasture and cut us a tree first thing in the morning. His mother has to be exhausted and in need of rest and time to get reacquainted with her son. You're needing rest yourself. Promise me that you'll all stay until the holidays are past."

"I'd be willing to do that," he said, "and it's my guess that July will as well."

She walked into the tack room as he spoke, returning with a large box. "I was so hoping you would return before Christmas that I got you a present. I made myself think that by doing so it would somehow make it more likely you would come home." She handed him the box.

"But it ain't Christmas yet."

"It feels like it to me," Sister said.

He lifted the lid and looked into the box, then began to laugh. "I know a number of folks who'll say it's about time." He placed the new hat on his head. "Seems it fits."

"Yes," she said, "seems it does." She turned to go back up to the house. When she reached the barn door she stopped and turned to him. "I'm proud of you, you know. And your daddy would have been as well."

Thad Taylor tipped his new hat and smiled as she walked into the night.

Afterword

Spring 1911

He was just a teenager when he'd written his story of the gruesome discovery at the Benders' way station. In the almost forty years that had passed, however, Ashley Ambrose's career path had taken him from the weekly *Thayer Observer* to a prominent position at the *Kansas City Star*. His writing had greatly improved with age and experience, and his regular column had become the best read in the state.

He had become something of a celebrity. He won prizes for his work and he was regularly invited to speak at political functions and enjoyed a first-name relationship with many of the state's wheelers and dealers. To his credit, however, he never strayed far from his roots.

When he learned that Brantley Thorntree, by then in his nineties, was near death, Ambrose immediately left for Thayer to say good-bye to his old friend.

In the town's new hospital, the writer sat at Thorntree's bedside and shared old memories with the former marshal.

"I learned way back in the day never to tell a newspaperman how to do his business," Thorntree said in a raspy, labored voice, "lest I get my britches burned. But since it makes no matter now, I've got a suggestion I'd like you to think on."

"And what's that?"

"A book. A true story after talking with folks and getting all the facts," he said. "Not that make-believe hogwash that Ned Buntline writes."

"A book about what?" Ambrose asked.

"The story of what Tater Barclay and Thad Taylor done as they traveled to Texas back in '73. I can't say I know all about what happened, but I know enough to tell you it's one of the greatest stories ever to come out of these parts. Think on it."

"A project like that would take a great amount of time and research," Ambrose said. "I'm not sure I'd even know where to start."

"You can start with me. Taylor told me enough when he returned so's I could point you in the right direction. He spoke of the places they visited and people they encountered. Never heard him so talkative before or since. It was like he was trying to remove the Devil from his heart. I'm not saying that he was all that good on detail, but I still find myself thinking back on the story he told.

"I was you, I'd see about speaking with the woman they saved from the Indians first. July Barstow's still living out on the place Tater willed to her 'fore he died. Her boy's now took my old job as marshal, you know." Thorntree's voice was growing weak.

"What can you tell me about her?"

The old marshal's breathing was labored, and it was a

minute before he continued. "She just retired from teaching at the school a few years back. The rest you likely already know. Her husband was killed by the Comanches and she was taken away. Thad and Tater went looking and found her. She's pretty much stayed to herself since settling here. I know for a while the Weatherby brothers tried to court her—first Jason, then Mason—but she apparently had no interest in 'em. Which, by the way, don't surprise me none. Since the stage now comes through Thayer, I think she and her boy occasionally travel to Independence to visit Taylor's sister. Long as you're in the area, maybe you ought to pay her a visit."

July Barstow was working in her garden when Ambrose arrived in his buggy the next afternoon. She shaded her eyes with one hand, brushed a strand of gray hair away with the other, and nodded at the man wearing a suit and tie. "You must be lost or selling something," she said.

Once he'd introduced himself and explained the purpose of his visit, she invited him to sit with her on the porch. She went into the house and returned with two glasses of lemonade. "I should go into town and see Marshal Thorntree," she said. "I wasn't aware he was in such a bad way."

"Since you were such a big part of the story," Ambrose said, "I'm wondering if you would consider telling me about it. I'm sure even now there are things you would just as soon not recall, but to do the story justice I'd need your cooperation."

"What you're talking about took place a long time ago," she said. "Things were different then, and not often very pretty. I've not even spoken of those days with my own son, much less to a complete stranger. I'd have to do some serious thinking about it."

She sipped at her lemonade. "Will you be speaking to Thad Taylor?"

"If I can locate him."

"Last time I saw him, he was riding off to return to Texas. I think he'd found himself a lady friend down there. What he did for me and my boy, I'll never be able to repay. I still pray for him every night. And, on occasion, I ride over to where Mr. Barclay's buried and give him my thanks as well."

"I've taken advantage of your hospitality enough," Ambrose said as he rose to leave. "I hope you'll consider what I've proposed."

"If you do see Thad, I'd appreciate you passing along my good wishes and telling him I still think of him fondly. And if he decides to tell you what you're wanting to know, come back to see me and maybe we'll talk some more."

Brantley Thorntree died two days after Ambrose's visit. But the idea he'd planted remained. A week after attending Thorntree's funeral, Ambrose surprised his boss by announcing that he was taking time off from the paper.

For weeks he followed the trail the two men had long ago traveled, imagining what the landscape had looked like back then. He visited the Cookson Hills, where he learned that Big Boone Stallings had died years earlier, choking to death on a chicken bone during what would be his last meal. Now only moonshiners remained hidden away in the infamous hills.

He visited reservations, hoping to find anyone who might

recall a white woman who once led a renegade band and claimed to be able to speak with the dead. He found no one willing to talk.

In Waco, he walked the streets and stayed a night at the Captain's Place. Its owner, Eli Stampley, he was told, had simply disappeared years earlier, never to be heard from again.

Six-Shooter City still thrived, and those old enough to remember Kole Guinn had nothing good to say except that they were glad he got himself shot and killed by a drunk and jealous husband who was also serving as the town marshal at the time. As Guinn had no living relatives or partners, his ranch became property of the county. His magnificent house mysteriously burned, his huge herd of longhorns was sold, and his property was divided into small farms where cotton now grew.

Finally, on a day that must have been much like the one when Taylor and Barclay first visited there, Ambrose arrived in Dawson's Ridge.

What Taylor had long ago described to Marshal Thorntree as a small settlement had grown into a thriving town. On the main street a long line of buildings housed a pharmacy, a general store, two cafés, a barbershop, and a doctor's office. Several new houses were being built near the creek, and a stagecoach was pulling away from a hotel as Ambrose arrived.

He asked a group of children playing in the street where he might find Thad Taylor. They pointed in the direction of the small church. "His wife'll know where he's at," one of them said.

Joy Taylor stopped putting hymnals in place along the

pews and smiled at the visitor as he entered Jerusalem's House. Ambrose removed his hat as he stepped into the sanctuary and introduced himself. "Mrs. Taylor? I'm looking for your husband, hoping to have a word with him."

"This time of day you'll likely find him down at the Social Center," she said.

He made the short walk to what was still the largest building in town, greeted along the way by smiling people and friendly merchants. Inside, he approached a group of men drinking coffee, and again stated his purpose.

One of the men turned and called out to a table near the back of the room, "Mayor Taylor," he said, "you've got a visitor."

Aside from the specks of gray in his red hair, Thad Taylor had changed little since Ambrose met him that dark afternoon at the Bender place years earlier. After introducing himself, the newspaperman explained Marshal Thorntree's deathbed wish that he write a book, then passed along July Barstow's best wishes and recounted his recent travels.

"I'm sorry that you've come so far," Taylor said, "just to hear me say I'm not interested in talking about things I'd just as soon forget. What me and Tater Barclay done had very little plan to it. That it worked out well in some instances was mostly pure luck. Tater, he might have been a hero—I'm of a mind he was—but I was just young and not real smart in those days. Lucky not to get myself killed." There was a finality in his tone.

Ambrose slumped in his chair. "Well . . . I can't deny I'm disappointed. But I'll respect your wishes. I'll not pursue the matter further."

"Long as you're here," Taylor said, "have a cup of coffee and a piece of pie. I'd admire to hear how July and her boy are doing. And learn more about what Marshal Thorntree done in his later years. And it seems you've done right well."

Late into the afternoon they talked, not as interviewer and subject, but two men simply enjoying each other's company. Ambrose told of how his career as a newspaperman had taken him from Thayer to Kansas City, with several stops in between. Taylor explained that he'd served as Dawson Ridge's marshal until the town's founder had died of a heart attack on the very day the first stagecoach arrived in town.

"My wife, who's been preaching here even before we were married, had decided it was high time for me to quit being a lawman and set about campaigning to get me elected as the new mayor," he said. "I figgered why not? My horse had got old and passed, same with my dog. I haven't had a drink since my weddin' day. And I'm not gettin' no younger.

"Truth be known, I'm gettin' to where I kinda like the peaceful life."

Ambrose smiled as he rose to his feet, extending his hand to the mayor. "No chance at all that you might change your mind?"

"I 'spect not," Taylor said as he stood up. "Now, if you'll excuse me, I've gotta get over to the church to get my little one, Barclay Junior, where his grandma's been watching him. I promised him we'd walk over and watch the train come in."

"Little one? But your wife must be . . ." Ambrose frowned. "Barclay Junior? I don't understand. . . ."

Taylor's smile disappeared, and his voice softened. "His daddy, Barclay Senior, died in Cuba, chargin' up San Juan

Hill with Teddy Roosevelt. Never saw his little boy—shipped out before he was born. And his mama died giving birth. Bark was the only child we had, so wasn't nothing else to do but raise his son ourselves." He chuckled. "And you know what's funny? He reminds me more of Tater each day."

With that, he turned and walked down the sidewalk.

Read on for an excerpt from
the next Ralph Compton Western adventure

THE DANGEROUS LAND

By Marcus Galloway
Available from Signet in paperback and
e-book in September 2014.

Colorado, 1886

In his life, Paul Meakes had been plenty of things. When he was inclined to boast, he would mention his time spent as half a lawman working as a deputy for a marshal in Kansas. Those had been an exciting couple of months but hadn't amounted to much apart from riding on a few posses without ever being offered steady employment. He'd had a few lucky strikes as a miner while panning in the rivers of Wyoming and California, but plenty of men had stories like those. During his younger days, he'd been a trapper on the Nebraska plains skinning buffalo and dragging their hides from one trading post to another in search of the best price.

Paul didn't have much use for boasting anymore. Some years ago, he worked a few cattle ranches and picked up odd jobs in mining camps on his way into the southeastern portion of Colorado. Once there, he'd met a lovely little woman named Joanna and opened a little general store that stocked bits and pieces the locals weren't likely to find anywhere else. He kept one of the best-stocked selections of books in the county and was known throughout his town for the oddities displayed in his front window. Residents of Keystone Pass knew where to go for blankets, oats, shoes, or tools. When they wanted something to read, a newspaper from any of a number of bigger towns, or fashions left behind by merchants on their way to New York or San Francisco, they went to Meakes Mercantile.

Before long, Paul's little store had acquired something of a reputation throughout Colorado. Those in favor of his place regarded it as a haven for fine goods and intellectual delights. Those who weren't feeling so generous called the shop a dumping ground for yellow-back novels and wares from every snake oil salesman who'd dared showed his face east of the Rockies. Either way, Paul made a decent living. He was a far cry from being rich, but he managed to keep his head above water when it came time to feeding his little family.

Joanna was a beautiful woman. Short and a bit stout in stature, she stole Paul's heart the instant he saw her smile. When he worked up the nerve to ask her to a dance, hold her in his arms, smell her soft blond curls, marriage was a foregone conclusion. She was a caring wife and patient mother.

Was.

Paul thought of her often, so his brief respite while arranging the books for sale in his store was nothing new. Neither was the pinch at the corner of his eyes or the grief that stabbed at his heart when he thought of her in terms of *was* or *used to be*. She'd passed fourteen months ago. Fourteen months during which he'd felt the passage of every single moment. The whole town missed her. Joanna was the sort of woman who took it upon herself to remember folks by name and ask about their young ones whenever they passed in the street. Paul, on the other hand, was more likely to nod to familiar faces in a friendly way without being overly enthusiastic about it. Without Joanna at his side, he was only left with silent nods from partial strangers.

For the most part, that suited Paul just fine. He'd spent most of his life roaming from one spot to another, one job to another, surrounded by a fair number of other people or none at all. When he was alone, he enjoyed the silence. When he was part of a community, he knew it was only a matter of time before he'd break away to become part of another. More than likely, folks remembered him fondly but not very often. Since he remembered them the same way, Paul was content to let things remain that way.

Whenever his spirits needed lifting, he only had to look at the faces of his two children. Abigail and David were both the spitting images of their mother, even though he'd been told the nine-year-old boy bore a mighty large resemblance to his father. If he wanted to be reminded of himself, Paul would look into a mirror, so he chose to only see them for what they were and as fond reminders of his sweet Joanna.

Standing with a pile of books cradled in his arms, Paul hadn't realized he'd been lost in his thoughts until it was pointed out to him by the young woman looking through a small stack of dresses that had arrived all the way from New Mexico earlier that week. She was in her early teens and a bit tall for her age. Long, light brown hair was braided and draped over one shoulder to display a yellow ribbon tied at the end. Rolling her eyes, she rooted through the clothing with exaggerated vigor and let out a pronounced sigh.

"What's wrong now, Daddy?" she asked.

Paul shrugged and got back to stocking the bookshelf. "Why does anything have to be wrong?"

"You're staring at me."

"Because you're beautiful."

Abigail started to roll her eyes again but blinked and showed her father a smile instead. It was a halfhearted gesture, but served its purpose well enough. "Thank you for saying so."

After placing the last book upon its shelf, Paul walked over to the table displaying the store's most recently acquired articles of clothing and rubbed his daughter's shoulder. She was almost as tall as him even though she tended to stoop a bit to hide it. "I'm not just saying so. It's the truth."

"You're the only one who thinks so."

"I doubt that very much."

"Yes, well . . . thank you all the same."

Walking to the back of the store where a few crates had been opened, Paul said, "I imagine you could corral any boy you wanted."

Another sigh from the girl was followed by a series of stomping steps that led to the front of the store. "I don't want to talk about this with you."

"What about Michael Willis? Weren't you and Becky talking about him just the other day?"

Even from her new spot behind the cash register, Abigail managed to shoot a terse glare all the way back to where Paul was retrieving some more books. "You were spying on me and Becky?"

"You and Becky are almost always together and you talk quite a lot."

"What's that got to do with anything?"

Paul gathered another armful of books and carried them to the shelf at the front of the store. Although he wouldn't have dropped one volume in the middle of a hurricane, he fretted with them as a way to avoid his daughter's critical eye. "I have ears," he said. "They're not filled with wax. I hear things." He also saw things but decided not to embarrass her with those details.

"Becky's meeting me at Johansen's Bakery. Can I have some money?" she asked while already poking a key to open the cash register.

"Take fifty cents. Not a penny more."

"Fine."

Sliding each book into place and taking his time in the process, Paul waited until he heard his daughter walking to the front door before saying, "If you're still hungry, there's going to be a picnic after Sunday services."

"That's not for two days," she pointed out. "We're not eating until then?"

"Of course we are. It's just that . . . most everyone will be there. The Willis family, for certain."

Abigail lingered at the door with her hand on the knob. She closed her eyes and pressed her lips into a tight line in an expression of anxiety dating all the way back to when she'd been a baby worried about standing upright. "Michael doesn't care if I'm there or not."

"Do you know that for a fact?"

"Yes." When she finally looked over to her father to see his stern expression, Abigail sighed. "No."

"Then you should go to that picnic and ask him to dance."

"He should be the one to do the asking."

"Maybe he's shy," Paul said. "Boys get shy too, you know. And it's not such a terrible thing to ask one to dance. Many of them even like it that way."

"Sure they do," she scoffed. "That's less work for them."

Paul laughed and fell into an easier rhythm of placing the books in their proper order. After taking a moment to lift one to his nose so he could smell the musty pages, he said, "You're right about that, but it never hurts to meet someone halfway. If things go right, it won't hardly matter who took that first step."

"I guess I could go to the picnic . . . if Becky's going too."

"That's the spirit."

"You know what would make me feel better about going?" she asked.

"What's that?"

"If I had a new dress to wear."

"I couldn't agree more. Martha just sent over a few nice ones the other day," Paul told her. "They're hanging next to those waistcoats."

"I was thinking more about the fancy silk ones on the front display."

"I bet you were. Those will fetch a mighty good price, but not if they've already been worn. They'll be damn near worthless once you spill jam or soup on them."

"I won't spill on it, Daddy!" she insisted while coyly trying to shift her arms to hide the faded stain on the dress she now wore.

"You spill on just about everything, sweetie. It's part of your charm."

Judging by the way she stormed out of the store, Abigail did not share that sentiment or find it half as endearing as her father did.

Western Stowers 1291540

XX